Patterns of Love

Also by Robin Lee Hatcher

Coming to America Series
Book One: *Dear Lady*

Coming to America
Book 2

Robin Lee Hatcher

Patterns of Love

ZondervanPublishingHouse
Grand Rapids, Michigan

A Division of HarperCollinsPublishers

Patterns of Love
Copyright © 2001 by Robin Lee Hatcher

Requests for information should be addressed to:

♨ ZondervanPublishingHouse
Grand Rapids, Michigan 49530

ISBN: 0-7394-1764-9

Interior design by Todd Sprague

Printed in the United States of America

To those who came from far away to make America their home.
Especially in memory of my great-grandparents,
Andro T. and Selma Josephine Johnson,
who immigrated from Sweden in 1868 and settled in Iowa,
where nine of their thirteen children were born

~Acknowledgments

My thanks to Ingrid Kristensson and Margit Berglund, my cyberspace friends in Sweden. Thanks also to Marylee Woods and Diana Anderson, my cyberspace friends in Iowa, and to fellow author Cheryl St. John, who introduced me to Marylee and Diana. You were all so gracious and generous with your time and answered so many questions from a virtual stranger. I will be forever grateful.

For those familiar with Swedish names, please note that I have used the more common Americanized spellings in this book, including that of my heroine and her family (i.e. Linberg instead of Lindberg).

Any mistakes found herein are solely my own and not the fault of those who endeavored to keep me from making them.

~ Preface

To my readers:

Patterns of Love was written in 1997 for the general romance market and was published in 1998. Since then, God has called me into a deeper walk of faith, as well as calling me to use the talents he entrusted to me in a new and better way—writing novels that share my hope in Christ.

I was delighted when Zondervan expressed interest in revising and reissuing my Coming to America series, because I'm fond of these stories. While you will not find the faith message as overt in these books as you will find in the novels that I've written specifically for Christian publishing houses, I believe you will find the stories entertaining and uplifting.

One of my goals as a writer is to make my characters true to life, with all the faults and foibles that real people have. Unbelievers and Christians alike make mistakes, make foolish choices, fall into sin. I don't know any perfect Christians, and so I don't write about them. What I always hope to share is that we have Someone to call upon Who *is* perfect, Someone Who can take who we are and what we do and turn it into good when we trust in Him.

In His grip,

Robin Lee Hatcher

~ *Prologue*

Ellis Island, New York Harbor, April 1897

Jostled by the other immigrants disembarking from the ferry, Inga Linberg hurried down the gangway. There were some advantages to being tall, she thought as she looked over the heads of others, her gaze locked on solid ground. It seemed months rather than weeks since the steamship had left Southampton, even longer since she and her family had bade farewell to Göteborg, Sweden, and she wondered what it would feel like to stand on something that wasn't rolling beneath her feet.

She glanced over her shoulder, trying to catch a glimpse of her parents or sisters, but they had been swallowed up by the crowd. That she'd become separated from them was her own fault, of course. She'd wanted to get a better look at the federal immigration depot and had worked her way to the railing to stare at the building and watch while immigrants from other ferries were unloaded and ushered inside.

"Form a line! Form a line!" an official yelled in English. Another shouted the same in Swedish. Others yelled the command in a variety of languages.

Inga glanced at her bodice, making sure the numbered card that had been pinned there before she'd left the RMS *Teutonic* had not been lost in the rush to shore. The number matched Inga to the steamship's manifest. Without it, her processing through immigration could be held up for hours, perhaps even days.

"Saints be praised! Sure and I was afraid we wouldn't find you again."

Inga turned to find her shipboard friends, Mary Malone and Beth Wellington, standing behind her. *"Ja.* I am here. How are you feeling?"

"Tired." Mary touched the round swell of her stomach, as if to reassure the unborn child within.

"You remember what I told you?" Inga asked softly, so as not to be overheard.

Mary nodded. "I remember. They'll not hear it from me that I'm yet to be married. And 'tis married I am in me heart, so 'twon't be a lie. Seamus would never have come to America without me had he known about the babe." She touched Inga's arm. "We may become separated inside and not see each other again. 'Tis thanks I owe for all the help you've been to us. I'll have you know it."

Beth smiled sadly. "Mary's right. Without your help and advice, we would have been frightfully ignorant about so many things. You have become the dearest of friends, Inga. I shall miss you a great deal. Remember, we all promised to write to one another as soon as we're settled."

The line started moving forward. "I will not forget," Inga promised quickly, her throat tight with emotion.

In all of Inga's life, she had never had any truly close friends. Not like Beth and Mary. But the three of them had become inseparable, almost from the moment they'd met in Southampton. Inga was going to miss them more than she dared admit, even to herself.

"Check your belongings in the baggage room," a man yelled as she entered the depot. "Check your parcels here, then proceed up the stairs."

After leaving her bags where she was told, Inga glanced behind her, only to discover Mary's prediction had proven true. Her friends had disappeared into the sea of immigrants filling the vast room. She wondered if she would ever have an opportunity to hug them and say a proper farewell before they went their separate ways.

But she hadn't time to allow feelings of melancholy to overtake her. This was her first day in America. Even the examination process of Ellis Island, which everyone seemed to dread, wouldn't spoil it for her. She was determined to savor every moment of this great adventure until the Linbergs reached their new home in Iowa. She suspected that once they were living in the parsonage in Uppsala, the adventure would end, and her life as the pastor's eldest and most dutiful daughter would return to the same familiar routine she had known in Sweden.

What else could possibly await her?

~ One

Uppsala, Iowa, December 1897

Dirk Bridger drew the wool collar up around his ears, but the wind was bitter cold and his coat was too thin. He slapped the reins against the horses' rumps, hoping to hurry the ancient animals along, even though he knew the gesture was useless. Sunset and Robber had no more speed to give. They were worn out and used up, like far too many things on the Bridger dairy farm.

He frowned, remembering how his ma had used similar words about herself yesterday. "I'm no spring chicken, Dirk," she'd said. "I'm wore out. But if I could just get me some rest, I'd be right as rain in no time."

Only Dr. Swenson didn't seem to think so. He thought Hattie Bridger's illness was much more serious than that.

And so Dirk had decided to put pride behind him and seek some much-needed help.

"You go see that Reverend Linberg," Ma had told him this morning. "He'll know who we can hire to mind the girls."

But who would want to work for what little Dirk could afford to pay? And what would happen if he couldn't find someone willing to help out? His ma was ailing—perhaps dying, if the doctor knew what he was talking about—and Dirk couldn't take care of Ma, his orphaned nieces, and the farm all by himself.

An icy wind buffeted him from behind. He closed his eyes and, for just a moment, allowed himself to remember those last few weeks he'd spent out West. Summer. Hot and dusty. Cowboys with fast horses and shiny guns strapped to their thighs.

He gave his head a shake and returned his gaze to the road before him. Daydreams were for young boys and men with no responsibilities. They weren't for him. Not anymore. Not for a long time.

The Prärieblomman Lutheran Church came into view, its tall white steeple piercing the cloudless blue of the sky. Beside the church was the two-story parsonage where the Linbergs lived. Dirk hadn't met the minister or his family, even though they'd arrived in Uppsala last May. The Bridger dairy farm was more than an hour's ride outside of Uppsala, and Dirk limited his trips into town to once or twice a month. As for Sundays, Dirk Bridger hadn't darkened the door of a church—*any* church—in many years.

He didn't figure God had missed him.

Dirk drew back on the reins, stopping the team in front of the clapboard parsonage. He dropped the lap robe onto the floor of the wagon, then hopped to the ground. With a few long strides, he crossed the yard and climbed the steps to the porch. Quickly, he rapped his glove-covered knuckles against the door.

Within moments, the door opened, revealing a pretty teenage girl with golden hair and dark blue eyes.

"Hello. Is the pastor in?"

She smiled shyly. *"Ja.* Come in, please."

Dirk whipped off his wool cap as he stepped into the warmth of the house. The girl motioned toward the parlor, and he followed her into the room.

"I will get Pappa," she said, a flush coloring her cheeks.

Dirk waited until she'd disappeared before allowing his gaze to roam. Although sparsely furnished, the room had a warm, welcoming feel to it. Lace doilies covered a small round table; a lamp sat on top of it. A colorful quilt was draped over the back of the couch, another over the arm of a chair. Framed photographs lined the mantel, women with hair worn tight to their heads, their mouths set in grim lines, men with long mustaches and half smiles.

"Those are members of our family in Sweden," a man said from behind Dirk. His voice was heavily accented with the singsong rhythm peculiar to the Swedes.

Dirk turned.

"I am Olaf Linberg." The pastor held out his hand. "Welcome to our home."

"I'm Dirk Bridger," he said, relieved the man obviously spoke and understood English. "I run a dairy farm west of here."

Dirk guessed the pastor was about sixty years old. His hair and long beard were completely white, but his stance was unbent and his face only slightly lined. When they shook hands, he discovered the pastor's grip was firm.

"I believe I know the farm, Mr. Bridger. Sven Gerhard is your neighbor." Olaf released Dirk's hand and motioned toward the sofa. "Please, sit down."

As he accepted the pastor's invitation, Dirk sought the right words to say next. It wasn't easy, asking for help. He'd been taking care of his own for most of his life.

Olaf's smile was both kind and patient. "Whatever has brought you here, young man, I will do my best to be of service."

"I feel a bit strange coming to you, the Bridgers not being members of your church and all. My ma's a Methodist."

"Believers in Christ are all members of God's family." The pastor chuckled softly. "Even Methodists."

Dirk shrugged. Then he raked the fingers of one hand through his hair and said, "Reverend, I guess there's nothin' else for me to do but come right out with it. I need to hire a woman to take care of my ailin' ma and watch after my nieces while I work the farm."

"You are not married, Mr. Bridger?"

"No. The dairy used to belong to my brother, John. He and his wife, Margaret, died nigh on two years ago now. That's when I came here to run the place while Ma took care of John's little girls. But now she's sick, and the doctor says she's got to stay in bed if she's gonna get well. We thought you might know of someone who'd be willing to work for us. I can't pay much. We barely get by as it is."

Olaf Linberg steepled his hands in front of his chin. "I see."

"Whoever we find's got to be willin' to live in. The house is fair-sized, and she'd have a room of her own. Wouldn't have to share with the girls or Ma. We'd need her to cook and clean, as well as mindin' to Ma and the little ones. It's not gonna be an easy job." He looked down at his hands, now clasped together, his forearms resting on his thighs. "It was Ma's idea I come to see you, Reverend Linberg. She figured you'd know most everyone around Uppsala, most of 'em goin' to your church and all."

"How old are your nieces, Mr. Bridger?"

"Martha's five. Suzanne's three."

The pastor shook his head. "So young to have lost their parents."

"Yeah."

Olaf rose from his chair and strode to the window where he gazed out at the lead gray sky. "I have five daughters of my own." After a few moments of silence, he glanced over his shoulder. "Your nieces are fortunate they have you to care for them."

Dirk felt a stab of guilt. He was fond of Martha and Suzanne in his own way, but there were times he resented them, too. Sometimes he was even angry at John and Margaret for dying. As if they'd had any choice in the matter. But Dirk had wanted other things for his life than to be stuck on a farm in Iowa, milking cows and mucking manure, and he couldn't seem to rid himself of the bitterness. From the time he'd learned to read, he'd been planning and plotting to see the world, to sail the seven seas, to go to the Orient and Africa and South America. Shoot, if it weren't for his family and the farm, he could've been part of the rush to the Klondike goldfields. Maybe he'd have already struck it rich if he weren't stuck here, raising his orphaned nieces.

Drawing a deep breath while suppressing those dark emotions, he stood. "There's one more thing, Reverend. Ma and I don't know but a few words of Swedish. Whoever we find has to understand English."

Olaf nodded. "I encourage all members of my congregation to speak English, Mr. Bridger. Language will not be a problem in finding someone to work for you."

⸺

"He is the most handsome man I have ever seen," fourteen-year-old Kirsten repeated for the fourth time. "When I opened the door and saw him, I forgot to breathe." She flopped backward on the bed, her arms spread out at her sides as she stared up at the ceiling. "Dirk Bridger." She said his name on a sigh. "Have you ever heard such a wonderful name?"

"Is Pappa still with him?" sixteen-year-old Gunda asked.

"*Ja,* I think so."

Thea, seventeen and the prettiest of all the Linberg sisters, shook her head. "He could not possibly be more handsome than Karl." Immediately, her eyes filled with tears and her expression turned forlorn. "I should have refused to leave Jönköping. I should have told Pappa I would not go."

Inga laid a comforting hand on her sister's shoulder. "I am sure Karl will find a way to come to America, Thea," she whispered. "You will see."

"Of course he will," Thea said with a sniff. "He loves me."

Ignoring Thea, fifteen-year-old Astrid asked Kirsten, "Are you certain you overheard his name right? Are you certain he has never been to Pappa's church?"

Seated on the end of the bed, Gunda nudged Kirsten's foot. "Why did you not talk to him *before* you went for Pappa? What a goose you are."

Inga had had enough. "Listen to all of you," she said as she rose from her bed. "Gunda is right. You are like a gaggle of geese, clucking and waving your feathers. And you, too, Gunda. Have none of you ever seen a handsome man before? With Mamma out paying calls, did any of you remember Pappa would need someone to serve coffee to his guest?"

Gunda and Astrid jumped to their feet, simultaneously saying, "I will do it."

"No." Inga headed for the door. "You would only embarrass Pappa. You would spend all your time staring at his visitor instead of minding your duty. I will see to it."

There was no further argument. Inga hadn't expected there would be. After all, everyone knew it was her responsibility to act as Pappa's hostess in the absence of their mamma. Everyone knew Inga, the oldest and most levelheaded sister, would always live at home, helping their pappa in his Christian work. It had long been understood by the entire family that she would never marry.

As she descended the narrow staircase, Inga tried to ignore the sudden tightness in her chest. She knew she should gracefully accept her destiny. She was his right hand, Pappa would say. He would be lost without her. She was more sensible than any of her flighty, flirtatious sisters, he often added, and her intelligence should not be wasted. When Pappa said such things, it made Inga ashamed of the secret fears she harbored in her heart: a fear that nothing exciting or unexpected would ever happen to her and a fear that she was unlovable as a woman.

Such fears made her feel guilty, for they were so contrary to the faith she professed. So she pretended they didn't exist. She pretended to be happy and content with who and what she was.

Still, when she looked at Thea or Gunda or Astrid or Kirsten—all of them golden girls, bubbling over with feminine charm, petite, and oh-so-pretty—Inga couldn't help wondering why she had been born so plain, so tall, so thin. She couldn't help wondering what it might have been like to giggle and whisper and flirt, to fuss with her hair and her clothes, to have a young man—like Thea's Karl—try to steal a kiss and proclaim her too pretty to resist.

"Now who is being the goose?" she scolded herself.

And then she stepped into the parlor doorway and saw him, the stranger visiting her father. In that instant before Pappa knew she was there, Inga realized Kirsten had been right. Dirk Bridger was undoubtedly a most handsome man, and her longing to be different became almost tangible.

Perhaps she made a sound, for he looked up. His eyes were dark brown, the darkest brown eyes she had ever seen. The color of Mamma's strong coffee.

"Ah, here is Inga," Pappa said. "Inga is my eldest daughter."

She knew she shouldn't stare. She was acting as silly as Kirsten. But she seemed unable to wrest her gaze from him.

Dirk Bridger stood, and once again, her heart skittered. He was tall, so tall she had to look up at him to maintain eye contact. She couldn't remember the last time that had happened.

Pappa continued, "This is Mr. Bridger. He has come to us for help."

"Help?" she echoed inanely.

Dirk Bridger nodded. "I need a woman to stay at our farm and tend to two little girls and my mother."

"Your mother is ill?" She wondered whether he had a wife. "Yes."

She wished to comfort him, this stranger. Instead, she asked, "How old are your daughters, Mr. Bridger?"

"They aren't my daughters. They're my nieces. Their folks're dead."

Impulsively, Inga turned toward her father and said, "Perhaps I should go with Mr. Bridger."

There was a flicker of surprise on the pastor's face. Then he began stroking his beard, and Inga knew he was giving her suggestion serious consideration. She didn't know why, but she wanted desperately for her father to agree.

"I can't pay much, Miss Linberg," Dirk said. "You should know that up front. And the work'll be hard."

She kept her gaze on her father as she replied, "I am sure whatever you pay would be fair, Mr. Bridger, and I am not afraid of hard work. I am much stronger than I look."

"You probably need to talk this over with your pa before you decide for sure."

She heard Dirk take a couple of steps toward the doorway. "Pappa?" she asked hurriedly.

"*Ja.*" Her father nodded. "You could be a help to the Bridgers, I think."

Inga felt a warm pleasure flood through her. She told herself it was because she was doing a good work for someone in need. But she had helped others in the past and never felt this same elation. Perhaps it would be better not to know why she felt this way.

She turned toward her new employer. "It will only take me a short while to pack my things, Mr. Bridger. Would you like a cup of coffee while you wait? It might brace you for the cold trip back to your farm."

Looking a little surprised, he answered, "Yeah, I guess I wouldn't mind somethin' hot before we head out."

"I will see to it, then."

Dirk stared at the doorway through which Inga Linberg had disappeared. He wasn't sure how it had happened, but it seemed he'd hired himself a housekeeper.

The pastor cleared his throat. "Inga will take good care of your mother and nieces, Mr. Bridger."

Dirk turned around. "I wasn't expectin' to find someone this quick."

"It is surely God's will that brought you here. There is no other woman in my congregation more suitable for this duty than Inga. She is accomplished at running a household. You will find her quite sensible in all her decisions. She will do all she can for you and your family."

"We still didn't talk money."

Olaf shook his head. "When your mother is well, then you may pay Inga what you can. My daughter is not doing this for the wages she will earn. It is no more than her Christian duty to help a neighbor in need."

Great. Just what he needed. A bona fide saint living in his house. Maybe he'd made a mistake, coming here for help.

The rattle of china drew his gaze back to the doorway. A moment later, another Linberg daughter appeared, carrying a tray with cups, saucers, and a delicate china pot, steam drifting up from its spout. Dirk guessed this girl was slightly older than the one who had opened the door for him upon his arrival. Her hair was the same shade of gold, her eyes the same dark blue, her skin porcelain smooth.

"Inga told me to serve coffee, Pappa," she said as she slipped past Dirk, casting a sideways glance at him through thick golden lashes.

"Thank you, Astrid. Just set the tray on the table."

Before Dirk could move, another blond beauty stepped into the room, this one carrying a basket of sweet breads. She blushed as her eyes met with his, then she dropped her gaze to the floor and hurried forward.

"Ah, Gunda, how thoughtful. Mr. Bridger, come have your coffee and something to eat. You have a long journey back to your farm."

Dirk had just sat down as instructed when two more sisters appeared.

"Is it true, Pappa?" the girl who had let him into the house asked. "Is Inga really going away?"

"It is true, Kirsten," the pastor replied. "But not so very far we won't be able to see her on Sundays. Mr. Bridger, allow me to introduce you to my other daughters, who, it seems, are plagued by curiosity to the point of forgetting their manners."

Dirk again rose from the sofa, thinking that he'd never been in the same room with so many lovely females. Not even in that saloon in Montana. And these were unmistakably sisters, from the color of their hair and eyes to their petite and very feminine figures.

"This is Thea," Olaf Linberg continued, pausing after each name, "Gunda, Astrid, and Kirsten. My dears, say hello to Mr. Bridger."

They did so in unison. *"Goddag."*

"Pleased to meet all of you," he replied with a nod and a smile.

"May I pour your coffee?" Astrid reached for the china pot.

Gunda held up the basket. "And some bread, *Herr* Bridger?"

He opened his mouth to answer but was once again interrupted, this time by the return of Inga.

"I am ready, Pappa."

Dirk was immediately struck by how different she was from her younger sisters. Where their hair was golden blond, hers was as pale as wheat at harvest time. Where their eyes were dark blue, hers were the light blue of a robin's eggs. Where they were small and shapely, she was tall and reedlike. They were all sparkling smiles and innocent flirtation. Inga was ...

Inga was not.

And something in the way she was watching Dirk told him she knew what he was thinking.

He cleared his throat as he turned toward the pastor. "We'd best be on our way, sir. I've got plenty of chores waiting back at the farm."

"Of course." Olaf rose and walked to where Inga stood near the door. He put his hands on her shoulders. "We will miss you, *dotter.*"

"And I will miss you, Pappa," she whispered. "Give Mamma my love. I will see you all on Sundays."

Her father kissed her cheek. Then he turned to look at Dirk. "Mr. Bridger, I am entrusting Inga to you. I expect you will not abuse that trust."

Dirk understood the man's meaning. He could have told him he had no interest in taking any liberties with his daughter. Not with any of them. Not even the ones who had cast flirtatious glances in his direction. And certainly not the one who was coming with him because she deemed it her duty.

"I'll see she comes to no harm, Reverend Linberg," he answered.

In her heart, Inga heard what Dirk Bridger hadn't said as clearly as what he had. As always, she schooled her expression not to reveal her hurt. To do so would change nothing. It would not make her pretty or sure of herself.

She moved her gaze to her sisters. "Good-bye."

"Godspeed, Inga," Gunda said softly, offering an encouraging smile.

Inga gave each of her sisters a hug, then picked up her portmanteau and valise and said, "I am ready, Mr. Bridger."

A few minutes later, they were seated in his wagon and driving away from the parsonage. Inga stared at the road ahead of them, her hands tucked into the muffler her mother had made two winters ago.

She wondered again what had possessed her to volunteer to go with this man. She had never been the impulsive sort like her sisters. Perhaps she'd done it because, just as she'd feared on the day they'd arrived in America, her life had settled into a familiar routine, and this was her chance to alter it a bit. She wondered if that was a good thing.

"Tell me about your nieces, Mr. Bridger?" she inquired softly.

"Martha's five. Suzanne's three. They're good girls. Won't cause you more trouble than most young'uns, I reckon."

"How did their parents die?"

His frown deepened. Bitterness darkened his eyes, and his shoulders seemed burdened by the weight of the world. "John,

my brother, and Margaret were comin' back from Chicago.
They were crossin' a river on a ferry when it capsized in a
storm. The river was runnin' high from all the rain. Most folks
on board were lost."

What about you, Mr. Bridger? Were you lost, too?

He glanced at her, as if he'd heard her silent question, and
his eyes somehow answered her. Yes, they seemed to say, he'd
been lost, too.

There were more questions she wanted to ask, but she
sensed he didn't want her questions, and discretion won over
curiosity.

Lapsing into silence, she stared across the farmland. Iowa
was not like Sweden. Her native land was a country of lush
emerald forests and clear, cold lakes. Iowa was a prairie, sometimes flat, sometimes rolling. While the river valley to the west
was heavily wooded, here there were only the trees that farmers had planted for windbreaks. Most of the ground was under
cultivation, trees giving way to crops.

Still, despite the differences, she had grown fond of this
new land and its people. Uppsala, Iowa—and much of the rest
of the county—had been settled by Swedes who were hungry
for land of their own. They had immigrated to America,
worked hard, and prospered. Those in town had thriving busi-
nesses. They had built their church and brought a minister to
Uppsala to shepherd them. They had remembered the tradi-
tions of their native land, but had made themselves a part of
their new country as well.

There were others, of course. Like Dirk Bridger. He wasn't
from Sweden nor did he or his family attend the
Prärieblomman Lutheran Church as did nearly everyone else
in this part of the county. And because of that, Inga could have
gone her entire life without ever making his acquaintance.

Surreptitiously, she glanced his way again, studying his profile. He was, indeed, as handsome as she'd first thought him.

He had a farmer's face, the skin darkened by sun and wind. She guessed he was close to his thirtieth year. The corners of his eyes and mouth were crinkled with lines that long days and many worries—not age—had etched there. His thick hair, neatly trimmed, was dark brown, like his eyes. His clean-shaven jaw suggested determination and a strength of character that appealed to her.

Somewhere, deep in her heart, she believed she would have regretted not knowing him. She didn't understand why, and she chose not to analyze the feeling but simply to acknowledge that it was true.

His head turned and their eyes met, their gazes held. Then one of his eyebrows rose slightly, and he asked, "Why did you do this, Miss Linberg? Come to work for me, I mean."

"I do not know, Mr. Bridger. Your mother is very ill. *Ja?*"

His expression hardened. "Yeah."

"Then we must pray she will get well soon."

"Yeah," he said as he looked forward again. "Right."

The impulse to reach out, touch his arm, assure him prayers could make a difference was nearly irresistible.

As if to keep her from giving into her instincts, he said, "Your English is good, Miss Linberg. You been in America long?"

"Only eight months. But Pappa always believed in education for his daughters. I learned English when I was but five years old, as did all my sisters."

Dirk nodded, as if considering what she was saying, but Inga suspected his thoughts had drifted away before she'd even opened her mouth. He didn't ask any more questions, and she didn't offer any more information.

Instead, they continued the journey in silence.

~Two

Hattie Bridger saw the wagon while it was still some distance down the road. It was none too soon, she thought.

Martha did her best to look after Suzanne, but there was little that could control the rambunctious three-year-old when she was in one of her moods. Today had been one of those days, and Hattie was exhausted.

When she realized her son was not alone in the wagon, she sagged onto a nearby chair and uttered a soft, "Thank the good Lord. He's found someone."

"It's Uncle Dirk!" Martha exclaimed.

Suzanne ran over to the window. "Unca Dirk! Unca Dirk!" she echoed as she hopped up and down, then raced for the front door.

"Suzanne!" Hattie cried, but the child was already outside before she could rise from the chair. "Martha, get your sister. Quick! And put your coat on," she added hastily as she brushed aside the window curtain to see where the littlest one had gone.

Suzanne's chubby legs carried her like lightning right toward the big workhorses pulling the wagon. It was amazing how fast she could move into the path of danger. Hattie's heart caught in her throat.

Thankfully, Dirk saw Suzanne and drew back on the reins. Then he shouted something at the child that caused her to stop in her tracks. The next moment, Martha caught up with her, grabbed hold of one of Suzanne's long braids, and yanked her out of the wagon's way. Even with the door closed, Hattie could hear Suzanne's sharp wails of protest.

Oh, mercy. This was not a very good beginning. The children were acting like a couple of hooligans.

But instead of demanding Dirk take her straight back to town, the woman climbed down from the wagon seat and walked toward Martha and the screaming Suzanne. She was wearing a heavy coat and her head was wrapped in a thick knit scarf, hiding much of her face from view. Hattie couldn't tell how old she was, but she walked with a long, easy stride. When she reached the girls, she knelt down so that she was at eye level with them. After a moment, Martha nodded, then glanced over her shoulder toward the house. Suzanne never stopped shrieking her rage.

Rising from the chair, Hattie grabbed her coat from the rack and threw it over her shoulders, then opened the door and stepped out onto the front porch. With one hand, she shaded her eyes against the sun and winter wind.

"Please, child," she whispered. "Please be good just long enough for her t'get to know you."

Miraculously, Suzanne quieted, and a moment later, the woman took hold of the youngster's hand and started toward the house, Martha leading the way. When she was close enough for Hattie to see her face, the young woman—for Hattie could see now that she was young—offered a shy smile.

"Goddag."

"Hello."

"I am Inga Linberg." She tipped her head to one side. "And this must be Suzanne?"

"Sure is," Hattie answered, then asked a question of her own. "You the pastor's daughter?"

"*Ja*, his eldest. I hope you do not mind. I gave the young ones a sweet. I thought it might make our first meeting easier."

Hattie could see now that both children had something in their mouths and were rolling the candies with their tongues like cows chewing their cuds. "Don't mind at all. I was wonderin' what shut Suzanne up so quick-like. She's been into mischief all day."

"I have four younger sisters. I know how they can be."

"Ah." Hattie nodded. "Come inside 'fore we catch our death, and we'll get to know one another. I take it you've come to stay with us a spell."

"*Ja*, if you want me to stay."

She chuckled dryly. "Oh, we want you all right."

Hattie didn't say so, but right now she'd be tempted to let the devil himself into her house if it meant she could get a bit of rest.

—

An hour later, with Hattie lying down for a nap and Suzanne doing the same, Inga stood in the large, airy kitchen with Martha. Despite the icy wind buffeting the Bridger house, this room seemed warm and friendly. It wasn't just the fire burning in the stove. It had more to do with the white lace curtains framing the three windows and the yellow gingham tablecloth covering the table. She wondered if it was Hattie or her daughter-in-law who had made them.

"D'ya know how to cook?" Martha asked with a fair amount of skepticism, interrupting Inga's musings.

"*Ja*." She smiled as she glanced down at the child. "My mamma taught me when I was no more than your age. You are five, *ja*?"

"I'll be six come January."

"So old already? And what have you learned to cook? Maybe you make pancakes for your uncle and grandmamma. *Ja*?"

Martha frowned, causing the freckles across the bridge of her nose to blend together. "Grandma doesn't let me be 'round the stove. She says I might get burned."

"But you can do other things. Come. Show me the root cellar. We do not want your uncle returning and finding nothing to eat."

"Oh, he won't be in for a long time yet. Lotsa chores t'do." Martha opened the cellar door, then looked over her shoulder. "You ever lived on a farm?"

"*Nej.*" Inga picked up the lamp on the table and followed after the girl. "We have always lived in town."

"In Uppsala?"

They started down the steep steps into the cellar.

"*Nej,*" Inga replied again. "I grew up in Sweden. We have been in America only a short while."

"You like it here?"

"*Ja,* very much."

Martha stopped at the bottom of the stairs. "You gonna be Uncle Dirk's wife?"

Dumbfounded, Inga couldn't form a reply.

"Grandma says he needs one."

Swallowing, she said, "I did not come to be your uncle's wife. I am here to help care for your grandmamma and you and your sister."

Martha seemed to forget her question as quickly as she'd asked it, but it lingered in Inga's mind as she selected potatoes, onions, and carrots for their supper.

You gonna be Uncle Dirk's wife?

What would it be like, she wondered, to be married? To spend every day of her life preparing meals in a bright kitchen like the one upstairs? To listen for a man's footsteps as he returned from his chores, his broad shoulders wearied from his hard labors?

As she climbed the stairs, Martha in front of her, she thought of her shipboard friend, Beth Wellington. Only her name wasn't Wellington any longer. Beth had a husband now. Beth had said she would never marry, but now she was Mrs. Steele, and in May, she would have a child of her own.

Perhaps . . .

Nej, Inga mentally chided herself before the wishful thought could even form. She shouldn't hope for such a thing to happen to her. There was one enormous difference between Inga and her friend. Beth was beautiful. Extraordinarily so. She had been sought after in England. Aboard ship, she had drawn more than a few looks of interest. It was no wonder she'd married so soon after her arrival in Montana. What man wouldn't want a woman like Beth?

Inga, in contrast, was not beautiful. Her face was no more than ordinary, and when compared to her pretty sisters or the exquisite Beth, she was rendered plain. She was also much too tall for most men's liking. Pappa said she could be too headstrong and willful—not the most feminine of qualities—and her sisters said she was much too forthright and sensible for her own good. They told her she needed to learn to flatter and flirt.

She gave her head a small shake as she set the vegetables on the counter. This was unlike her, having such thoughts, and she didn't much care for them. Long ago, she had learned to accept herself the way she was. She wasn't going to start wishing for the moon now.

With more vigor than required, she primed the pump, then filled the sink with water. Glancing over her shoulder, she asked Martha, "Do you have a stool to stand on?"

"Yeah." She pointed. "Over there."

"If you bring it here, you could help me wash the vegetables."

Martha immediately did so, carrying the small step stool over to the sink and setting it on the floor beside Inga. As she stood on it, she looked up and said, "You're real tall for a girl, ain'tcha?"

"*Ja.*"

"My ma was real purty. She had red hair just like mine and Suzanne's."

Inga paused and looked down at the child. "Do you remember your mamma?"

Martha nodded, then tears suddenly swam before her eyes as she shook her head. "Not really," she whispered.

Inga's heart squeezed painfully.

"I got a picture of her and Pa, but it don't show that her hair's red." She sniffed. "I sure wish it did."

"It must have been very beautiful," Inga said as she lightly touched Martha's hair, "if it was like yours."

"You s'pose I'm awful 'cause I can't remember her better than I do?"

Inga cupped Martha's cheek with one hand and leaned toward her. "*Nej,* I do not think so. I believe such things are meant to fade so our hearts do not hurt so much. It is enough to remember that you loved your mamma and pappa."

Unnoticed, Dirk watched from the dim hallway. He saw Inga tenderly caress Martha's cheek and heard her comfort the child with words. He was grateful, for he never knew what to do or say in these situations. He always felt helpless. Too often he realized he was a miserable substitute for their father.

Inga gave Martha a peck on the cheek, then straightened and returned to her work. Martha quickly did the same, her tears forgotten, the look of sorrow erased from her face. It seemed this minister's daughter knew something about children.

During the trip back to the farm, Dirk had silently questioned the wisdom of bringing her here. Inga didn't look strong enough to handle the work that would be required of her. But Ma seemed to have taken to her right off, and so had the children. He reckoned that was all that mattered.

"I wonder if . . ." Inga began as she turned toward the table. Her voice died when she saw Dirk standing in the shadows. "Oh . . . Mr. Bridger . . . I did not hear you."

"Just came in to check on Ma."

"She is asleep."

"Yeah. I know. I already looked in."

Inga touched his niece's shoulder. "Martha and I are preparing supper."

"So I see."

For just a moment, he felt warm inside. Almost content. It was an odd, unexpected sensation, a foreign one.

A blush rose in Inga's cheeks as he continued to stare at her. "Is there something you needed, Mr. Bridger?"

He gave his head a quick shake, and the feeling fled. "No." He spun on his heel and strode down the hall.

Cold air slammed into him as he stepped outside. He shivered and hunched inside his coat. *Blast!* How he hated this weather! How he hated this farm! He wasn't meant to be here, stuck in this life.

He stepped off the porch and headed toward the barn, running over the chores he still needed to finish before milking time. An endless list of chores, because no matter how much he got done, there would be other things added to the list tomorrow. And the next day. And the next. And the next . . .

Feelings of guilt returned. This farm had been his brother's dream. Heaven only knew why. As far as Dirk was concerned, no man in his right mind would want to be a dairy farmer. But John had loved everything about this life. He'd put everything he had into it. He had planned on staying right here with Margaret and their daughters. He had wanted more children.

He'd hoped for a son—or perhaps several sons—who would work the farm with him and inherit it one day.

Now John was dead. There would be no sons, no more children. His life had ended while he was yet a young man, and his dreams had ended with him.

Inside the barn, Dirk sank onto a bale of straw, cursing softly. His dreams had ended, too, with John's death, and it seemed the bitterness grew sharper with each passing month. And the bitterness only served to increase his guilt. After all, he was alive and his brother was dead. He would only have to stay until the girls were raised, then he could leave. John didn't have any more chances.

But Suzanne wasn't yet four. It could be another fourteen or fifteen years before he could leave Iowa. He would be in his forties by then. Who was he kidding? He'd be too old to start life over again. The world was changing with amazing swiftness. Things would be different in fifteen years. It would be the twentieth century by then!

He leaned forward and rested his forehead in his hands, his elbows braced on his thighs. He was a lousy son, a lousy brother, a lousy uncle. His ma was ailing, and his nieces needed love and attention, and all he could think about were the things he'd wanted, the places he'd counted on seeing—the Orient, the Swiss Alps, the jungles of darkest Africa—wherever the winds of chance might have blown him.

"Mr. Bridger?"

He straightened abruptly, surprised Inga had entered the barn without his hearing the door open.

"I brought you some coffee and a sandwich. I thought you might need something, since supper will be late."

He wasn't hungry, but he did recognize her thoughtfulness. "Thanks." He rose to his feet and watched as she walked toward him, her movements fluid and willowy, like a tree swaying in a gentle breeze.

It had been a long time since he'd had the opportunity or the energy to notice the way a woman moved. It surprised him that he'd noticed Inga Linberg. His preference had always run toward dark-haired women with eyes to match. Fiery little things like the gal in Montana he'd been with the night before he received the telegram about John. Women with a thirst for life who didn't want to tie a man down. Certainly not the saintly daughter of some minister.

He met Inga's gaze as she stopped in front of him, and once again he suspected she knew exactly what he'd been thinking. He didn't like the way that made him feel either. But then, it wasn't his fault she'd been born tall and fair-haired, not to mention a minister's daughter. And even if she were his type, he wouldn't be interested. He didn't want or need any more obligations or complications in his life.

"It is just cold beef, Mr. Bridger." She handed him the tray, her gaze unwavering, her posture straight and her head held high and proud.

"Thanks."

"Is there anything particular you would like me to do before supper is ready?"

"No."

"Very well." She turned to go.

"Miss Linberg?"

She looked back at him. *"Ja?"*

"Thanks for comin' to help us."

Her smile was tender, and it softened the sharp angles of her face. *"Ingen orsak."* Apparently remembering herself, she repeated the words in English. "You are welcome, Mr. Bridger." Then she walked out of the barn with the same long, sure steps that had carried her into it.

Wednesday, December 1, 1897
Uppsala, Iowa

My dear Beth,

I received your letter of one month ago and was delighted with your joyous news, as were my parents and sisters. I pray you will have an easy confinement.

I write to you with some surprising news of my own. I am not living at the parsonage at present. I have taken employment in the home of a dairy farmer, caring for his widowed mother, who is ill, and his young nieces, who lost their parents in an accident nearly two years ago. I had not had the opportunity to meet Mr. Bridger before this morning as he and his family do not attend Pappa's church.

While you came to America knowing you would be a teacher in Montana, I have never imagined that I should be employed in any capacity other than as Pappa's assistant. The decision to take employment surprised everyone, including me. I am certain my sisters never expected me to leave home, even in a temporary manner.

My employer seems an unhappy man, though I suppose that is not surprising, given the hardship the family has endured. Yet that he loves his mother and his nieces is evident. I feel he has a great capacity for kindness within him.

Hattie Bridger, his mother, is quite easy to like. I knew this the moment I met her. Although she does not say so, I suspect she suffers great pain for she moves with care and uncertain steps. But mostly it is weariness and worry I see in her face.

Not that anyone wouldn't be wearied by her two granddaughters. Martha, who is nearly six, is a darling child, inquisitive and bright beyond her years. I think her mamma's absence has left an emptiness in her heart that is hard to fill. I shall do my best to do so as long as I am able. Suzanne, who will celebrate her fourth birthday in January, is like all children her age. Active and imaginative. This I have already learned in just one day with the family. I think I shall have my hands full with little Suzanne, but I also think I shall grow to love her and her sister in no time at all.

I have begun work on your baby's quilt. I hope to have it finished soon so you might receive it before the birth. I think you shall be pleased with it, for I have tried to tell the story of how you came to America, met Mr. Steele, and learned to love him. I have used not only what you told me on board the ship but your letters from Montana to create the quilt.

I think of you and our friend Mary so often, remembering the weeks we were together with great fondness.

You may write to me in care of the Bridger Farm, General Delivery, Uppsala, Iowa.

Affectionately,
Inga Linberg

~Three

Inga awakened to the sound of creaking boards. At first she thought it was only the never-ending wind continuing to assault the house. Then, as she grew more alert, she realized it was footsteps on the stairs she had heard.

"Äsch!" she muttered as she tossed aside the thick covering of blankets and sat up. How could she have overslept her first morning here? What would Dirk Bridger think of her?

Rising from the bed, she smacked her shin against a chair. She winced and swallowed a groan. To make matters worse, the bedroom was icy cold. Gooseflesh puckered on her arms and legs, and her teeth began to chatter before she could even light the lamp.

She made hasty work of her morning ablutions, dressing quickly and brushing her hair into a simple bun at the nape. Then, still shivering from the cold, she left her bedroom and hurried down the stairs.

A lamp burned brightly in the kitchen, and its light spilled into the hall, serving as a beacon for Inga. When she reached the doorway, she paused and looked about the room. Much to her relief and delight, blessed warmth emanated from the wood stove on the far wall. A pot gurgled and boiled on top of the stove, and already the enticing scent of brewing coffee was filling the room.

Her employer, with his back toward her, bent down and shoved another piece of wood into the fire. Afterward, he closed the black iron door, straightened, and turned. Stubble darkened his jaw and chin, his hair was mussed, and sleepiness lingered in his brown eyes. But none of it lessened his dark good looks.

All of this Inga realized in the instant before he noticed her standing there.

Dirk cocked an eyebrow. "You're an early riser, I see, Miss Linberg."

"Only reluctantly, Mr. Bridger," she answered honestly. She entered the kitchen and stepped over to the stove. "I am sorry not to have your breakfast ready."

He stifled a yawn, then grunted and said, "Too early to eat. It's coffee I want at this time of day, and I can fix that myself." He jerked his head toward the speckled blue pot on the stove. "Always do."

Inga felt a sudden shyness as she looked into his eyes, realizing how close she was standing to him in her quest for warmth from the fire. Her heart did a funny little dance in her chest, and her mouth felt as dry as cotton.

"You'll get used to how we do things around here quick enough, I reckon. Just ask Ma if you got questions." He glanced once again at the coffee pot, which continued to rattle and shake as the water boiled inside.

Released from his gaze, Inga took a step backward, trying to still her racing pulse. She was surprised and more than a little unnerved by the way she reacted whenever she was near Dirk Bridger. One would think she was a silly schoolgirl instead of a mature woman of twenty-two years.

Dirk looked over his shoulder. "Join me?" he asked, lifting the pot with a towel around the handle.

She nodded. *"Ja. Tack."* She gave her head a small shake, trying to clear her thoughts, then repeated in English, "Thank you."

Dirk filled two mugs with coffee and carried them both to the table. "Sit here," he said as he pulled out a chair. "It's closest to the stove. You'll be warm in no time."

She forced a smile, feeling awkward that he had guessed her discomfort.

"House is always plenty cold when I first get up." He walked around the table. "But cows don't wait to be milked, no matter the weather." He pulled out his own chair and sat down.

Inga did the same. Then she wrapped her hands around the mug and stared at the steam rising from the dark liquid within. Her sense of awkwardness increased as silence filled the room. She couldn't think of a time when she'd been alone like this with a man—except her pappa, of course. It seemed somehow . . . intimate, the two of them seated at the kitchen table when the sun had yet to rise.

"Ma's mighty grateful to have you here," Dirk said, breaking the silence. "So am I."

She felt a tiny skip in her heart. "I hope I will be of help to you all."

"Already have been. Ma looked more rested at supper last night than I've seen her in a long spell." He took a sip of coffee, then added, "You're a good cook, too."

"Thank you." She lowered her gaze to the center of the table, feeling that wretched shyness again, along with a flush of pleasure.

Outside, the wind whistled around the corners of the house. Here in the kitchen, there was only the friendly sound of a crackling fire in the stove.

Inga lifted her gaze just enough to look at Dirk's hands. Strong hands. Work-worn and callused. The hands of a man who labored long hours to provide for his family. Hands that could cradle little Suzanne with tenderness as he carried her, sleeping, to her bed as Inga had seen Dirk do last night.

She had a sudden vision of those same hands touching her arm. She could almost feel the warmth of them, pressed against the cotton fabric of her sleeve.

What might it be like . . .

She closed her eyes and took another drink of the strong, dark brew. What fanciful thoughts! And Pappa had always called her the sensible one. Surely, if her father knew what she was thinking, he would no longer believe she had any sense at all.

"Well . . ." Dirk set down his mug, scooted the chair back from the table, then stood. "Better see to the milkin' 'fore it gets any later."

Inga glanced up, her heart quickening as she looked him full in the face again. "You will want breakfast when you return, Mr. Bridger. *Ja?*"

"Yes, ma'am. I sure will." Then without another word, he turned on his heel and headed out of the kitchen.

—

"Poor Inga," Gunda said as she smoothed the quilt her sister had made. "She will be miserable, being away from home. Pappa should have sent me to work for Mr. Bridger."

"You?" Thea straightened from making her own bed and stared at Gunda. "Pappa would never be so foolish."

"And why *not* me?"

"Because, Gunda, you flirt with every male over the age of fifteen. That is why."

"I do not!"

Thea laughed. "Of course you do. Ask anyone."

"And *you* don't?" Gunda plopped herself down on the edge of her bed. "Besides, no one could have blamed me if I flirted a little with *Herr* Bridger. He really is *so* handsome."

"Perhaps." Thea turned toward the window, staring out at the lead gray skies. In her mind, she imagined Karl, saw his sun-gold hair and icy blue eyes and pale, close-trimmed beard. No one would ever be as handsome as Karl Gustav. She knew she would feel that way until her dying day. But Karl was in Sweden and Thea was in America, and nothing had ever seemed as hopeless in her seventeen years as her love for Karl.

"You're wishing you'd run off with Karl, aren't you?"

Thea glanced over her shoulder. *"Ja."* She whispered the reply, as if afraid her father would hear.

"Karl promised he would come."

"Of course he will come. But it will take him so long to save enough for the passage. It could be years." It was all so unfair. Why hadn't her pappa understood?

Gunda ran a brush over her hair. "At least Karl loves you. It could be worse."

"Ja, it could be worse. I could be an old maid like Inga." As soon as the words were out of her mouth, she couldn't help laughing at the ridiculous nature of the statement. She was the prettiest of all the Linberg sisters. She could have had her pick of any of the young men in Jönköping or in Uppsala.

"Shame on you, Thea. That was a very unkind thing to say."

Thea harrumphed as she lay down on her sister's just-made bed, her hands cupped behind her head. "Perhaps, but it is true, and you and I both know it."

Gunda nodded. As much as they loved their oldest sister, they both knew there had never been a boy in Jönköping who had asked to pay calls on her. All the boys and young men had come to see the younger Linberg sisters, never Inga.

"It's because Inga has never shown any interest in marriage," Gunda offered in her sister's defense. "She's too involved in helping Pappa with his work and acting like a second mother to the rest of us. Besides, she wouldn't know how to catch a man." After a moment's pause, she grinned. "Now if it were me working for *Herr* Bridger, I would have myself a husband in no time."

Thea thought about chiding her sister but, instead, got up and returned to the window. What would be the point, after all? There was little danger of Gunda making a fool of herself over Dirk Bridger. The man's farm was a long way from Uppsala, and since he didn't attend Pappa's church, their paths weren't likely to cross any time soon. Being the silly coquette she was, Gunda would forget him as soon as she was around some other eligible male.

If only Thea could as easily quit thinking about Karl. Perhaps then she wouldn't feel this constant ache in her chest or this overwhelming sadness that made it such an effort to smile. If only Pappa had let her marry Karl and stay in Sweden. But Pappa had said she was too young to marry and that Karl, only seventeen at the time, could not provide for her, being the youngest of six sons with nothing to inherit.

"If he loves you as he says," Pappa had said the night she and Karl had gone to him, asking for his permission to marry, "he will find a way to come to America. True love is not diminished by distance."

That had been almost a year ago. It seemed even longer, and Thea felt eons older. She believed Pappa had thought she would forget Karl, but she hadn't. She would never forget Karl. She would die first. Like Shakespeare's Juliet, she would die before she would forget her Romeo, her Karl.

It was all so terribly tragic and romantic.

By the time Dirk had finished with the milking, he'd cursed every cow in the barn, several of the cats who made their home in the loft—and who constantly pestered him for a squirt of milk—and one old plow horse that the girls called Chief. Chief, who had done nothing wrong in particular that morning, was included for good measure.

A bitter wind slammed into Dirk as he stepped out of the barn, a bucket of milk in each hand. He leaned into it and headed toward the back door, feeling tired already even though the day had just begun. He purposely didn't look at the house. He knew if he did he would see at least a dozen things that needed repairs. Like the shutter at his mother's bedroom window that had a loose hinge or the porch banister that needed to be replaced or . . .

He muttered an oath—the sort his mother had washed his mouth out with soap for when he was a boy. Come to think of it, if she'd heard what he'd said, she'd probably threaten to do it again.

When he opened the door into the kitchen, laughter spilled through it, along with warmth from the fire and the tempting odors of fried eggs and sausage. He lifted his gaze as he kicked the toe of one boot against the step, knocking off straw and mud. His glance took in both of his nieces and his mother, seated around the table, and Inga Linberg standing near the stove, dishing breakfast onto a large platter.

"Here's Dirk," Hattie said, still smiling from whatever had caused them all to laugh moments before. There were patches of color on her cheeks, and her eyes twinkled with merriment.

Dirk hadn't seen her looking like this in more than a year.

He stepped inside, closing the door behind him, then set the buckets of milk on the nearby counter. "Hope you haven't been waitin' on me."

"*Nej,*" Inga replied. "Your breakfast is only now ready. Come and eat while it is hot."

Dirk nodded. "I'll wash up."

"Inga was tellin' us about her trip to America," his mother said. "I can't imagine goin' so far from home, myself."

He shoved his hands into a pail of sudsy water in the sink, thinking, *I can.*

"Pappa says there's much of our seagoing ancestors in me." Inga set the platter in the center of the kitchen table. "I thought the voyage was wonderful, but my mother and sisters suffered from seasickness, especially when there were storms."

Dirk grabbed a towel and dried his hands. "I've never seen the ocean myself, but I've been to the Rocky Mountains." He turned. "If you haven't seen 'em, you can't imagine 'em. Air so thin at the top a man can't scarcely breathe. Trees like nothin' in Iowa. Streams so fresh and cold they'll make your teeth chatter."

"You'll go back some day, son," Hattie said softly. All remnants of her smile vanished, and her gaze filled with sorrow.

"Doesn't matter, Ma." He pulled out his chair from the table and sat down. "I've been there once."

He wished he'd kept his mouth shut. It didn't serve any purpose, thinking about his brief time out West, except to make him want what he couldn't have and make his ma feel responsible for it. He would have thought, after two years, he'd be used to being here in Iowa, that he would've accepted his lot in life. The world was full of people who never made it more than a few miles in any direction from the place where they were born. He'd at least done more than that. He ought to be thankful for it.

"Mr. Bridger?"

He looked at Inga. "Yeah?"

"Perhaps this afternoon you would be kind enough to show me around the farm."

"Sure. Whenever you want."

After Hattie said the blessing, the Bridger family and their new housekeeper ate in relative peace for about ten minutes. Dirk got to hear about the immigration depot on Ellis Island and about Inga's first impression of New York City. Despite himself, he was interested in hearing it, even though listening made him yearn for the same type of experiences.

Then Suzanne spilled her milk and immediately began to cry. Quickly, Inga sopped up the liquid with a towel while crooning words of reassurance to the girl. As if jealous of the attention her younger sister was receiving, Martha knocked her plate on the floor, splattering eggs and sausage everywhere. Her face turned red, and her eyes filled with tears as she bit her lower lip. Suzanne's wails increased in volume.

Dirk wolfed down his last few bites, then mumbled, "I'd better get back to the chores," and rushed out of the house into the cold, preferring the frigid conditions outside to the current indoor chaos.

Inga glanced up as the door slammed closed.

"He's still not used to children," Hattie said, sounding apologetic.

Inga shrugged, ignoring the disappointment his departure caused as she lifted Suzanne into her arms. "Pappa always hid in his study when things got too noisy for him." She swayed and shushed and stroked the child's back with one hand. As Suzanne began to quiet, Inga kissed the tip of her nose. "I suppose your uncle is not so different from my pappa. What do you think, *prinsessa?* Do you think he is hiding like my pappa did when my sisters and I made too much noise?"

Suzanne stuck out her bottom lip as she drew in tiny gasps of breath.

Inga looked down at Martha. "What do you think, *kattunge?*"

Martha frowned. "What's that mean?"

"*Kattunge?* It means kitten." She set Suzanne back on her chair, then retrieved the broom and swept up the spilled food.

"What'dja call me that for?" Martha persisted.

Inga smiled. "It is habit, I suppose. I had pet names for each of my sisters when they were little." She paused and met Martha's gaze. "Do you mind?"

Sounding a lot like her uncle, the girl answered, "Don't reckon I do." She actually looked pleased as she slid off her chair and helped Inga clear the breakfast dishes from the table.

"You've a way with children, Miss Linberg," Hattie commented.

The words gladdened Inga more than she'd have thought they would. But her pleasure was fleeting. When she looked at Hattie Bridger, she was alarmed by the sudden pallor of the older woman's face.

As if she'd read Inga's thoughts, Hattie rose from her chair, saying, "I'd best lie down for a spell. I'm feelin' a bit peaked."

"Do you need—"

Hattie waved away her offer of help before she could make it. "I'll be fine now that we've got you t'look after the young'uns. Don't worry 'bout me none."

But her footsteps were shuffling as she made her way out of the kitchen, and Inga continued to worry. She knew Hattie wasn't well. That was, after all, why she had come here—because Hattie was no longer strong enough to care for herself and her family. But still . . .

Inga gave her head a quick shake. She was borrowing trouble. A nap and some time away from the commotion of young children would likely have Hattie feeling refreshed and strong once again. Inga would check on her later. For now, there was much to be done.

First, she washed the breakfast dishes, and when she was finished, she heated more water on the stove and filled the washtub. After the children were bathed and dressed in clean clothes, she sat them down on a blanket near the stove so their hair would dry quickly.

At midmorning, she took a cup of hot tea to Hattie. The woman apologized profusely for her weakness. Inga insisted she remain in bed the rest of the day, and Hattie did not seem inclined to argue with her.

To keep them occupied, Inga asked the girls to sort the quilting scraps she had brought with her from home into separate piles, depending upon color. She was certain she would have to reorganize them again at another time, but the purpose was to keep the children quietly occupied so their grandmother could sleep.

Once Martha and Suzanne understood what was expected of them, Inga returned to the kitchen, filled a pail with water, and began giving the room a thorough cleaning, something she suspected it hadn't had in many months. Time fled, and before she knew it, she heard the stomping of boots just before the back door opened and Dirk reentered the house.

Inga, scrubbing the floor on her hands and knees, felt a sting of embarrassment. She could feel rings of perspiration under her arms and a stripe of moisture along her spine. Her skirt was wet from the wash water. She sat back on her heels and swept her straggling hair from her face, knowing she must look a sight.

But despite whatever work he'd been doing, despite the redness of his cheeks from the cold winter air and the wildness of his windblown hair, Dirk Bridger looked even more handsome than she'd thought him this morning.

She blushed and could only hope and pray he would mistakenly think it was caused by heat from the stove.

"Where is everybody?" he asked as he shucked off his coat.

"Your mother is lying down. The children are in their room."

He raised an eyebrow, as if doubting the truth of her reply.

Inga dropped the scrub brush into the murky water in the bucket and rose from the floor. Nervously, she ran the palms of her hands down the front of her skirt. "I am afraid I have forgotten the time. I haven't prepared a noon meal."

His gaze swept over the room, but he didn't comment on what he saw or on what she'd said.

He had the most amazing eyes. Rich and dark. Yesterday she had thought them like coffee. Today she thought them more the color of baker's chocolate. They seemed to take in everything around him, yet revealed nothing to others. She wished she knew what lay behind them. She wished she knew what he was thinking.

Her heart began to hammer wildly. Suddenly light-headed, she found it almost impossible to draw a breath. The room seemed far too warm. What was the matter with her? Was she ill? Only illness could explain the odd way she felt.

She turned her back toward Dirk. "I will make your dinner now."

"No hurry. I'll just look in on Ma. See how she's feelin'."

She heard him walking across the kitchen, felt the sudden emptiness of the room the moment he was gone. Her pulse slowed, her breathing became easier, the light-headedness vanished.

Being the sensible sort—just as her pappa expected her to be—Inga could not deny the truth. It wasn't illness she'd been feeling, but an emotional and physical reaction to this man's presence. She knew, of course, that the reaction was absurd. She had always thought her sisters silly when they would giggle and whisper about some boy. That such a thing should happen to her now, at her age, was disconcerting, to say the least.

"Well, it simply must stop," she whispered with conviction as she set about making dinner, foolishly believing she could control the way Dirk Bridger made her feel.

Four

Dirk hadn't been particularly enthusiastic about bringing a stranger into the Bridger home, but after a couple of days, he was forced to admit that Inga Linberg had made a difference. A difference for the better.

The house was cleaner and the meals were tasty. His ma looked more rested than she had in months. He'd actually heard her humming. Even his nieces looked tidy, their curly red hair captured in braids. Come to think of it, little Suzanne seemed less inclined to throw one of her temper tantrums, and Martha smiled more often than before. Funny, he hadn't really thought about the girls' behavior until he'd seen the changes in them.

On Saturday evening, after a supper of fried pork and potato griddle cakes—what Inga called *raggmunkar eller rårakor*— Dirk sat down at the kitchen table with his logbook and financial records. He thought sometimes that he hated this task even more than milking cows in the wee hours of the morning, perhaps because it was obvious to him when he saw how little money they had that he was failing everyone. His brother had managed to make a profit when he was living. Dirk was lucky to break even from year to year.

He didn't know how long he'd been going over the figures and making entries before he became aware of soft voices coming from the living room. He twisted on his chair and looked through the open doorway at the cozy scene.

His mother was in her favorite overstuffed chair, the one closest to the fireplace. Her eyes were closed, but he knew she was awake because she was smiling. Inga sat in the rocking chair John had made for Margaret when she was expecting Martha. A partially completed quilt lay in her lap, and she was taking small stitches in the fabric as she talked to Martha, who was kneeling beside the chair, watching intently. Suzanne lay on the rug near Inga's feet. Unlike her grandmother, she had drifted off to sleep.

"It's sorta like a painting, isn't it?" Martha said.

"*Ja.* A little."

"And you just make it up as you go?"

Inga nodded. "As I go. *Ja.*"

Martha pointed at the quilt. "What's that?"

"It is England. That is where my friend Beth is from."

"Do you s'pose you could make a quilt for me?"

"Martha," Hattie scolded without opening her eyes.

"It is all right, Mrs. Bridger," Inga responded. "I would very much like to make quilts for the children." She set her sewing in her lap and touched Martha's cheek with her left hand. "But I will need to know you better before I can do so. I must know the story I need to tell before I begin. That will take some time."

Curious, Dirk got up and went into the living room.

"Uncle Dirk," Martha said when she saw him, "come look. Miss Inga tells stories with her quilts. See? This one shows the steamship she came to America on. And this one is the train her friend rode to get to Montana. The quilt's for her friend's new baby."

Dirk wasn't much of a judge of such things, but even he could see that Inga's quilting skills were unique. She had used different colors of cloth—carefully cut and layered atop each other—and fancy embroidery to make her pictures. There was a feeling of real movement in each quilt block.

In the first block was a large green and brown island, shaped like England. It was surrounded by a sea of blue fabric, tiny whitecaps embroidered to make the ocean. There was even a small steamship, departing a western port. Inga had captured the detail so perfectly that it was easy to imagine the ship was actually at sea. The second block showed a train rolling across tiny gray tracks, steam belching from the engine's smokestack, tiny faces at the windows of the passenger car.

"Isn't it pretty?" Martha asked.

"Sure is," Dirk replied softly.

Inga glanced up with a hesitant smile, a tint of pink in her ivory cheeks. For an instant, he caught a glimpse of . . .

"Are you finished with your figurin', son?"

Whatever he'd seen in her expression disappeared. Inga dropped her gaze and resumed sewing. With a shake of his head, Dirk turned toward his mother. "Yeah. I'm finished."

Hattie looked at him, and he knew she understood how worried he was. He wished she didn't know. She shouldn't have to worry about money, on top of everything else.

"Well . . ." She pushed herself up from her chair. "I think it's about time I took these tired old bones off to bed." She stepped toward him, laying her hand against his chest. "Don't fret, son," she said softly. "It'll work out. God'll provide. You'll see."

He caught his mother's hand and squeezed it gently, thinking how like parchment her skin felt, how fragile the bones of her fingers. At one time, Hattie Bridger had been a plump woman, but no longer. Now she seemed to be wasting away right before his eyes. If only there was more he could do for her.

She turned from him. "Carry Suzanne up to her bed, will you, son?"

His throat felt tight as he answered, "Sure, Ma."

"Good night, Inga."

"Good night, Mrs. Bridger."

Dirk watched his mother walk to her first floor bedroom and knew real despair. She might look better than she had before Inga Linberg had come to help, but she still wasn't well, still wasn't strong. Dirk wanted to think the doctor's prognosis was wrong, but he knew he was only trying to fool himself. His ma was dying. Dying by inches and trying hard not to let any of them see the pain she was feeling.

"Mr. Bridger?"

He turned, surprised to find Inga standing close behind him.

As their gazes met, mutual understanding passed between them. He saw sympathy in her pale blue eyes, felt it almost like a balm. For just that moment, it seemed the ever-present sense of heaviness lifted from his shoulders.

"I will see if she needs anything," Inga told him.

He nodded, the tightness in his throat returning.

Inga moved passed him. He noted that she, too, was slight of build. But unlike his mother's, Inga Linberg's willowy figure disguised a surprising strength.

Anger sparked suddenly to life. It wasn't fair! His ma was only fifty-seven. She shouldn't look so old. She shouldn't be dying. She should have a long life stretching before her. If she hadn't had to work so hard, trying to hold everything together for her family . . .

He turned around and crossed to the sleeping child on the floor. Frustration made his voice gruffer than he'd intended as he said, "Time for bed, Martha." He bent down and lifted Suzanne into his arms. "Now!"

———

"You needn't fuss over me, Inga," Hattie protested weakly as she sank onto the stool in front of the dresser.

"I want to help, Mrs. Bridger." She pulled back the covers on the bed and fluffed the pillows.

The older woman let out a long sigh. "You have been a godsend, young woman. But what will happen after I'm—" She stopped abruptly.

Inga turned to meet Hattie's gaze in the dressing table mirror. "Mrs. Bridger," she whispered, "you must not worry. Your son will see to everything."

"I can't seem t'help it. We all know I'm dyin'. There's no point in tryin' to deny it. But what's gonna happen to Dirk and the girls when I'm gone? Dear God, what's gonna happen to them?" She covered her face with her hands. She made no sound, but her shoulders shook as she began to cry.

Inga crossed the room and sat on the stool beside Hattie, taking her into her arms as she would have done one of the children. "You must not worry," she crooned. "It will be all right. You must not worry."

It was several minutes before Hattie stilled. Finally, she sat up straight and dried her tears, staring all the while at her reflection. "My son is so unhappy," she said, the sound of a mother's broken heart in her words. "He had such big dreams, and they've all been stripped from him, one by one."

"He does not blame you."

"No." Hattie shook her head. "He doesn't blame me. But all the same, it's killed somethin' inside him, bein' stuck here on this farm. He's dyin' just as sure as I am. If he'd turn to God for help, he might find release. Only he refuses."

Inga felt her own heart breaking as she listened. She longed to comfort this woman. She longed to comfort this woman's son. She hadn't known, when she volunteered to come here, that this family needed so much more than a housekeeper, and she wondered how she could help them in the way they needed most.

Hattie's eyes looked watery. "He was always the dreamer, my Dirk. Always the one wantin' to do other things, go other places. When my husband was alive, Dirk was always tellin' him how much more there was to see in the world than just our farm in Ohio. If his father hadn't taken ill, he'd have been halfway around the world by the time he was eighteen." She drew a ragged breath. "I admit I was hopin' he'd get married and settle down, have himself a family of his own. He was keepin' company with a young widow a few years back, and I thought . . . Well, I thought if he'd just fall in love, maybe it would stop his yearnin' for wanderin'. Maybe he did love her. Maybe she wouldn't have him. I don't know. All I know is, the bitterness is eatin' at him, and he's hurtin' because of it."

"You are tired, Mrs. Bridger. You should be in bed."

"He hates this place, Inga. My, how he hates it. But he's a man of honor, my Dirk, and he'll never shirk his duty. He'll stay here till those girls are grown and married, and by then . . ." Her voice trailed off into silence.

"Wait here," Inga said softly as she rose from the stool. "I will get a stone from the hearth and then help you to bed. You will feel better after a good night's sleep."

"A good night's sleep," the older woman repeated, as if not understanding the meaning.

Silently, Inga prayed for wisdom and words of comfort as she went after the warming stone.

Over the years, she had often accompanied her pappa when he'd gone to pray for the sick and the dying, and she had helped her mamma prepare food to take to distraught families. It wasn't as if she were unacquainted with such situations. Only tonight, the suffering had become personal to her.

By the time she returned to Hattie's bedroom, the woman had already gotten into her bed. Inga placed the heated stone near her feet, then pulled the blankets up and tucked them around her shoulders.

"God bless you," Hattie said, her voice weak.

"And you, Mrs. Bridger."

Hattie's eyelids drifted closed, and within moments, she slept.

Inga sighed, then extinguished the lamp before turning to leave the room. She stopped with a gasp of surprise when she spied Dirk observing her from the doorway, his face obscured in shadows.

When her heart slowed its riotous beating, she said, "She is asleep."

"You've been mighty good to her."

"I have done what I can."

"No, you've done more than that."

She wasn't certain what he meant, but she hadn't an opportunity to ask before he turned and walked away.

⟶

Dirk leaned his forearms on the top rail of the stall and stared at the cow inside. The Jersey was dry now, awaiting the birth of a calf in about six weeks.

He would have liked to let all the cows go dry in the fall and not start milking again until after calving in the spring, the way it used to be done when everything depended upon pasturage and dairymen didn't feed their cows silage and grain throughout the winter months. But his brother had intended this to be a modern dairy farm with all the most recent inventions, and John had gone to great lengths and expense to make it so. Trouble was, he'd invested all his money in the barn and cows and had put nothing into the house or other livestock. There'd been no money left in reserve at the time of his death.

Because of it, his children would go hungry if Dirk didn't sell milk the whole year round.

He closed his eyes and rested his forehead on the back of his hands.

What was he going to do when his ma died? How was he going to run this place and take care of John's daughters?

Maybe he should sell the farm. Except he couldn't do that. This land and house were the only legacy Martha and Suzanne had of their father and mother. If Dirk sold it, he would be betraying the trust his brother had had in him.

The Jersey mooed, and Dirk opened his eyes to look at her. Flower, the girls called the fawn-colored milk cow. The day Dirk had first arrived at the Bridger farm in the winter of 'ninety-six, Flower had gone into labor. There had been a raging blizzard that night with temperatures dropping far below zero, and the birth had been a difficult one. He'd spent the night in the barn, trying to save both cow and calf. That had been his introduction to life on a dairy farm.

And there'd been similar scenes in the twenty-two months he'd lived here. More than he cared to remember. He would probably repeat them countless times before Martha and Suzanne were grown.

He shoved off from the fence, striding toward the barn door. As he stepped outside, he stopped and looked up at the sky. Not a star could be seen because of the clouds hovering low in the sky. There was a nip in the air that told him it would probably snow tonight.

Snow. And he still hadn't repaired that broken runner on the sleigh. He'd have to get to it first thing tomorrow. It wouldn't do for them to be without transportation. Not with his mother ailing.

He started toward the house, mentally ticking off a list of more things he needed to do before the next day was done. Then he glanced up, and his footsteps slowed.

In the glow of the lamplight, he saw Inga's silhouette against the curtains of her upstairs bedroom. She was special, this Swedish minister's daughter. Her sweet spirit had brought something to their home that had been absent too long.

He looked away quickly. Just what he didn't need. To think of Inga as anything other than what she was—the hired help.

Bending into the wind, he headed toward the house.

———

Inga knelt beside her bed—hands clasped, eyes closed, head bowed—and whispered her evening prayers. First she prayed for Hattie Bridger, for an easing of the woman's pain. Next she prayed for Martha and Suzanne, asking God for wisdom and patience that she might be able to give them the love and guidance they needed. Then she lifted Dirk Bridger's name before the Almighty.

But she didn't know exactly what to pray for. Memories of him from the previous three days replayed in her mind. She saw the way he watched his mother and his nieces, understood his worries and concerns. She felt his weariness, his unrest. What words could she say on behalf of such a man?

Finally, she whispered, "Give him peace, Father God. Just let him know peace."

A squeaky board on the staircase told her that the man in her prayers was climbing to his room at that very moment. Her breath caught in her throat, and her heartbeat quickened. Her prayers evaporated like a mist over the ocean at dawn. She heard each step he took, seemed to feel his nearness as he moved past her room and into his own. She didn't let out her breath until she heard his door close.

And then she uttered one last prayer.

"Oh Lord, my heart is in danger. Protect me."

But it was already too late for that particular cry for help, and Inga knew it. She was falling in love with Dirk Bridger.

Hastily, she extinguished her lamp and crawled into bed, burrowing down beneath the blankets, as if trying to escape her discovery.

How could this be? She had met him scarcely three days before. A woman didn't fall in love as quickly as that. Love took months, even years to grow, and many women never experienced love—not even for their husbands. Most were content if they shared a common regard. Everyone knew that. Everyone. Even a spinster of twenty-two like Inga.

Besides, Dirk Bridger wasn't her kind. He didn't attend her church or share her faith in God. He could be sullen and taciturn. He was angry and bitter. He hated Iowa, hated this farm, wanted to go far away. Until the children were grown, he was trapped. He stayed only because of them. He was not a man who wanted to be loved or would love in return.

She rolled onto her side and squeezed her eyes closed.

Even if he *wanted* to fall in love, it wouldn't be with her. Men wanted girls like her sisters. Men fell in love with the pretty Mary Malones and the beautiful Beth Wellingtons of this world. Not with the ordinary Inga Linbergs. Not with Inga.

"Oh, Pappa ... What have I done?"

Five

The family awakened the next morning to six inches of snow on the ground with more snow falling and the wind blowing even deeper drifts.

"Won't be able to take you into town for church," Dirk told Inga when he returned from the barn. "Not in this storm. Doesn't show any signs of lettin' up. Sorry. Besides, the sleigh needs repairs, and I haven't got to 'em yet."

Inga purposely kept her gaze on the skillet. "I understand. It is all right." She was almost relieved. She couldn't imagine sitting beside him in a sleigh for more than an hour each way. Not after her revelation of last night.

Dirk stepped over to the sink and washed his hands in the basin. Despite her better judgment, she cast a surreptitious glance in his direction. He had yet to shave, and the stubble of his beard darkened his jaw. His eyes still carried the look of sleep about them. When he'd removed his hat, he must have smoothed his thick brown hair back with his hands, for it had a finger-raked look about it that she had already become fond of.

She'd known what would happen if she looked at him. Her heart raced. Her knees weakened. Her fingers began to quiver. "What am I to do?" she whispered to herself as she stirred the diced potatoes, ham, and onions in the frying pan.

"Did you say something?" He looked over her shoulder. "Mmm. Hash. My favorite breakfast."

Her heart thumped so loud she thought he must surely hear it. "I know. Your mother told me." Her voice sounded hoarse.

"So what do you call this dish in Sweden?"

She wished he would move away. His cheek was much too close to her own. She couldn't breathe with him so close, couldn't think. *"Pytt i panna."*

"Be ready soon?"

"Ja. Soon."

"Okay. Back in a jiff." He turned and strode out of the kitchen.

Inga scarcely had a moment to pull her ragged nerves together before she heard the sound of children's feet on the stairs. She stirred the hash again, then turned toward the doorway as the two girls rushed through it.

Wisps of wild, red hair—pulled free from their braids as they'd slept—curled around their freckled faces. Their green eyes, the color of unripened apples, were sleep-filled, just like their uncle's had been. They were still wearing their nightgowns, and their feet were bare.

"I'm hungry," Suzanne announced.

"Good. Breakfast is nearly ready. But you must get dressed before we eat. It is too cold for bare feet." She felt her equilibrium returning. She could deal with the children much better than with their uncle. "Get your things and you can dress beside the stove where it is warm."

Martha yawned, rubbed her eyes with her knuckles, then said, "Our room is freezin'."

"Mine, too." Inga smiled at them. "Did you know it snowed in the night?"

Sleepiness vanished in an instant. Both of the girls dashed to the window.

"Look at that!" Martha exclaimed.

"Snow! Snow!" Suzanne chimed in.

"Let's make a snowman." Martha glanced over her shoulder at Inga. "Can we?"

"A snowman?" It had been many years since she'd made a *snögubbe*. Perhaps as many as twelve or more. There had always been so much work to do, she'd had little time for play. While her younger sisters had romped in the snow, Inga had been helping their pappa. Suddenly, she realized how much she had missed it. *"Ja,"* she answered, "we will make a snowman."

Suzanne jumped up and down. "A snowman! A snowman!"

"But we must wait until the snowfall stops. For now you must both get dressed so we can eat our breakfast. Go on with you. Get your clothes."

"Come on, Suzanne. Let's hurry."

The children raced away, scampering up the stairs, sounding like a stampeding herd of reindeer.

Inga turned to the stove and stirred the hash again, smiling to herself in anticipation.

A moment later, Hattie entered the kitchen. "Mornin'."

Inga lifted the skillet, holding the cast iron handle with a towel. "Did we wake you?" she asked as she turned toward the table.

"No. I've been awake for some time now. Just didn't want to get up."

"The children are excited about the snow."

"I know. I heard." Hattie sank onto a chair. There were dark circles beneath her eyes, and her coloring seemed sallow. Still she was able to smile as she said, "I'm surprised Martha remembers about makin' a snowman. Last time would've been with her daddy. As for Dirk ..." She left the sentence unfinished.

Inga's heart skipped a beat at the sound of his name. Trying to ignore the reaction, she scooped the hash onto plates already set on the table. "It has been a long time for me, too."

The older woman glanced up. "You're a special young woman, Inga Linberg. The way you and the girls've taken to each other."

"*Nej,* I am not special." She carried the skillet to the sink. "It is not hard to . . . take to . . . Martha and Suzanne."

Hattie chuckled. "They've got their days."

The children returned, and on their heels came their uncle. He had shaved while he was upstairs. His hair was freshly combed and had been dampened with water. Inga's mind went blank of everything except for the pure pleasure of looking at him.

Suzanne grabbed hold of Inga's hand and tugged on it. "Help me get dressed, Miss Inga. I wanna make a snowman now."

Dirk's gaze met hers. "A snowman?"

She nodded. "But not until the snowfall has stopped."

He glanced at the children. "Ought to be fun."

"Will you help us?" Martha asked.

"No, I—"

"Please, Uncle Dirk. Please help us."

"Help us, Unca Dirk," Suzanne chimed in. "Help us."

"Sorry. Too much work to do." He looked at Inga again. "Got that sleigh to repair."

"Of course." Inga turned her attention to Suzanne, pulling the nightgown over her head, then replacing it with a day dress and stockings.

She told herself it was silly to feel such disappointment over his refusal. If Martha hadn't suggested it, Inga would never have thought of his joining them. And she didn't want him to, she decided. Whenever he was nearby, she had a difficult time thinking clearly.

"You're lookin' better this morning, Ma." Dirk stepped over to where his mother was seated and kissed the top of her head, then he slid onto his own chair.

"And you're lookin' tired, son. Seems to me you could use a little enjoyment."

He released a humorless laugh.

Inga glanced up as she laced Suzanne's shoe. She saw Hattie lay her hand over Dirk's and look at him with worried eyes.

"The girls want you to help them build that snowman."

"Ma, I—"

"Please, son."

He sighed. "All right, Ma. If it's what you want."

Inga felt a trill of pleasure in her chest, followed by a shiver of apprehension.

"Thank you," Hattie whispered.

Confused and flustered by her contrary emotions, Inga finished tying Suzanne's shoe, silently praying no one would ever guess how much she had wanted him to join them—or how much she dreaded it now that he was going to do just that.

⌒

"'And be not conformed to this world: but be ye transformed by the renewing of your mind, that ye may prove what is that good, and acceptable, and perfect, will of God …'"

Thea had a difficult time concentrating on what her pappa said from his pulpit. Constantly, she cast covert glances toward the back of the church, hoping to see Inga's arrival.

"'Let love be without dissimulation. Abhor that which is evil; cleave to that which is good …'"

She needed desperately to talk to her older sister. Inga could always be counted on to give good advice. She wasn't scatterbrained like the others.

"'Be kindly affectioned one to another with brotherly love; in honour preferring one another …'"

But it seemed the snowstorm had kept Inga from church, as Mamma had predicted it would. Thea didn't know how long she would have to wait before she could meet with Inga. Perhaps another entire week.

"'Rejoicing in hope; patient in tribulation; continuing instant in prayer . . .'"

A week? She couldn't wait that long. She would go mad if she had to wait that long. She had to know what to write back to Karl.

"'Distributing to the necessity of saints; given to hospitality . . .'"

Karl . . . He would arrive in three months. He was coming to America, as he had said he would. He'd written to say he had the promise of employment in a clothing factory in New York City, and he wanted her to join him there. He wanted them to be married.

"'Bless them which persecute you: bless, and curse not . . .'"

It was truly romantic, the very way she'd imagined it would be for them. Karl, leaving Sweden because of his undying love for her. She would have a charming wedding in a small church in New York City. When they walked down the street, arm in arm, people would look and comment on what a beautiful couple they made. Karl would bring her gifts every night when he came home from work because he loved her so dearly.

Oh, Karl . . .

"'Rejoice with them that do rejoice, and weep with them that weep . . .'"

But if Pappa knew of her plans, he would stop her. She knew he would. Pappa didn't approve of Karl. He thought Karl too young to marry and provide for a family. He thought Karl's and her love was only an infatuation. He didn't understand. Would never understand. Couldn't understand. He was too old and too staid to understand how Thea felt.

"'Be of the same mind one toward another . . .'"

Not that Inga would understand either. Inga had never been in love, would never be in love. But at least Inga liked Karl. Unlike Pappa, she seemed to understand that Thea and Karl belonged together.

"'If it be possible, as much as lieth in you, live peaceably with all men . . .'"

No, Thea could not wait another week to talk to Inga. She would have to go out to the Bridger farm. Somehow she would have to convince her pappa that they must visit her sister soon. Today. She must see her today.

"'Be not overcome of evil, but overcome evil with good . . .'"
Today. This very day.

———

The snowstorm let up just before noon, and by one o'clock, the children were bundled in coats, scarves, and mittens, as was Inga. While Hattie watched from a chair set near the kitchen window, the three of them went out the back door.

A cloud of mist formed in front of Inga's mouth as she instructed the girls how to make a ball from the wet snow, then roll it around the yard until it became the base for a snowman. Martha quickly caught on, but Suzanne seemed more intent on falling face-first into the blanket of snow.

"You will never make a *snögubbe* that way, *prinsessa*," Inga said, laughing as she stood the child upright for the fourth time.

"Here, Miss Linberg. Let me help Suzanne."

Inga's laughter died instantly as she looked up to find Dirk standing nearby. *"Ja."* She moved the child a few steps forward. "Suzanne, your uncle will help you now."

He packed some snow into a large ball, then set it on the ground in front of Suzanne. "Don't know how I got talked into this." Together, they began to roll the ball of snow. "Not like I've got the time for it."

Inga watched uncle and niece as they moved away from her. Her heart tightened at the sight of them, although she didn't know why it affected her so. Perhaps it was the tender way he guided the little girl, a tenderness quite in contrast to his frequent frowns and constant complaints about time and work.

"Is this big enough, Miss Inga?" Martha asked, interrupting her musings.

She turned and found Martha standing beside an enormous snowball, reaching higher than the girl's waist. Inga's laughter returned. *"Ja,* I think that is big enough, *kattunge.* Now we must make another one, but smaller or we will never be able to lift it."

"Uncle Dirk can lift it now that he's here. Can't you, Uncle Dirk?"

"Sure, but you two had better hurry. Suzanne and I are gonna get our snowman made first."

"It's a race!" Martha shouted with excitement. "Come on, Miss Inga. Let's hurry!"

For the next half hour, the two adults and two children were embroiled in a contest of speed and agility. No one seemed aware of the cold as they crisscrossed the barnyard, rolling the balls of snow before them. Laughter and shouts echoed between the barn and the house.

When it came time to stack the second section of their snowman onto the bottom section, Inga wasn't about to ask Dirk for help. It had been too long since she competed with anyone in any manner, and she wanted to win.

Since Dirk was handicapped by the littler of the two nieces, it seemed almost a certainty that Martha and Inga would complete their snowman first. More than once, Suzanne tripped her uncle, and he was soon as dusted with snow as she was.

As Inga set the head of the snowman in place, she sent Martha after some branches to use for arms. Then she glanced behind her to see how far ahead they were of Dirk and Suzanne. She was just in time to see Dirk scoop the three-year-old up from the ground and toss her into the air. The smile he wore and the sound of his deep laughter stole Inga's breath away.

There was no point in arguing with herself, no point in trying to reason away her feelings with logic. It didn't matter that love was supposed to take time to grow. It didn't matter that she had known this man less than a week. She *was* falling in love with him, *had* fallen in love with him already. She only had to look at him to see here was a man to be admired. He had set aside his own plans in order to care for his mother and nieces. Despite his own desires for his life, he had put the needs of others first.

If it were in her power, she would grant him what he wished for most in that instant. Whatever he might want, she would have given it to him gladly.

Because she loved him.

Dirk set Suzanne on her feet, turned, and his gaze met with Inga's. For one horrible moment, she feared he might read her feelings in her eyes. Then she was saved by the sounds of jangling harness.

—

He couldn't have said why, but Dirk was oddly disturbed by the look that had passed between them before Olaf Linberg and the rest of the pastor's family drove into the yard. But there was no time for Dirk to figure it out before Inga broke eye contact and rushed toward the sleigh.

As soon as the horse came to a halt, all four of the Linberg girls tumbled, giggling, out of the sleigh.

"We've missed you, Inga."

"Pappa can't find anything in his study."

"Do you like it here?"

"Have you heard about the Johnson boy? He broke his wrist when he fell on a patch of ice outside the school."

As they chattered, they each hugged Inga, acting as if they hadn't seen her in months instead of a few days.

Dirk waited until the pastor and his wife disembarked from the sleigh before walking toward the family. His nieces beat him there.

"Everyone," Inga said, "I want you to meet Martha and Suzanne."

"Goddag," the Linberg sisters said in unison.

"You're all so pretty," Martha declared. Looking up at Inga, she added, "You don't look much like 'em, do you?"

Dirk thought there was a hint of sadness in Inga's smile as she shook her head and answered, *"Nej.* We are very different, my sisters and I."

It wasn't as if he hadn't noticed the difference himself. Still, he wished Martha hadn't spoken so frankly.

As Dirk stepped up beside her, Inga motioned toward him without looking. "Mamma, this is Mr. Bridger. Mr. Bridger, this is my mother."

"Pleasure, Mrs. Linberg," he said, touching the brim of his hat.

"Goddag, Mr. Bridger," Bernadotte Linberg replied. "I have been eager to make your acquaintance. It was quite a surprise for me to find Inga gone from our house when I returned there last week."

Reverend Linberg glanced toward the snowmen. "It looks as if we have spoiled your fun." Then he glanced at Inga. "I hope that was not what kept you from worship this morning, *dotter."*

"No, Pappa. I . . . we—"

"That was my doin'," Dirk interrupted. "The runner on my sleigh is broke."

Her father raised an eyebrow—as if to say that was a poor excuse for missing church—but said nothing more on the matter.

Dirk cleared his throat. "I reckon we'd better go inside. Ma will be itchin' to meet all of you."

As the Linbergs, Martha, and Suzanne trooped through the snow toward the back door of the house, Dirk's gaze remained on Inga. Maybe she wasn't pretty in the same vein as her sisters. But the more he was around her, the more he thought she—

"Hurry up, Uncle Dirk," Martha shouted at him.

He gave his head a brief shake, then started after them, the image having slipped away without quite becoming clear to him.

———

"Inga, what am I to do?" Thea repeated in an anxious whisper.

Inga glanced at her sister as the two of them walked toward the barn, ostensibly because Thea had an overwhelming urge to see the cows. Inga could scarcely believe what her sister had just told her, and now Thea wanted her advice.

"Inga?"

"I don't know, Thea."

"But you must help me find a way to get to New York City. You have always been the smartest one. You will know how I should do it."

"Oh, Thea . . ."

"Karl is coming to America to marry me. I must be there when he arrives. I must go to New York City and be there to meet his ship."

Inga opened the barn door, and the two young women stepped inside. "Why don't you talk to—"

"Pappa will not talk about this. He would only stop me from going." Thea grabbed Inga's arm. "I know you don't understand what it is like to be in love, but you must try. Please, help me. If I don't go, I will die. I will simply die."

You don't understand what it is like to be in love. Thea would never know how wrong she was, Inga thought as she stared into her sister's frantic gaze. Because she did understand. She knew how being in love stole her breath away, stole her ability to reason or think clearly. She knew how it made her heart race and her blood run hot, how it made everything seem possible and impossible at the same time.

"Inga, you must not tell me I am too young. You must not tell me to forget Karl. I could never forget him."

She shook her head. *"Nej,* I will not say that."

"Then you *will* help me?"

"I should not. I should do what Pappa would do. I should do the sensible thing and forbid you to go. New York City is full of danger. You could come to some harm. I should refuse." She thought of Dirk. "But . . ."

Thea held her breath.

"Ja, kära du, I will help you. I do not know how, but I will find some way to help you."

Her sister threw her arms around Inga and hugged her tightly. "I knew I could count on you. I just knew it. You are my favorite sister."

"I am sure I shall regret this." She drew back so she could look at Thea. "But all I care is that *you* never regret it." She kissed the younger woman's cheek.

"I won't, Inga. I promise you, I won't."

The barn door swung open a second time, and Gunda peeked inside. "What secrets are you telling each other?" she asked as she entered.

"No secrets," Thea said hastily. "I have been asking Inga how she feels about working for the Bridgers."

Gunda closed the door. "I know how I would feel." She hugged herself. "Dizzy."

"Dizzy?" Inga repeated.

"Mmm." Gunda closed her eyes. "Whenever *Herr* Bridger was near, I would go weak in the knees and my head would swim. He is so handsome, Inga. How do you bear it?"

Inga felt her cheeks growing warm. Quickly, she turned and walked deeper into the barn, hoping the dim light would hide her reaction to her sister's question. It would never do for anyone to guess she felt exactly the way Gunda had described.

See, she scolded herself. *These are the feelings of a silly schoolgirl. I only have to look at Gunda to know it. The feelings will not last.*

"Hush," she heard Thea say. "Don't you know Inga is only here to help the Bridgers? She would never be as silly as you."

Inga wanted to ask why she would never be like Gunda. Why did everyone assume she would never fall in love, would never get dizzy or go weak in the knees over a man? Was she really so different from the rest of them?

She looked behind her in time to see Gunda give her head a sassy shake.

"I don't care what you say, Thea Matilda Linberg. I am going to visit Inga as often as I can, and I *will* make *Herr* Bridger notice me."

Inga felt her stomach sink. Gunda was so pretty, so vibrant. Of course Dirk would notice her. What man wouldn't notice a girl like her? And if Gunda had her mind set on it—

"And what about the Dolk twins?" Thea interrupted. "I thought you liked one of them."

Gunda grinned. "I like them both. And they *do* live in town. I cannot avoid seeing them. Can I help it if they like me, too?"

"What are you doing in here?" Kirsten asked as she and Astrid entered the barn.

Astrid wrinkled her nose. "Ooh, it smells."

"Of course it smells." Kirsten poked Astrid with an elbow. "It's a *barn*."

Inga had a sudden urge to defend the barn for the way it looked, the way it smelled. And just as suddenly, she knew she felt that way because it was Dirk's barn.

There was no doubt about it. She *was* becoming as silly as Gunda. The next thing she would know, she'd find herself flirting with Dirk.

And that was the most preposterous thought of all.

———

Later that evening, after the children were asleep in their beds, Hattie settled back in her chair near the fireplace and closed her eyes. It was pleasant—the warmth of the fire, the peace and quiet of the house, Inga's company nearby.

"It was real nice gettin' to meet all your family," Hattie said after a lengthy but companionable silence. "You must miss them."

"Sometimes. But I fear their visit wearied you."

She felt Inga lay a blanket over her lap. "Thank you, dear." Then she smiled. "I enjoyed the snowman race, too."

"We never finished."

She opened her eyes. "Didn't you see? Dirk finished them both."

"He did?" Inga glanced toward the back door.

It was then that Dirk came inside, stomping his feet to shake off the snow from his boots before he stepped onto the clean floor. A tiny smile curved the corners of Inga's mouth as she watched him.

Hattie looked from their new housekeeper to her son, then back again. *Could it be?* she wondered. *Was it possible?*

"It's startin' to snow again." Dirk removed his hat, then shrugged out of his coat. "My guess is we're in for a long winter."

"All winters're long," Hattie replied, her gaze continuing to shift between the two young people.

Inga set her sewing aside and rose from her chair. "Let me get you something hot to drink, Mr. Bridger."

There had been a time when Hattie was more than eager to do anything to make her husband, Joseph, comfortable after a hard day's work. Was it possible those were the same feelings Inga had for Joseph's son? Or was she merely showing him the same concern she showed for everyone in the Bridger family?

If Dirk were to know the love of a woman, perhaps then his heart would find peace. Hattie knew he continued to long for other things, for the life he'd wanted since he was a boy. He did his duty for his family because that's the sort of man he was. But if love should find him . . .

"It is black. The way you like it." Inga held the steaming mug of hot coffee out toward Dirk.

Hattie was right. Inga had fallen in love with her son. But it was also plain to see, as Dirk took the mug from Inga's hands, that he hadn't discovered it yet.

Don't be blind, Son, she wanted to say to him. *Look at the happiness that's starin' you right in the face.*

He walked into the living room, crossing to where Hattie was sitting. He leaned down and kissed her forehead. "I'm turnin' in, Ma. You need anything?"

"No, son. I'm fine."

"Well, good night then."

"Good night."

He headed for the stairs, then as an afterthought, glanced back and said, "Good night, Miss Linberg."

"*Godnatt,* Mr. Bridger."

Hattie's time was short. She had accepted it. She didn't know how many days on this earth had been allotted to her, but she knew there weren't many of them left.

Lord, I'd sure count it a blessing if I could go to my rest believin' Dirk's gonna be happy. The kinda happiness that only comes from lovin' and bein' loved in a good marriage. I reckon if you do your part and I do mine, we just might see it happen for my boy.

"Amen," she whispered, then smiled to herself.

It was going to be okay. She had a feeling it was all going to be okay now that Inga Linberg was here.

Six

Snow continued to fall off and on for several days, and when at last the series of storms passed, shortly after noon on the third day, the dark clouds drifted away, revealing a startling blue sky overhead. Icy crystals reflected the rays of the distant winter sun, turning the landscape into a sparkling wonderland that was almost blinding in its brilliance.

"But why can't we make another snowman?" Martha demanded as she turned from the window.

"Because it is freezing outside," Inga replied while rinsing a kettle in the sink. "The snow is so cold it will not pack."

"Can't we go out to the barn and see what Uncle Dirk is doin', then? Maybe he'll take us for a sleigh ride."

"Your uncle is busy with his chores."

Martha plopped onto a kitchen chair. "He's *always* busy. He's never got time to play with me and Suzanne."

Inga's gaze went to the window. "Your uncle has to work hard, Martha, in order to provide for all of you. And, remember, he did take the time on Sunday to help with our snowmen." She glanced back at the child. "While Suzanne is napping, why don't you help me with some Saint Lucia's Day preparations? It is less than a week away, and I have done nothing."

"Who's Saint Lucia?"

For a moment, Inga was silent, surprised by the question. She'd never known anyone who didn't celebrate Saint Lucia's Day. Then she realized it would be the perfect diversion for the children.

"In Sweden, it is the day the yule celebrations begin." She joined Martha at the table while drying her hands on a towel. She sat on a chair opposite the girl. "Lucia was a Christian maiden who was martyred during the time of the Roman emperor Diocletian. Do you know what martyred means?"

Martha shook her head.

"It means she died for her faith, for the things she believed in. In honor of Saint Lucia and her day, the eldest daughter of the house dresses up as the Lucia bride. Wearing a flowing gown of white, she places a wreath of greenery with lighted candles on her head, and then she visits all the bedrooms of the family, serving coffee and Lucia buns and cakes."

"I don't have a white dress."

"Then we must make you one. This is a great honor."

"Were you the Lucia bride?"

Inga smiled. *"Ja,* ever since I was your age. I always felt pretty on that morning," she added softly, remembering.

"Will I look as pretty as you?"

She was warmed by the words. "Oh, Martha, you will be much prettier than I." She rose from her chair. "Come. I am certain I have some white fabric we can use." She took the child by the hand and drew her out of the kitchen.

As they climbed the stairs, Inga made a mental note to thank her mamma again for bringing the large trunk—full of Inga's fabric, clothes, books, and keepsakes—to the Bridger farm last Sunday. When Inga left the parsonage, she had packed in such haste, she hadn't given thought to many of the things she might need or want during her stay. But her mamma had.

When they entered Inga's bedroom, she led Martha to the battered old trunk, and together they knelt on the floor in front of it. The hinges creaked softly as Inga opened the top. It didn't take her long to find what she was looking for.

"Here it is." She pulled out a length of white organdy. "This will make a lovely dress for you."

"You'd make a dress for me outta this? But it's so fine!"

Inga was about to reply when her heart skipped a beat and the back of her neck began to tingle. She turned her head, somehow knowing she would find Dirk standing in the doorway, watching them.

———

The sight of Inga, kneeling beside the open trunk, wearing a yellow gown—the shade of just-churned butter—touched Dirk's heart in an unexpected way. Bright winter sunlight streamed through the bedroom window, forming a halo around Inga's pale hair. It caressed her porcelain-smooth cheeks and emphasized the length of her swanlike neck. He felt frozen in place, captivated, unable to look away, not wanting to even if he could.

"Uncle Dirk, look!" Martha exclaimed when she saw him. "Miss Inga's gonna make me a Saint Lucia's dress. I'm gonna be a bride!"

He glanced at the girl. "A bride?" His gaze shifted from his niece to Inga. With the sunlight gilding her, she looked like a bride herself.

She blushed, as she often did when speaking to him. "It is a Swedish custom, Mr. Bridger. The celebration of Saint Lucia's Day. I hope you do not mind."

"Nah. I don't mind."

She rose, and he was again mindful of the gracefulness with which she carried herself. He thought of her sisters, how very different she was from them. He remembered thinking, only a week ago, that they were all so gay, so sparkling and pretty, and she was not. But he'd been mistaken. Inga Linberg's loveliness was of a different kind, that was all. Maybe it was the goodness of her heart. From the moment she'd come here, she'd shown nothing but affection and kindness toward his nieces and his mother. And toward him, too, for that matter.

Funny, he'd always hankered after brunettes with big brown eyes. Tiny and curvaceous girls who flirted and laughed. Young women full of sass. Just like Clara Keene, the widow he'd worked for in Kentucky, and Pearl, the little barmaid in Montana.

Inga was none of those things. Inga was—

"Was there something you needed, Mr. Bridger?" she asked as the silence stretched between them.

He was surprised by the direction his thoughts had taken. Right now, he couldn't remember why he'd come upstairs. "No. Nothing." He turned and headed down the stairs.

"Mr. Bridger?"

He stopped on the bottom step and glanced behind him.

"May I speak to you a moment?"

Since he could see no way of avoiding it, he shrugged. "Sure."

She started down the steps toward him, moving with a certain elegance.

He swallowed hard.

Speaking in a soft voice as she drew near, she said, "It is about Christmas, Mr. Bridger."

"Christmas?"

"*Ja*. I was wondering ... well ... I needed to know what your family's customs are."

His own sense of failure slammed into him. "Can't say as we have any," he answered gruffly.

She stared at him with wide eyes, the look both questioning and tender.

"There's no money for presents for the girls."

"Oh. But—"

"Look, maybe we oughta skip Christmas this year."

"*Skip* Christmas?"

He couldn't stand to look into her eyes a minute longer. Couldn't bear to see his deficiencies mirrored there. He turned his back toward her.

"Mr. Bridger, there are many ways to celebrate this blessed season." Her admonition was gentle, yet it only served to stir up more anger and bitterness in his heart.

"What's to celebrate?" he demanded.

"Why, the birth of our Lord, of course."

He glanced over his shoulder. "Look, from what I've seen, God doesn't care what we're doing down here. If he did—"

She placed her hand on his arm, causing him to face her again. "But you are wrong, Mr. Bridger. He cares very much."

"Then why's Ma dyin' before her time?" He shrugged off her hand. "Look, you go on believin' if that's what you want. You and Ma both. Just don't expect me to."

Softly, "What caused you to lose your faith?"

He headed for the door. "Maybe I never had any."

"How very sad."

He grabbed his coat off the rack. "Do whatever you want about Christmas, Miss Linberg. Makes no difference to me." Then he stomped outside without waiting to hear her reply.

Dirk plowed his way through the snow to the barn, allowing his anger to grow and multiply. What *did* he have to celebrate? he silently demanded again. Why was he supposed to be glad when he was unable to do the simplest things for his family? And if God had wanted his thanks, then he should have let John and Margaret live. He shouldn't be taking his ma before her time. If God cared so much, he wouldn't have punished Dirk by bringing him to this dairy farm where all he could do was fail.

He slammed closed the barn door behind him, then kicked at an empty milk pail.

Cows and horses raised their heads and stared at him with accusing eyes.

He sank onto a workbench, his anger dissipating. The bitterness, however, lingered in his soul as his future stretched grimly before him, failure after failure after failure.

Throughout the day, Inga recalled the expression on Dirk's face before he'd turned and walked out of the house. She'd wanted to comfort him, to find a way to reassure him, to make him understand that all was not as bleak as he thought. She wondered why he couldn't see how much he was loved by his nieces, and because of their love, how very rich he truly was. She prayed she might find a way to help him discover the truth.

Certainly she wasn't going to allow this family to miss Christmas simply because money was in short supply. So in the afternoon, she and the girls began work on gifts for their grandmother and their uncle. They worked upstairs in Inga's room, the door closed for privacy, both of the children having sworn to keep what they were doing a secret. Suzanne was given the task of stringing together a collection of old beads and buttons for a necklace for Grandma Hattie. Martha chose the more difficult task of making a new cap for Uncle Dirk.

As for the girls themselves, Inga decided to make them each a doll from a pattern Bernadotte Linberg had used for her daughters. Inga had nearly everything she would need in her trunk, except for the yarn. She would have to go into town for that. And there were a few items she needed from the general store for their Christmas dinner.

It wasn't until evening, after both the children were in bed and Hattie had retired for the night, that Inga found the courage to again bring up the matter of Christmas with Dirk.

He was seated at the kitchen table, account books and log-books spread out before him. His forehead was creased in concentration, and he rubbed the furrows with the fingertips of his right hand as he stared at the columns of numbers entered in the books.

"Mr. Bridger? May I trouble you for a moment?"

His frown deepened as he turned to look at her.

She wanted to tell him she loved him, and her heart thumped crazily in her chest because of it.

"What is it, Miss Linberg?"

"I . . . it's about Christmas."

He sighed. "I thought we finished this discussion. I told you to do whatever you wanted."

"*Ja.*" She drew closer to the table, feeling her heart quicken even more in response to his nearness. "I was hoping you might be able to kill a goose for Christmas dinner. I have nearly everything else. Your mamma has told me you enjoy sweet potatoes, and these we have in the cellar. I will need only a few items from the general store, but I promise the expense will not be great."

"So you want me to take you into town?"

"That is not necessary. I am able to drive myself, if you would not mind me doing so." She sat down on one of the chairs, purposely not looking at him. "Unless, of course, you would want to go with me," she added, thinking she sounded a trifle breathless.

He didn't reply.

After what seemed a long silence, she glanced up to find him staring at her.

"You're a persistent woman, Miss Linberg."

"*Ja,* I have been told so, Mr. Bridger."

His voice dropped to a near whisper. "I reckon it's to be Ma's last Christmas."

"*Ja.*"

"She'd probably like a tree. I didn't bother with one last year."

"I could make decorations for it."

His smile was filled with sadness. "Thanks, Miss Linberg."

"It is not so much." She longed to touch his cheek, to feel the stubble of his dark beard beneath her fingertips, to wipe away those creases in his forehead.

"You're wrong. It's a great deal."

"You carry much on your shoulders. I am happy to help where I am able."

Dirk leaned back in his chair, holding her gaze with his own a moment longer before asking, "Why aren't you married, Inga?"

Her heart skipped a beat at the sound of her given name falling from his lips. "Because I have never been asked," she answered honestly. Heat rushed to her cheeks. "I expect my calling is to help Pappa in his church work."

"A pity. You're a right good cook, and I've never seen this place look so clean. You'd probably make some man a good wife."

He had described nothing more than a housekeeper, and yet she was pleased by what praise he had given. She wanted to say that she would make *him* a good wife. Instead, she asked a question of her own. "Why have *you* never married?"

"Never wanted to." His eyes took on a faraway look. "There were other things I wanted more."

"Tell me," she encouraged gently—and was surprised when he did.

"I used to read a lot when I was a boy. John always teased me about it, sayin' I'd ruin my eyes, but I didn't pay him any mind. My favorite books were about other countries, different cultures. Like China and India and Africa. My dad thought it was a waste of time, fillin' my head with things I didn't need to know, makin' myself want things I wasn't ever going to have, but I kept right on readin' and dreamin', just the same. I was determined to go to all those places I'd read about." The thoughtful expression vanished, turning to one of resignation. "But my dad took sick and I had to stay on and work the farm for him. We lived in Ohio then. Raised corn mostly. Some wheat, too. After Dad died, Ma sold the farm and came here to live with John and Margaret. As for me, I was gonna work my way around the world." He gave a humorless laugh. "You can see where I ended up, though. Guess Dad was right. Dreams are a waste of time."

Dirk Bridger was in every way a man. He was tall and muscular. His shoulders were broad. His face had been creased by hard work and worry. His eyes held wisdom that only time could dispense. And yet, as he'd spoken, Inga had caught a glimpse of the boy he had once been. She'd felt his disillusionment, understood what he had lost, wished she could give it back to him.

Her heart nearly broke in two as she said, *"Nej,* Mr. Bridger. Dreams are not a waste. They should be nurtured. God wants us to dream, I think."

"Do you?"

"Ja."

"What makes you so sure there even is a God, Miss Linberg?" Somewhat sarcastically, he added, "Other than because your pa's a preacher and you're expected to, that is."

"That is easy," she answered with assurance. "Because I can hear my Lord's voice in the wind and see his love all around me." She laid her hand over her heart. "It begins in here, a person's faith in Christ." She touched her right temple. "Not in here." She paused, then said, "That is how I know, Mr. Bridger."

He stared at her again, and she was so afraid he would see how much she loved him that she rose from her chair and turned her back. She walked to the sink, where she pretended to wipe crumbs off the counter. She heard the scrape of chair legs against the floor, knew that he stood.

"Do you have dreams for the future, Miss Linberg? Beyond helpin' your pa, I mean."

"I did not use to," she answered, immediately wishing she hadn't.

"But you do now?"

"*Ja.*" Her voice fell to a whisper. "Very private ones."

"I'm sorry. Didn't mean to pry."

Foolishly, she turned around. She met his dark gaze, felt all the familiar emotions looking at him always caused. "You need not apologize. You asked no more than I did myself. It was I who was prying, I fear, and I who must apologize."

As had happened earlier in the day, Dirk found himself looking at Miss Inga Linberg and seeing her in a slightly different light than before. She wasn't beautiful, and yet there were moments when she seemed beyond lovely. At times, she seemed uncertain, even shy, and then he would recognize she had a strength of character and a faith that were unshakable.

He wished she had told him what dreams she had for herself. He had a sudden desire to know her better, although he couldn't explain the reason for it.

"So you will allow me to take the sleigh into Uppsala tomorrow?" she asked softly.

Stubborn was too mild a word for her, he thought, then laughed aloud. "Persistent *and* tenacious, aren't you, Miss Linberg?"

She smiled. *"Ja,* when I need to be."

"All right. I know when I'm whipped. I'll take you. We'll go right after the driver from the milk plant comes. He's usually here by eleven on Thursdays, unless the snow slows him down."

"The children and I will be ready when you are."

There was a moment—with the two of them standing there in the kitchen, looking at one another, laughter still lingering in the air—when Dirk felt the heaviness lift from his shoulders, when his bitterness did not taste so acrid on his tongue.

Then Inga's smile faded. "The hour is late. I had best retire."

As she walked by him, he caught a whiff of her lemon verbena toilet water. The fragrance was like her, he thought. Fresh, subtle, clean, alive.

But once she was gone, his gaze fell on the table and his log and account books. Reality reasserted itself. If he was going to be spending money at the general store tomorrow, he'd better find out tonight where it was going to come from. That wasn't going to be an easy task.

Inga was wrong about dreams. They were a waste of time.

~Seven

When John Bridger designed his dairy farm, he'd done it with an eye toward the future and modernization. He had studied and planned in order to make his operation successful in every way. He had looked for land close enough to a milk plant in Des Moines that processed raw milk into both condensed and pasteurized milk, then he had quickly become one of their most reliable suppliers. He'd built an airy, rectangular barn and put in a cement floor with stalls for the cows. A milk house was attached to the barn, with facilities for washing utensils as well as for packaging the milk for shipment to the plant. He'd bought the finest livestock he could find, choosing the Jersey over other breeds as the best for his type of operation. He'd fed his stock only high quality hay and silage, and he'd kept his cows free of disease by following the most modern practices known to dairymen.

Problem was, John's methods took more time and were more costly besides. John had made the extra effort and gone to the extra expense because he'd loved this place. He'd loved the old house and the land it sat on. He'd loved the new barn and the scattered outbuildings. He'd loved the livestock—cows and pigs and horses and chickens. He'd loved growing crops to feed both family and animals. He'd probably even loved milking the stupid bovines morning and night.

Dirk didn't doubt John would have continued to make this place a success, just as he'd planned, given the time to do so. But he'd died too soon. He'd invested everything he'd made back into the farm, and he'd had no money in reserve. He'd left only an outstanding mortgage at the bank in Des Moines.

Now it was Dirk who was expected to carry on in his brother's behalf. He did his best to run the dairy exactly as John had intended, but it was never easy, and he was always aware of his failures. When a cow took sick, he knew it was his fault. When a calf died, he knew it was his fault. When milk production fell, he knew it was his fault.

As Dirk sat on the stool the next morning, milking cow number six out of thirteen—for that was how he counted them off each morning and evening—he thought about his brother's goals for this farm. It occurred to him for the first time that John had been as big a dreamer, in his own way, as Dirk had been. Only John's dreams had been of the sort that had made sense to their father. Often, while he was still alive, Joseph Bridger had wished aloud that his younger son were more like his elder.

Dirk pressed up closer to the side of the Jersey, trying to borrow some of her warmth as he tugged on her teats, squirting milk into the pail.

Yeah, his dad had probably been right. He should have been more like John. But who would have guessed Dirk would be forced to live John's life instead of his own?

Get your head out of the clouds, Son, he could still hear his dad saying. *Be more like your brother. Build something that will last.*

"Something that will last," Dirk muttered. "Like what?"

It wasn't that he was afraid of hard work or that he minded getting by with little. He didn't need much for himself. But when he saw his ma or his nieces needing things he couldn't provide, it ate at him, taunted him: *failure, failure, failure.*

If only he'd had a chance to prove himself anywhere else but here. If only . . .

A blast of cold air hit him, alerting him to the opening of the door.

"Mr. Bridger?" Inga called out.

"Over here, Miss Linberg."

In a few moments, her face appeared above the top rail of the stall. *"Goddag."* Her head was covered in a black shawl. Her cheeks were rosy from the cold.

"Mornin'." He wondered what had brought her out to the barn so early, but he didn't ask. He wasn't feeling exactly charitable toward her this morning. It was her fault that he'd been thinking about John's plans for this farm and about his own plans, too. She'd said dreams were good, and he'd found himself remembering all the unfulfilled ones he'd once entertained.

She cleared her throat. "Mr. Bridger, it occurred to me last night, after I went to bed, that I could be of more help to you than I have been. It is obvious you need help with the dairy as well as with the home. It is too much for one man. Even I can see that. But I am sure I could learn to milk the cows. Will you teach me?"

His hands had stilled in the midst of her speech. He thought of her dignified father and of her ladylike mother and of her four vivacious sisters, and he could not imagine them approving of Inga sitting in an icy cold barn in the middle of winter, milking cows.

"I came to help. Let me do it however I can."

It was true. He could use a hand. If he had even a quarter fewer of the cows to milk, he could use that time for other chores. But . . .

"I am able to do this," she continued quickly.

"You're already workin' mighty hard."

"I would not allow my other duties to suffer."

"I never thought you would."

She opened the gate and stepped into the stall. "Then show me what I can do out here."

There was a part of him that continued to resist. Having the woman who had been hired to be their housekeeper and a nurse for his mother milking the cows seemed to point out all the more clearly the ways he had failed. Yet there was another part of him that would welcome her presence, not just for the help she would be but for the company itself.

Seemingly out of the blue, he realized the hours he spent working in the barn were lonely ones. Maybe it was because he had too much time to let his mind wander. Whatever the reason, he wouldn't object to a diversion or two.

"Mr. Bridger?"

He wasn't fool enough to refuse the offer. If she wanted to milk cows, who was he to stop her? He rose from the stool and motioned for her to sit there. "Sure, Miss Linberg. If you want to learn, I'll teach you how."

Her smile was sweet as she moved into place.

"You'll have to take off your gloves," he said.

She did so.

"Now, scoot in close. That's right." He hunkered down beside her, then took hold of one of her hands. "Now, wrap your fingers around a teat like this. That's right. Now, sort of squeeze and roll down at the same time. Firm but gentle-like. No, a little harder. Now, try and get a rhythm going with both your hands. Left and right. Left and right. There you go."

Milk squirted into the pail. *Splash. Splash. Splash.*

Inga laughed softly in delight. The sound drew Dirk's gaze to her face.

Before sitting down, she had pushed the black shawl from her head. Now she rested her left cheek against the Jersey's fawn-colored side. Loose strands of pale yellow hair feathered near her right cheek and against her neck. He felt an unexpected urge to sweep the freed tresses away from her face, to feel for himself whether or not they were as silken as they looked.

As if sensing his gaze upon her, she looked up. Her smile instantly vanished, and he realized how sorry he was to see it go.

"You've got the hang of it now, Miss Linberg." His voice sounded hoarse to his ears. He cleared his throat as he stood. "I'll get busy with the next one. Holler if you got any questions."

"I will," she whispered in response.

—

It wasn't until Dirk was out of the stall that Inga found herself able to breathe comfortably again. She'd thought she had experienced all the physical reactions his nearness could cause, but she'd been wrong. She had known breathlessness in his presence. She had been left dizzy and weak in the knees. She had felt her mind go blank more than once. But this time, when she'd met his gaze, there had been a nearly overwhelming urge to throw her arms around his neck and kiss him.

That he did not feel the same urge was more than apparent by his actions. It was obvious kissing her was the last thing on his mind.

She wished she had paid more attention to her sisters. Even Kirsten, at fourteen, would know how to make a man want to kiss her. Inga was pitifully ignorant of such things. Whether by chance or by her own design, she had never known a boy or a man she would want to kiss or to be kissed by. But she very much wanted Dirk's kisses. She wanted to belong with him. She wanted him to want her.

Her vision became blurred by tears as she stared down into the milk pail.

More the fool I, she scolded herself silently. Hadn't Dirk told her he'd never wanted a wife? He had other plans for himself. Some women, her sisters probably amongst them, would know how to change a man's mind, would know how to make a man *think* he wanted marriage even if he didn't. But Inga didn't know how. Nor was she sure she'd want to obtain a husband in such a manner. If Dirk didn't want her of his own volition, then . . .

Glory! What a fantasy she was weaving in her head! Two weeks ago, she hadn't met Dirk Bridger or his family. Now here she was, daydreaming about becoming his wife.

Silly goose. That's what she was. A silly goose. Sillier than her sisters, because at least they were pretty. Men were drawn to them like bees to buttercups. It often seemed to Inga that the other Linberg daughters had been born knowing how to dress in the manner men liked and how to walk so that men took notice and how to listen with a look of pure rapture that men found so appealing. All were talents Inga severely lacked, talents she'd never wanted until now.

She blinked away her tears, scolding herself once again. She had come to the barn to be of help to Dirk, not to flirt with him—which she didn't even know how to do. She had best pay attention to the milking and forget the foolish path her thoughts were taking.

She began making a mental list of things she would buy at the general store when Dirk took her into town. She would ask him to stop at the parsonage. She was certain there were some extra decorations for the Christmas tree she could borrow from her mamma.

And perhaps, if she was lucky, she would find a moment when she could ask Thea what a woman could do to make a man want to kiss her. Perhaps she would ask Thea—but only if she found the courage to let these new feelings be known to anyone other than herself.

———

The proprietors of Dolk's General Store, Bjorn and Sonja, and their strapping nineteen-year-old identical twin sons, Vilhelm and Valdemar, were a smiling, friendly, well-liked foursome, and their store was a popular gathering place for the citizens of Uppsala, Iowa. The inside of the store was crammed full of every imaginable item, from tooth powder to saw blades, from satin ribbons to plowshares.

When Inga ushered her two small charges into the general store early that afternoon, she was greeted by an exclamation of delight from Sonja Dolk. "Ah, Inga Linberg, how glad I am to see you!"

"*Goddag, Fru* Dolk," Inga replied, uncertain why the woman was showing such delight. It wasn't as if she was an intimate friend.

The portly matron whisked through the aisles with surprising agility. "All these months you have lived in Uppsala, and I did not know about your quilts. Why was I never told? Why did you never show me?"

"My quilts?"

"I would like to sell them in the store. I will pay you quite handsomely for your efforts."

Inga blinked. "I have never sold any of my quilts before."

"But you should, Inga. You must."

She didn't know how to reply. Her quilts had always been something she did for enjoyment. She wasn't sure she wanted to sell them. They were personal expressions, telling stories of things that had happened to her or to someone she cared about, each panel unique and special in some way. She enjoyed giving the quilts for gifts, but selling them seemed somehow a betrayal of the pleasure she received in the making of them.

"Please," Sonja said, "do not refuse me out of hand. Give it some thought, at least." Then, as if she'd forgotten the matter already, she looked at the children. "And these must be the Bridger girls."

"*Ja.*"

Sonja Dolk leaned down. "Would you like a peppermint stick?"

"Yes!" Martha quickly replied.

"Come with me." Sonja held out her hands to the children. "We will find you each a candy while Miss Linberg does her shopping."

Martha glanced at Inga with a question in her eyes.

Inga smiled. "It is all right. You may go with Mrs. Dolk."

She watched as the proprietress guided the girls toward the counter, then she turned and went in search of the yarn for the dolls she planned to make for Christmas. On her way down the aisle, her gaze fell on a shelf full of books for sale. She stopped, arrested by the sight. Her thoughts returned to last night, to the glimpse she'd had of a young boy who had loved to read about faraway places, the boy who had still known how to dream.

One by one, she picked up the books and looked through them. She didn't know what she was searching for until she found it. A novel by Jules Verne, *Around the World in Eighty Days.* A Christmas present for Dirk. If she sold just one quilt, she would be able to afford this and more.

She would do it. She would offer some of her quilts for sale.

The front door opened, and she heard Dirk's deep laughter mingled with that of another. The sound caused her heart to quicken. Holding the book against her chest, she turned to look as the two men entered the store.

"He's a fine yearling, Hansen," Dirk said, still grinning. "You did well."

"I wouldn't have without your advice," Erik Hansen replied as he clapped Dirk on the back. "No one around Uppsala knows horses the way you do."

Dirk shrugged off the plaudit, although it came from the wealthiest man in the county. "Glad I could help."

"Perhaps you wouldn't mind having a look at the mare I purchased?"

"Be glad to." Dirk turned his head, sweeping his gaze around the large store until he spied his nieces, sitting on the back counter, each of them sucking on a peppermint stick. Then he looked again at Erik Hansen. "Seems like the girls have found what they wanted when they came inside. Listen, I'll try to come out to your place some time next week. How will that be?"

"Good."

Inga realized she'd completely forgotten her young charges, as well as her shopping, while she'd stood there, staring at Dirk. She dropped the novel into her basket. Why was it the mere sight of him could cause her to act so uncharacteristically absentminded? Why was it the sound of his laughter could make her lose her wits and the sight of his smile could make everything in her world come to a complete halt?

With a shake of her head, she hurried toward the piece goods, where she selected a skein of yellow yarn and another of black. Then she continued to move through the aisles, selecting the cooking and baking supplies she would need for the coming holidays.

Fortunately, by the time she reached the counter, Martha had dragged her uncle and sister over to a toy display near the entry, giving Inga an opportunity to speak privately with Sonja Dolk.

"I will offer my quilts for sale in your store, *Fru* Dolk," she told the proprietress, "if you will allow me to take this book and the yarn now, to be paid for out of my first earnings."

Sonja didn't hesitate. "Agreed. You will make far more than the price of those things, I promise you."

Inga thought the woman was being overly optimistic but didn't say so.

"How soon can you deliver the first one?"

"I will have Mamma bring one tomorrow."

Sonja beamed. "Wonderful!"

"Please, could you wrap the book and yarn so they will not be seen? They are for Christmas."

"Ah, I understand."

But Inga was quite certain Sonja Dolk did not understand. Not really. And it was for the best that she didn't, because when the day came for Inga to return to the parsonage, she would just as soon her love for Dirk Bridger not make her the subject of gossip or ridicule.

A broken heart would be enough for her to deal with.

———

Thea stared at the half-written letter on the table. There was so much she wanted to say to Karl, but all she seemed able to write was how very much she missed him.

Then the bedroom door opened, and Inga stepped into the room. Thea immediately laid the pen aside and rose to give her sister a hug.

"Have you come up with a plan for me?" she asked the moment she released Inga.

"*Nej,* not yet."

Thea felt her heart drop. She sank onto the edge of her bed. "What am I to do? I must be there when he arrives. He is coming all this way just for me."

"Do not despair, Thea. We will get you to New York City in time."

"It's easy for you to believe all will be well. It isn't your heart that is breaking because you are kept from the one you love."

Inga sat down beside her. "Perhaps not," she whispered, sounding sad.

Thea regretted her snappish retort. Still, it was true. Inga couldn't know how terrible it was for Thea to be separated from Karl. Inga had never had a beau.

She felt her skin growing hot with frustration. She had to get to Karl. She had to be with him. Nothing else mattered. Not obedience to her parents. Not her close ties to her sisters. Nothing and no one mattered except Karl. She didn't care if Pappa said she had a rebellious spirit. She knew what she wanted, and she meant to have it.

"Thea?"

She didn't look at Inga. *"Ja."*

"How did you ... When was it you knew you loved Karl? Was it after he kissed you?"

Thea knew her cheeks were flaming for a different reason now. "I knew even before that."

"Did he guess how you felt when the two of you first kissed?"

She remembered that furtive exchange in the hallway of her parents' house in Jönköping. Their lips had scarcely brushed, but her palms had been sweaty and she'd giggled nervously. She remembered the way Karl's blue eyes had seemed to look right into her heart afterward. "I suppose he did."

"Oh. I see."

Thea turned and grabbed hold of both of Inga's hands. "You mustn't think badly of me, Inga, for letting him kiss me.

I love him so much. Oh, how can I expect you to understand what it's like?"

For what seemed an endless moment, their gazes locked, but Inga's eyes were so serious, so searching, that finally Thea had to look away.

"You might be surprised what I understand," Inga said gently. "I would never think badly of you for loving Karl." She squeezed Thea's hands, then released them and stood. "Now, I must speak to Mamma about some of my quilts that are packed away in trunks in the attic."

It wasn't until after Inga left the room that Thea wondered at her sister's comment. Then she forgot it as she returned to her letter to Karl.

After all, it was impossible Inga could understand, having never been in love.

~ Eight

Dirk wasn't unaware of the changes Inga's presence had made in the Bridger household. Laughter seemed to linger in the halls, like a breath of warm summer air. The children blossomed a little more every day in the loving atmosphere she'd created, Martha becoming less serious, Suzanne no longer throwing tantrums. Even his mother, while growing more frail due to her illness, had an aura of peace about her, perhaps even joy.

Dirk knew it was because of Inga Linberg.

Often he would enter the house to the sounds of singing. Usually the songs were Christmas carols or hymns. Inga had a sweet, clear voice, but it was often obscured beneath the boisterous and occasionally off-key caroling of his nieces.

The kitchen became the center of activity. Martha and Suzanne were often seated at the table, working on some project or another. When he came into the room, Martha would demand he cover his eyes. Christmas presents, his mother explained to him with a smile. They were secret, these things, and he mustn't peek. So he didn't.

While the children and Hattie worked on those secret gifts, Inga cooked and baked. Delicious scents wafted through the house. Smoked sausage, limpa and saffron breads, coffee and spice cakes, gingersnaps and crullers. Dirk gladly sampled everything that was offered to him, and he proclaimed each new dish better than the last.

Inga was never idle. No matter when he saw her, she was busy: washing, ironing, cleaning, sewing, baking. Regardless how early he arose, she was up, too. When he went to bed, there was usually a sliver of light showing beneath her bedroom door. He wondered when—or if—she slept.

Now, in addition to everything else, Inga went with Dirk to the barn to help with the milking. He was amazed by how much faster the job was accomplished with two of them working. It didn't make him any more fond of the cows or the chore itself. It didn't make him dislike dairy farming any less than he had before, but he didn't seem to dread the start of each new day quite so much either.

Dirk would always remember the morning of December thirteenth of that year. Although he was awake, he was still in bed, for it wasn't yet time for the milking to begin. It was black as pitch outside his window, and a cold, mournful wind whistled around the eaves of the house. Suddenly, his door opened and flickering candlelight spilled into his bedroom. He sat up, surprised and thinking something must be wrong.

Then in walked Martha, swathed in a shimmering white ankle-length robe. A wreath of greenery sat atop her head, and in that wreath were lighted candles. The child's smile, however, outshone the tapers a hundred times over. She walked toward his bed, smiling all the while, carrying a tray with coffee, buns, and cakes on it.

"Happy Saint Lucia's Day, Uncle Dirk." Then she giggled as she glanced over her shoulder and back at him.

Her enthusiasm was infectious, and he returned it, grinning at her. He leaned against the wall at his back and let the pageant play out.

"I've brought you Lucia cats," she told him. "See? The buns are shaped like a cat's head. That's what they do in Sweden. And the gingerbread is in the shape of a goat. See?"

"I see." He looked toward the doorway where Inga stood. She was holding Suzanne's hand in her own, and her other arm was draped lightly around Hattie's shoulders. All were smiling as broadly as Martha.

"I'm the Lucia bride 'cause I'm older'n Suzanne."

He looked at her again. "And a pretty bride you are, too." He reached out and took the tray from her, then rested it on his lap. "Mmm. Did you help make these?" he asked after taking a bite of a warm slice of gingerbread cake.

"Me and Suzanne did."

"I didn't know you were such a good cook, Martha."

"Miss Inga showed me how."

Once again his gaze flicked to the doorway. "She's pretty good at showin' us new things, isn't she?"

Inga's smile dimmed, but she didn't look away as she so often did when their glances met. Dirk found himself wondering how his family had managed without her. She'd brought Christmas back into their lives, and Dirk, despite his best attempts to avoid it, had caught some of her excitement. He hadn't felt this way in a long time. Too long.

"I think today's the day we oughta go lookin' for that Christmas tree," he offered.

Hattie clapped her hands together, drawing his gaze from Inga to her. "A tree? Oh, son! How wonderful!"

He should have done it for her last year, he thought when he saw the joy on his ma's face. For an instant, he caught a glimpse of a younger, healthier Hattie Bridger.

"Of course, a tree," he answered. "I know where there's a small stand of conifers not too far from here. Just the other side of the river and south a bit. If we get an early start, I reckon we can get one chopped down, brought back, and decorated in no time at all."

"Oh, boy!" Martha exclaimed as she looked behind her. "You hear that, Suzanne? We're goin' after a tree, like the ones Miss Inga told us about."

Once again, he looked at Inga, and once again, he wondered what they had ever done without her.

—

Bundled snugly in their coats, hats, and mittens, Martha and Suzanne settled onto the backseat of the sleigh, then lifted their arms as Inga tucked several blankets over and around them. Already their cheeks and noses were rosy with the cold. Their green eyes sparkled. Inga understood, for she felt the same excitement bubbling up inside her.

"Ready?" Dirk asked.

Her pulse jumped as she turned to watch him walk toward the sleigh. *"Ja,* we are ready."

"Then let's go. That Christmas tree's just waitin' for us to find it."

This smiling, carefree-sounding Dirk Bridger was a stranger to Inga, but she liked him a great deal. She hoped he would stay. She hoped . . .

He stopped in front of her, then took hold of her arm. "Here. Let me help you in."

She could scarcely hear him over the beating of her heart. She tried to smile, but she was certain the look she gave him was more daft than pleasing in appearance.

As he sat on the seat beside her, taking up the reins and looping them through his fingers, he said, "How about some of those carols you've all been singing lately?"

"Which one?" Martha asked.

"How about 'God Rest Ye Merry, Gentlemen'? I know that one."

"We do, too," his niece answered.

Dirk glanced at Inga. "Can you get us started on key?"

She nodded. "I think so." She forced herself to concentrate on the melody, then hummed the first note and began.

It was the first time she'd heard Dirk sing, and if she hadn't loved him already, she would have fallen in love with him at that precise moment. His was a deep, resonant voice, welling up from his chest and bursting forth with confidence.

The journey seemed to take no time at all as the team of horses trotted along the road, big clouds of steam in front of their nostrils, their tails flowing out behind them like banners, snow crunching beneath their big hooves. The runners glided over an alabaster landscape, whispering their passage, the faint sound drowned out by the joyous singing of the sleigh's passengers.

Going west, they crossed a wooden bridge high above the river. The surface was frozen solid, hiding the swift-flowing water from view. After crossing the bridge, the road turned south.

Dirk drove the horses into a densely wooded area with sloping hillsides and a spectacular view of the river valley to the east. All around them rose elm trees and maples, oak trees and hickories, although it was difficult to distinguish one species of tree from another, dressed as they were in their wintery garb. Bare, snow-laden limbs glittered gaily in the sunlight. Interspersed among the tall broad-leaved trees were small copses of conifers, their evergreen branches also blanketed by snow.

Even in the dead of winter, wildlife was in evidence in this woods. Before Dirk had a chance to stop the sleigh, they had spied three white-tailed deer bounding off into hiding and two blue jays watching them from a high branch. A moment later, several squirrels jumped from another tree, startling the blue jays and sending them flying into the sky while a sifting of snow floated to the ground.

"How about that one over there?" Dirk said, pointing with one hand while looping the reins with the other.

Inga's gaze darted in the direction he'd indicated, and she immediately found the tree he meant. *"Perfekt!"* she exclaimed.

He hopped out of the sleigh, then turned back to help her. She didn't hesitate before putting her hand in his. For today, at least, she allowed herself to pretend this was her family, that she belonged with them and to them, that Dirk loved her as much as she loved him. It was a wonderful fantasy; she didn't care that it wasn't sensible, realistic, or prudent. God had given her this day, and she was going to revel in it.

As soon as Inga was out of the sleigh, Dirk released her hand and reached for the children. Before long, all four of them were trudging through the snow toward a small juniper, Dirk with an ax resting on his shoulder.

"Wait here," he said when they were about ten feet away, then he moved on.

Inga found immense pleasure in watching him chop down the tree. Even layers of winter clothing couldn't disguise his strength. It was easy enough for her to imagine the flexing of his muscles as he swung the ax in a smooth rhythm, notching out tiny chips of wood, first from one side, then from the other. His breath formed in tiny clouds before his slightly parted lips, and before he was finished, trickles of sweat streaked the sides of his face.

With a loud crack, the trunk split and the six-foot tree toppled to the ground, a puff of snow rising around it.

Martha cheered, hopping up and down and clapping her hands, and Suzanne mimicked her.

With a grin, Dirk turned and looked toward Inga and the girls. "We have a Christmas tree."

How very much she loved this man. She had no right to love him, but she did anyway.

Suddenly, a snowball struck Dirk in the shoulder. His attention shifted to Martha, who was wearing a proud expression.

"Why, you little—" Dirk began, grinning wickedly.

The girl threw another one, barely missing his head. She squealed as her uncle leaned down and scraped snow into his hands, patiently shaping a perfect ball in his palms. Martha spun around and tried her best to run away. His snowball struck her between her shoulder blades. Quickly, he shaped another.

Before Inga knew what was happening, she found herself in the middle of a free-for-all. She tried to shield a giggling Suzanne from the flying spheres. Finally, in an act of self-preservation, she tossed a few snowballs of her own. Her aim was atrocious. Neither Martha nor Dirk were in any danger from Inga, and when they both realized it, they turned upon her with glee.

"Run, Suzanne!" she shouted, grabbing the child's hand.

Before she could take more than a couple of steps, she was pelted from behind. She stumbled to her knees. She started to rise, and suddenly, she felt Dirk's hand beneath her elbow.

"Sorry. Didn't mean to knock you down."

She looked into his face as she rose to her feet. Despite the cold, she felt overheated. He was so close. Too close. Her heart began to race. Her laughter was forgotten.

As his gaze met hers, his smile faded. His brows drew together in a puzzled frown. Time stood still, and Inga wondered what he could read in her eyes. Would he guess—

"We'd better get home," he said, his gaze still locked with hers. "Don't want you takin' sick from the cold." He released her arm, took a step back. "I'll get the tree while you put the children in the sleigh. Come on, Martha. Time to go."

"Aw, Uncle Dirk. Can't we—"

"No argument. Let's go."

Inga was sorry she'd fallen into the snow, sorry she'd caused the playful Dirk to go back into hiding. She wondered when she might see him again. She hoped it would be soon, then she hoped it would not. For seeing this happier side of him only made her heart love him more.

And that she did not need.

The trip home was more quiet than when they'd set out. Dirk knew he was responsible for the solemn mood, but he made no effort to change it. To be honest, he didn't know how.

He glanced at the woman beside him. She was a mystery. One moment he thought there was nothing particularly attractive about her. And then, he would look at her again and think . . .

He set his jaw as he stared at the snowy road before him.

Only a fool wouldn't realize Inga was not like the women in his past. She was sweet and wholesome, good and kind. A man couldn't dally with her for a few hours and then forget her. Especially not when she had a minister for a father!

Only a fool . . .

Dirk slapped the reins against the backsides of the horses, hurrying them along. He must have been crazy, taking the time away from his chores to go after a Christmas tree. A tree, for pity's sake!

But the idea had pleased his ma. He would long remember the look on her face when he'd mentioned it. And Martha and Suzanne had enjoyed themselves today, too. He supposed it was worth the time he'd taken from his chores.

Like it or not, his thoughts circled back to Inga, because it was she who had brought so many smiles into the Bridger household. He owed her his thanks and a lot more.

He glanced her way a second time. She was staring into the distance, her expression pensive, her thoughts taking her far away. Dirk studied the lines and angles of her fine-boned features and decided it was the sort of face that grew on a person, the sort that got prettier over time. He felt another twinge of unwanted attraction and was once again surprised and angered by it.

After all, he had more than his fair share of troubles as it was.

Monday, December 13, 1897
Uppsala, Iowa

My dear Beth,

I write to you in need of advice. I cannot go to my family. Certainly not to my parents, and my sisters would not understand. So I turn to you for help.

I have fallen in love with my employer, Dirk Bridger. It is an impossible situation, I am afraid. His heart yearns for many things, but a wife is not one of them.

What am I to do, my friend? How do I tell my heart not to love? I know to continue to feel this way will only lead to more pain later, and yet I do not know how to keep from feeling it.

Did I tell you that he is the most handsome man I have ever seen? He has eyes of darkest brown, like the rich Iowa soil. He is tall, so tall I must look up to see into those wondrous brown eyes. His hair is thick and always looks slightly mussed. It is brown, like his eyes, only it has golden streaks in it, as if kissed by sunshine. But beyond his handsome appearance, there is someone truly worth loving. Mr. Bridger is a man of honor and integrity. He values the needs of his family beyond his own wants. Even though he does not take easily to the parenting of two little girls, yet that he loves them is unmistakable.

I would do anything to give him happiness. Anything. I did not know love was like this, dear Beth. I never understood, when I received your letters, what it was you felt for your Mr. Steele. If I had, perhaps I might have been more sympathetic to your own struggles of the heart. It is bittersweet, this wanting, especially when I believe it is fruitless.

I am not sure if it makes matters better or worse, but I have also fallen in love with Mr. Bridger's nieces. This morning we celebrated Saint Lucia's Day. It does not seem to be of the same importance in America as it is in Sweden. I made Martha a white gown and a wreath for her head, and we baked cakes and buns to surprise her uncle. He was pleased, I think. I have never seen him smile so.

Only, I did not realize, until I was standing in his bedroom doorway, looking at him in his nightshirt, that perhaps it was inappropriate for me to do so. Beth, I felt so strange inside. It was an ache really. Nothing like I have ever felt before. I only knew I could have gone on, standing there, looking at him, forever if it had been possible.

Have you any advice for me, my friend? Or must I simply endure the broken heart which I know is to come?

Sincerely,

Inga Linberg

~Nine

D r. Swenson closed the door to Hattie's bedroom, then turned toward Dirk, who was standing in the living room, awaiting the physician's verdict. "I am sorry, Mr. Bridger. There is nothing more I can do for her. I have left laudanum to help dull the pain."

"How long?"

"The timing is in God's hands, young man. I cannot say for certain. But when her time comes, she will be free of the pain she is suffering now. That should give you some comfort."

Dirk leaned both palms against the fireplace mantel and stared into the flames. He felt both rage and despair. His mother was dying, and the best the doctor could do was offer platitudes. Platitudes that weren't welcome.

"Dr. Swenson?" Inga said softly from the kitchen doorway. "Will you stop by the parsonage and tell my father about Mrs. Bridger?"

"Of course, Miss Linberg."

"Tack."

The physician stepped over to Dirk and laid a hand on his shoulder. "I am sorry," he repeated.

Dirk didn't reply. The lump in his throat was too big. He could only nod his head.

"I'll return tomorrow." Dr. Swenson walked out of the living room and into the hall, followed by Inga.

Dirk heard them talking in muted voices before the front door opened. Cold air whisked down the hallway and into the living room, and he knew the doctor had departed.

He turned his back to the fire and stared at the Christmas tree, standing near the front window. It seemed years since he and Inga and the children had brought it back, but it had only been a week. His ma had been so pleased with the evergreen, proclaiming how wonderful it made the house smell. She'd sat in her chair by the fire and watched as Martha and Suzanne, with Inga's help, decorated the tree with bits of ribbon and strings of popcorn.

Dirk had almost believed his ma was going to prove the doctor wrong. For a couple of days, she'd looked better, seemed stronger, than he'd seen her in a long time. Then, just when he'd been getting used to her seeming improvement, she'd taken to her bed, no longer able to hide the pain she was in.

Drawing a deep breath, he walked to her bedroom and opened the door. The lamp was turned low, the window curtains drawn.

"Come in, son."

The lump in his throat threatened to choke him. He swallowed hard before entering the room. When he reached her bed, he took hold of her hand. "Ma."

Feebly, she tugged on his hand, urging him to sit on the bed beside her. "Did I tell you I got a letter from Margaret's cousin, Allison Trent? Only family Margaret had in the world, other'n us, after her folks died. Nice lady, Allison Trent. I met her once, back 'fore Suzanne was born. Real nice lady."

Dirk didn't know what Margaret or her cousin had to do with anything, but his ma seemed to want to talk about it, so he was ready to listen.

"Mr. Trent's some sort of diplomat. They've been livin' in Europe for years." She turned her head on the pillow. "Is it snowin' again?"

"No. The sun's out." He started to rise. "You want me to open the—"

"Don't go," she interrupted, her tenuous grip tightening.

"Okay. I'm not goin' anywhere, Ma." He settled back onto the edge of the bed.

Hattie met his gaze. "She said they'll be comin' for a visit in the spring."

"Who?"

"Allison Trent. Margaret's cousin. She and Mr. Trent will be comin' to see the girls." She sighed, glanced toward the window again. "I wish I could've seen her again. Margaret was mighty fond of her. The two of them were always writin' back and forth." She closed her eyes, then whispered, "I'd just like the Lord t'give me till Christmas. That'd be enough for me now. Just till Christmas."

Her words made him angry, and he was unable to hide it from her. "If you're askin' God for more time, why not ask for old age?"

"Dirk . . ." She waited until their gazes met before she continued. "Don't strain against the will of God so. You've lived off the land too long not to understand the meanin' of the passage that says everything's got its season, and everything under heaven's got its own purpose. It says there's a time t'be born and a time t'die, and I believe it. It's my time, Dirk. That's all."

"But it's *not* your time. You oughta have another twenty or thirty years. You're not old yet."

Hattie sighed deeply. "You know what else the good book says in that Scripture?" Her fingers tightened, squeezing his. "It says there's a time t'get and a time t'lose. A time t'weep and t'laugh. And there's a time t'love, son. It says God's made everything beautiful in his time. There's love and beauty all around us."

He knew she was seeking some way to comfort him, to make her dying not seem so wrong, but it wasn't working. He didn't want to hear what she was saying any more than he'd wanted to listen to the doctor's banalities.

"Maybe I've been wrong," she whispered, glancing away from him.

"About what?"

"I always thought it best t'let my boys discover what life had in store for 'em for themselves." She looked up. "But my time's runnin' out, Dirk, and if I'm ever gonna say what's in my heart, if I'm gonna be able to help you, I'm gonna have t'say it now, 'fore it's too late." A note of urgency entered her voice. "We don't always have t'go lookin' elsewhere for happiness, son. Sometimes, it comes knockin' on our own door. All we gotta do is just open that door and let the happiness in. This farm, these girls of John's and Margaret's, they're your life now."

"You know I'll take care of 'em, Ma."

She sighed again, and her voice returned to a near whisper. "Yes, son, I know you'll take care of 'em. But I want *more* for you. I want you to recognize the happiness that's starin' you in the face. Don't you see?"

He'd wanted more for himself, too, but he'd ended up on this farm instead. Of course, now wasn't the time to repeat those thoughts to her. Not now. Not with her dying.

"If you clutch that bitterness to your chest so hard, son, there'll come a time when you won't be able to let it go, even if you want to."

"I'll be okay, Ma," he answered. "Martha and Suzanne and me, we'll all be okay. They'll never want for anything. I'll make sure of that."

"I know that's what you believe," Hattie responded. "But you're still not hearing me, son. Please hear me."

"Ma, I don't know what—"

"I brought you and your brother up to trust God. I'm not sure when you chose to look elsewhere for the answers in life, but you won't find 'em anywheres outside Christ. I promise you that."

Dirk glanced away from her earnest gaze, uncomfortable with how it made him feel.

"I said a moment ago that you need to recognize the happiness that's starin' you in the face. But you need to know there's no real happiness if you don't have the Lord in your heart and put him first. Everything else ends up meaningless without him."

Dirk looked at his mother. He wanted to say something that would give her comfort, that would reassure her. Only there didn't seem to be any such words.

She returned his gaze for several heartbeats. Then, with another sigh, she closed her eyes. He watched her for a long while before realizing she'd fallen asleep.

Unbeknownst to Dirk, Inga had been listening from the doorway. She'd heard what Hattie had told her son. She'd also realized that he didn't understand. Her heart ached for him.

She moved into the room on silent footsteps, making her way to the foot of the bed. He seemed unaware of her presence.

"Mr. Bridger?" she whispered.

"Ma's asleep," he said without looking at her, his voice a monotone, revealing not just his weariness but also an emptiness of spirit.

"I think you should talk to Martha."

"About what?"

"She is frightened. She knows her grandmamma is dying. She needs your comfort."

Suddenly, his eyes blazed with anger. "What am I supposed to say to her?"

Tears burned Inga's eyes, and her throat ached. "Tell her you love her, Mr. Bridger. That would be enough."

"Would it?" He stood.

"*Ja,* it would."

He headed for the door. "I think I'm the wrong person for the job, Miss Linberg."

A few moments later, the back door slammed closed behind him.

"Inga?"

She looked toward the woman on the bed.

Awake again, Hattie was watching her with pain-filled eyes. "Promise me you'll stay on after I'm gone. The girls are gonna need you more'n ever." She paused, then added, "So's Dirk."

Inga slipped to the side of the bed. She took hold of Hattie's hand and leaned in close. "I will stay, Mrs. Bridger. As long as your son wants me to. As long as I can be of help. I promise."

"You love him." It wasn't a question.

Her chest hurt. "*Ja,* I love him."

"Give him time. He'll come around."

"He is angry with God. He is angry with himself."

"Remember a couple weeks back, when I told you Dirk was dyin' inside 'cause of all the dreams he'd had to give up? I thought there wasn't any hope for him t'find what he's been lookin' for. But I was wrong. He just doesn't know what it is he's supposed to find. He's chasin' the wrong dreams. The good Lord's got somethin' better in mind for him."

Inga smiled sadly. "If I could give him his dreams, I would. I will pray for him. I will ask God to help him."

"You're a lovely young woman. You've brought joy into this house like it hasn't seen in ages. I wish ... I wish I could've lived long enough t'see you and Dirk together. I believe God brought you to our home for Dirk and not me or the girls. The Lord'll finish what he started."

Inga hadn't the heart to disagree with Hattie. Why not let the woman die in peace, believing her son would find happiness without traveling the world over first? Inga was certain it was only wishful thinking, but if Hattie believed it, what would it hurt?

Dirk's mother closed her eyes. "You think I'm a foolish old woman, but some things are made clearer when your time on this earth nears its end. You'll see."

Hoping Hattie was right, Inga smoothed the blankets around the woman's shoulders.

Hattie opened her eyes again. "Promise me you won't give up on him. Promise me that, and I'll ask nothin' more."

"All right. I promise. I won't give up on him. Now close your eyes and get some rest."

"There'll be plenty of rest where I'm goin'." She turned her head and gazed toward the window. "Open the curtains for me, will you, Inga? I've a mind to see some sunshine. Pity it's winter. In the spring, I can see daffodils through this window. Margaret planted a large bed of bulbs there about five, maybe six years back. Right pretty when they all start bloomin'."

Inga hurried to pull back the curtains as asked.

"Sure hope I get t'see one more Christmas."

Outside, sunlight glittered over a crystalline landscape. Inside, the wintery bright rays cast dozens of little rainbows onto the bedroom ceiling and wall, thanks to the teardrop prisms hanging from the shade of the bedside lamp.

"Pappa says the rainbow is a promise from God," Inga said when she saw the reflected lights on the wall. "You have no daffodils, Mrs. Bridger, but see how many promises you have been given?"

But Hattie had fallen asleep without seeing them.

—

His ma was right. Dirk *was* bitter, and he was hanging onto that bitterness for all it was worth. Didn't he have a right to feel that way? His dad was sick for years before he died. His brother and sister-in-law were killed while still in their prime. Now his ma was dying, too. The only family left to him were two little girls that he didn't have the foggiest notion how to raise, and he was saddled with a dairy farm that he hated.

And Inga was right, too. It was *his* duty to talk to Martha, not hers. Trouble was, he didn't know how to offer the child comfort when he felt so comfortless himself. But he reckoned he'd better try.

He returned to the house, determined to do the best he could. When he opened the back door and stepped into the kitchen, he was greeted by the excited cry of his niece.

"Look what I'm makin', Unca Dirk!" Suzanne exclaimed as she showed him a piece of bright yellow cloth.

"What is it?"

Martha answered without looking up from the fabric she was cutting with scissors. "We're makin' daffodils for Grandma."

"Daffodils?" He glanced toward Inga.

"Your mother expressed a wish to see the flowers again. The children and I thought we would surprise her with some."

Dirk shrugged out of his coat, trying to ignore the lump in his throat. "That's real thoughtful."

"You look cold." Inga's pale eyes were filled with compassion. "I will get you some coffee."

"Thanks." He followed her with his gaze as she rose from her chair and went to the stove. Then, while Inga poured the coffee, Dirk turned to his nieces.

Little Suzanne was full of smiles and excitement over their latest project, and he knew she hadn't any real concept of what dying meant. But Martha, she had to understand. She had to know it meant she would never see her grandma again, just like she'd never seen her parents again.

Looking now at the older girl's wan face, he knew she'd been crying, and he understood that she was more than sad. She was scared.

He drew a deep breath as he crossed to the table and pulled out a chair next to Martha. "Your grandma's gonna like these," he told her.

The girl nodded but kept right on with her cutting, her mouth pursed in concentration.

"This is gonna be hard on all of us. We're all gonna miss her."

She looked up, her eyes suddenly swimming with tears.

Tell her you love her, Mr. Bridger. That would be enough.

He cleared his throat softly. "Martha—"

"Are you gonna die, too?" She hiccuped a tiny sob.

Dirk opened his arms. "Come here."

She almost fell off the chair in her rush to do exactly that.

A moment later, he was holding her against his chest. "I'm not gonna die, Martha," he whispered as he stroked his hand over her hair. "I'm gonna be right here, takin' care of you." He glanced up and saw Inga watching them.

Tell her you love her, Mr. Bridger. That would be enough.

He gave her a small nod, as if she'd actually spoken. Then he whispered, "I love you, Martha. I love you and Suzanne, and we're gonna be all right, the three of us. I swear to you, we're gonna be all right."

Strangely enough, he almost believed his promise. For just that moment, as he watched Inga smile gently at them from across the room, he felt a spark of hope.

—

When Inga opened the door the next morning and saw her parents standing on the porch, she felt a great flood of relief. Until then she hadn't realized how heavy her burden of worry for the Bridger family had become.

"Oh, Pappa, I'm so glad you are here." She kissed his cheek. Then, fighting unexpected tears, she embraced her mother. "Mamma."

"We have come to see Mrs. Bridger," her pappa said. "Dr. Swenson brought your message yesterday."

Inga nodded. "She will be glad you have come. Let me have your coats, and then I will take you to her. Mr. Bridger is out in the barn, but the children are in with their grandmamma now."

A few minutes later, she led the way to Hattie's room. "Mrs. Bridger, my parents have come to call."

The ailing woman turned her head on her pillow. "Reverend and Mrs. Linberg." Her voice was weak. "What a nice surprise." She smiled. "Do you see what my granddaughters have made for me? A garden of daffodils."

It was good Hattie had explained the patches of yellow and green fabric which had been pinned to the walls and the curtains. Only a very few of them resembled flowers. But it hadn't mattered to Hattie. She'd been delighted with them when she'd awakened this morning and discovered them there.

Bernadotte Linberg crossed the room to admire the cheery display, then she looked at the children. "This is a wonderful gift you have given your grandmamma."

"It was Miss Inga's idea," Martha volunteered.

Her mother glanced up. "I am not surprised." Then she asked the girls, "Will you show me how you made them?" She held out her hands. After only a moment's hesitation, Suzanne and Martha slid off the foot of their grandmother's bed, took Bernadotte's hands, and accompanied her from the room.

Inga had seen similar scenes in the past, and she knew this was her mother's way of leaving the pastor alone to pray with Hattie. As her father pulled a chair close to the side of the bed, Inga stepped out of the bedroom and closed the door. Then she turned and followed the children and her mother into the kitchen.

Martha was showing Bernadotte the paper pattern they had used to trace the flowers onto the fabric. "Miss Inga made these, but I did all the cuttin'."

"Will you show me?" Bernadotte asked again.

Martha glanced over her shoulder.

Inga nodded. "You know where I keep the sewing scraps."

Martha darted out of the kitchen, Suzanne not far behind. Inga smiled as she listened to the thunderous footsteps on the stairs.

"How are you faring, dear?"

She looked at her mother, her smile fading. "I did not know it would be this hard."

"You have come to care for this family."

"*Ja*, that is true."

"Dr. Swenson says Mrs. Bridger does not have long. Perhaps a few days at most."

"*Ja*. We have tried to prepare the children." She turned toward the kitchen window. She thought of Dirk, of the way he had held Martha last night, of how much she had wanted to hold both of them in her own arms.

"It is a difficult time for a family to go through. I'm glad you are able to help them." Bernadotte sat on one of the kitchen chairs. "But I will also be glad to have you at home again when your time here is done."

Inga had walked over to the window and was staring out at the barn, wondering what Dirk was doing, wondering if she should go out and tell him her parents had arrived. "I have promised Mrs. Bridger I will stay as long as I am needed."

"Inga, you cannot stay after Mrs. Bridger dies."

She turned to meet her mamma's gaze. "But I must. The children—"

"You cannot live in this house without at least the semblance of a chaperone. I realize Mrs. Bridger has been ill, but her presence protected you from those who would gossip. However, it would not be seemly for you to remain after she is gone."

Panic was the only way Inga could have described what she felt. It hadn't occurred to her, although it should have, that convention would demand she return to her own home after Hattie's death. "Mamma, what will Mr. Bridger do with the children if I do not stay? I will be needed more than ever."

"I am sorry for them, of course, but this cannot be helped. We are to avoid even the appearance of evil."

The girls returned at that moment, and Inga was glad for the interruption. She needed some time to collect her careening emotions. She'd known she wouldn't be able to stay forever, but she hadn't expected to be forced to leave so soon. And although she'd used the excuse of Dirk's need for her help with the children, Inga knew her panic had much more to do with her own need to be near him.

Bernadotte appeared to be paying close attention to Martha as the child explained how they had made the daffodils, but Inga caught the occasional worried glances her mamma sent her way. She could only hope she wouldn't guess the full extent of Inga's feelings, or she might very well insist her daughter return to the parsonage that very day.

—

Hattie Bridger's prayer was answered. She lived to see one more Christmas. She was there when Martha and Suzanne saw the dolls Inga had made for them and when Dirk removed the wrapping paper to reveal the Jules Verne novel. She was there to see the sunshine melting icicles hanging from the eaves outside her window and to admire one last time the garden of daffodils that had been so lovingly made for her. She was there to eat a few bites of the Christmas goose and sample the Swedish porridge. She was there to hear the family sing her favorite Christmas carols.

As dusk cast a blue-gray shadow over the snow-covered farmland, she held her son's hand and told him one more time that she was proud of him, that she loved him. She kissed her granddaughters on their rosy cheeks and bade them to be good. She told Inga she was glad she'd been given these weeks to know her and thanked her for all she had done.

Hattie Bridger died just as darkness announced the end of Christmas Day.

~Ten

Two days after Christmas, they buried Hattie Bridger beside her elder son and daughter-in-law. The sky was gray, the wind plaintive, the temperature icy and bone-chilling.

Considering the weather, there were a lot of people at the funeral: their neighbors, Sven and Frida Gerhard; Dr. Swenson; the Dolks and their strapping twin sons, Vilhelm and Valdemar; Erik and Josephine Hansen; Reverend Linberg, who conducted the short service, and his wife and daughters.

And Inga was there, holding Martha's and Suzanne's hands, and somehow sharing a gentle strength with Dirk, even in her silence.

Dirk had done most of his mourning in the days before his mother passed on, and after the funeral, he observed the remainder of the day as if from a distance, never feeling quite connected with any of it. Inga, always gracious and efficient, played the role of hostess, greeting those who had come to pay their respects and condolences, accepting their platters of food, hanging up their hats and coats.

It was late in the afternoon by the time the Linbergs, the last to leave, began gathering up their things. Dirk thanked the pastor and his family for their kindnesses, but secretly, he wouldn't be sorry to have the house silent again.

Then he turned and saw Inga coming down the stairs, wearing her coat, her two youngest sisters carrying her trunk between them.

"Inga?" he asked. "You're going?"

"I am sorry, Mr. Bridger. We must leave before it gets any later or we will be driving in the dark."

"But why? Where are you going?"

Her eyes widened as she drew closer. "I told you I cannot stay, Mr. Bridger. Don't you remember?" She glanced toward her parents. "Pappa won't allow it."

Dirk looked at the pastor. "Why not?"

It was Inga who answered. "Because I am an unmarried female, and you are an unmarried man." She blushed when his gaze swung back to her.

Had she told him she would be leaving? He didn't remember the conversation. If she had, surely he would have tried to persuade her to stay. How was he to manage without her? His nieces loved her, and they would need her more than ever now. *He* would need her.

But when he turned toward her father a second time, he realized it would be fruitless to plead with him. The pastor would never allow his daughter to remain in a situation that might lead to gossip and scandal, even though there would be no basis for either. It wouldn't have mattered to Reverend Linberg that nothing untoward had ever been shared between Dirk and Inga. Not so much as a touch or a kiss.

Perhaps Dirk had thought Inga pretty a time or two. Perhaps he had even felt a tug of desire. But those had been momentary, passing thoughts. Nothing he would have acted upon.

Inga leaned forward, her hand reaching out but not quite touching him. "You will let me know how the children are when you come to town?"

"Sure. Of course." What was he going to do? He couldn't manage the farm and the house and the children all by himself. Martha wasn't old enough to cook the meals or clean. She wasn't old enough to keep a proper eye on Suzanne.

"I told the girls good-bye when I was upstairs. They are in their room." Inga's voice dropped almost to a whisper. "You need to go up to them."

How could she walk out this way, when they needed her so much? Dirk had come to depend upon her. How could she pretend to care about his family and then just walk out?

Reverend Linberg opened the door. "Come along, everyone. It's getting late."

"We are sorry for your loss, Mr. Bridger," Bernadotte said before walking through the open doorway.

One by one, the Linberg girls followed behind their mother, each offering parting words of comfort. Inga, the last to go, hesitated a moment in front of him, as if she would say something, too. Then, bowing her head, her gaze on the ground, she followed after the others without speaking. As she passed her father, who remained beside the door, the pastor bid Dirk a final farewell, then departed, closing the door behind him.

With real despair, Dirk turned toward the stairs, wondering again how he was going to manage.

—

"Whatever is the matter with you, Inga?" Thea demanded. "All you have done for three days is stare out that window and sigh. You cannot possibly miss those little girls that much."

"But I do miss them that much," she answered. She missed their uncle even more.

"Well, I know Pappa is glad to have you back where you belong. He couldn't find anything in his office while you were away."

Back where you belong.

Inga wandered to the window and looked down at the snow-covered garden behind the parsonage. She could feel the cold through the glass, but her heart felt colder still. If she could have spoken to either of her parents about what she was feeling, about her love for Dirk Bridger, she knew they would have told her to pray for God's will to be done. Only she didn't want to pray that way. For what if what she wanted wasn't God's will? She wanted Dirk. Never had she wanted anything more.

"Inga?" Thea placed her hand on Inga's shoulder. "You aren't listening to me."

"I am sorry."

"What about Karl? Have you given it more thought? How I am to reach him?"

She shook her head even as she felt a spark of resentment. It would never occur to Thea that Inga might be heartbroken by her separation from the man she loved, just as Thea was herself. It would never occur to any of her sisters that Inga might want to be married, to be held and kissed by a husband, to have children and a home of her own. Everyone simply assumed her future was in the parsonage, helping her pappa. She knew they didn't mean to be cruel or thoughtless. After all, it had always been what she expected, too. But it *was* cruel and thoughtless, and it *did* hurt.

She might have told Thea everything right then if they hadn't been interrupted.

"Inga, you have a caller," Astrid announced as she entered the bedroom. "It is Mr. Bridger."

Her heart jumped wildly. She glanced at her reflection in the mirror, wishing she was wearing one of her newer gowns, wishing she had done something different with her hair, wishing . . .

"Gunda went to get Mr. Bridger some coffee." Astrid took a step backward into the hall. "Pappa is with him now."

"I will go right down." Inga swept passed her sister, only barely restraining herself from breaking into an all-out run.

It was difficult to think above the pounding in her chest. Her breaths came in tiny gulps, and her legs felt unsteady as she descended the stairs. Her careening emotions only worsened when she stepped into the parlor doorway and saw him, seated on the sofa.

Dirk glanced up, then rose to his feet. "Hello."

He looked wonderful. So darkly handsome. So strong and so tall. It seemed years—eons!—since she had seen him.

Tears sprang to her eyes, and she blinked them away. Pasting a smile on her lips, she moved into the room. *"Goddag,* Mr. Bridger. How are you? How are Martha and Suzanne?"

"That's why I'm here," he answered obliquely. He glanced toward her father, then back to her. "I was hopin' I might speak with you in private, Miss Linberg, if that'd be all right with the pastor."

Inga's excitement over seeing him faded somewhat, concern replacing it. Something was wrong. She should have realized it before. Why else would he come?

She looked at her pappa.

He nodded. "I have work to do on my sermon." Olaf picked up a sheaf of papers. "Come along, Astrid. Let's join Gunda in the kitchen. I could use some of that coffee."

A dozen possibilities of what could have brought Dirk to the parsonage raced through Inga's mind as her father and sister left the room. Could one of the girls be ill? Had there been an accident at the farm? Certainly, judging by Dirk's expression, whatever had brought him here was serious.

Once they were alone, he pointed toward the sofa. "Mind if we sit down?"

"Has something happened to one of the girls? Suzanne, has she—"

"No. They're both right enough, I reckon. I left 'em with Mrs. Gerhard while I came to town."

Her voice dropped to a hoarse whisper. "And you? Are you well?"

He pointed at the sofa again and waited until she was seated before answering, "I'm okay."

She relaxed slightly. "I am glad to hear it."

Dirk raked his fingers through his hair as was his habit. "I don't quite know how to go about sayin' what I came here to say, Miss Linberg. I've never been much good with words. I guess the best way is to just get it said."

"*Ja,* that is true."

He drew a deep breath. "The truth is, Miss Linberg, things aren't goin' very well at the farm. The girls miss their grandma, and they miss you, too. I'm a lousy cook, so nobody's eatin' like they should. The house is a mess. Laundry's piled up. Truth is, we need you."

Her heart fell. "Oh, Mr. Bridger, I wish I could help, but Pappa would never—"

"I've come to ask for your hand in marriage, Miss Linberg. I'd like us to get married right away. Tomorrow, if you're willin'."

She caught her breath, and her eyes widened as she stared at him in disbelief.

"Look, I know there's no love shared between us, but I think we get on well enough together. I'm not askin' you to . . . well . . . to share my bed. It wouldn't be a marriage in that respect, if you know what I mean."

She didn't know exactly what he meant, but she had a vague notion. She nodded.

"We could go on, like it was before Ma died. You'd still have your own room. The girls are right fond of you, and I know you'd always be good to them."

"Mr. Bridger, I—"

"I respect you, Miss Linberg, and I promise I'd never treat you ill. The work would be as hard as ever, but I think we'd manage well enough. You and me, we both want different things than what we've got now. I've always had a hankerin' to travel, and I expect there are things you'd like to do, too. If you'd stay with us until the girls're old enough to take care of themselves, that's all I'd ask. I promise you here and now that I wouldn't leave you in need when the time came for partin'. The farm, it'll go to the girls and the men they decide to marry, but I'd find some way to see that you were compensated fairly for the years you'd be givin' up."

"That wouldn't be—"

"No, that'd only be fair. And I'd swear before whatever court or judge was necessary that we'd had us a celibate marriage so you could get yourself an annulment. There wouldn't be the scandal of divorce. I'd take all the blame on myself so no one could point any fingers at you. It wouldn't be for all that long, you know. Suzanne's nearly four now. In another eight years, maybe ten, she'd be—"

"I accept, Mr. Bridger." Inga waited a heartbeat, then added, "I will marry you."

The room stilled. Only the ticking of the mantelpiece clock could be heard. Inga fought the urge to cry, not knowing if it was for joy or sorrow. She supposed it was for both reasons. She loved him. There was nothing she wanted more than to be his wife and to love him until the day she died. But he had proposed in order to have a housekeeper and a woman to care for his nieces, not because he wanted a wife, and knowing the truth hurt more than she thought anything could.

"Are you sure?" he asked softly, his dark eyes searching hers.

Actually, she was certain the wiser path would be to reject his offer. She knew Dirk longed for many things, just as he'd said. She understood the hopes he harbored. Marriage, a wife, a family had never been part of those dreams of the future. She was setting herself up for more heartache. But the children needed her, she rationalized. Dirk truly could not manage without someone to help him. And marriages were often made for exactly this reason. Widowers with children often sought new brides simply to have a woman to raise the offspring they already had. Women frequently married for nothing more than security. Sometimes they married complete strangers.

Dirk was no stranger. Dirk was the man she loved. If she married him, there was always the chance he might one day come to love her, too.

"Inga, are you sure?"

"*Ja,* I am sure ... Dirk." It felt strange to use his given name, despite how often she had secretly thought it. "But I have a request."

He raised an eyebrow.

"I would not have anyone know this is a marriage in name only. While it was never my plan to marry, Mamma ... she will want to think I marry for love."

"Sure." He shrugged. "I don't reckon it's anyone else's business but ours, yours and mine, for now. Later ... Well, we'll see to that when the time comes."

Ours. Yours and mine. Wonderful words, if only they meant what she longed for them to mean.

Dirk stood. "I guess I need to speak to the pastor."

She rose, too, and impulsively took hold of his hand. "We will do it together."

As she looked up at him, Dirk briefly thought about kissing her. He wasn't a complete fool. Even a proposal for a marriage of convenience should probably be sealed with a kiss. It wasn't as if he didn't think kissing her would be pleasant. Actually, he imagined he'd enjoy it. But before he could act on the impulse, Inga took a step away from him, pulling him along with her.

At her father's study, she rapped on the closed door, then leaned in close and said, "Pappa, may we come in?"

"*Ja,*" came the muffled reply.

Inga glanced over her shoulder. She gave Dirk a fleeting smile, then turned the knob and opened the door.

Olaf Linberg was seated behind his desk, holding a steaming mug of coffee to his lips. As they approached him, Dirk saw the surprise in the other man's eyes when Olaf noticed their joined hands. Dirk's grip tightened, and Inga looked at him. He realized then that she was nervous, perhaps even afraid of what her father's reaction would be.

"Pappa, we—"

"Reverend Linberg," Dirk interrupted, "I've asked your daughter to be my bride, and she's done me the honor of accepting. We'd like your blessing, sir, and want you to perform the ceremony."

Olaf's gaze flicked back and forth between Dirk and Inga. "Marriage?"

"We'd like you to marry us tomorrow, Reverend."

Her father stood, his gaze locked on his daughter. "Is there reason for such haste?"

"*Ja,*" she answered.

Surprised, Dirk looked at her. Didn't she understand what her father was suggesting?

"We do not want to be apart, Pappa. I am needed there, by Mr.—by Dirk, and by the children, too. I want to be with them. That is the reason for our haste." Her gaze didn't waver as she met her father's watchful eyes. She stood straight, chin tilted stubbornly, and her voice was strong and certain. "Time will not change my decision to marry, Pappa. It is your blessing we seek, not your permission."

The minister glanced toward Dirk. "These are your feelings, too, Mr. Bridger?"

"I've never taken liberties with your daughter, if that's what you're gettin' at, Reverend Linberg. I took proper care of her when she was with us before, and I'll take proper care of her now. You've got my word on that."

"You mistake me, young man," her father replied. "I know what it is to be young and in love, although it is always difficult for the young to believe that of their elders. But if love is real, it will survive a time of separation." He looked at his daughter again. "I would never mean to imply that Inga would deport herself in any way but an acceptable one."

"Pappa—"

Olaf raised his hand to halt her words. "It is not necessary to argue with me, Inga. I have not been your pappa for all these years without learning many things about you. You are kind to those near to you. You are tender and loving to those who need nurturing, and you are generous with all that is yours, always looking for ways to help others. All good qualities, I might add." His smile was tolerant. "You are also more stubborn than a mule, *kära du,* and when I see that expression on your face, I know it is useless to try to reason with you."

What Dirk saw was a glimmer of tears in her eyes, not stubbornness, and he felt something tighten in his chest in response.

"Mr. Bridger," the pastor continued, still gazing at his daughter, "I foolishly thought I would be allowed to keep Inga at home with me and her mamma. When I get too old to shepherd my congregation, I always envisioned having long philosophical and religious discussions with her, for she is intelligent, this daughter of mine. I should have known her heart held too much love not to give it away to the man she would want to marry." Now he looked at Dirk. "You are fortunate, Mr. Bridger, that she has agreed to be your wife. You must also be a man of fine character to have won her heart. She would never agree to marry you otherwise."

Dirk felt like a fraud.

"Will you perform the ceremony tomorrow morning, Pappa?"

"*Ja.* I will agree to dispense with the reading of the banns. But your mamma is not going to like this haste. She will want to do more."

"Thank you, Pappa," Inga whispered, and again there were tears in her eyes.

Dirk had a strange wish to fold her in his arms and make her tears go away. He wanted to prove he was the man Reverend Linberg thought he was. He almost wished he and Inga were marrying for all the reasons her father thought. But they weren't, and that was the way Dirk preferred it to stay. Loving folks tied a man down, held him captive when he yearned to roam. Besides, loving someone only brought pain when they died.

And they so often died.

Olaf offered his hand to Dirk. "I wish you happiness, young man, and God's blessings on your marriage."

"Thanks."

Inga's hand slipped from Dirk's as her father turned toward her, his arms outstretched. They embraced, Olaf whispering softly in his native tongue.

Dirk wondered if he was making a terrible mistake, taking Inga from her father and the rest of her family. Would a man of fine character take a woman from a warm and loving home to the harsh life he had to offer? It wasn't fair to her. But what other choice did he have?

"Now," the pastor said as he stepped backward, "I believe you should bid each other a good day. Then, Inga, you and I must go and tell your mamma. She is with Mrs. Jansson this afternoon. The widow's rheumatism has been causing her great distress. But we must not wait until your mamma comes home to tell her your plans for tomorrow morning. She will think of much to be done before then, if I know my wife."

Inga nodded, then glanced at Dirk. "I will walk you to the door."

"Goddag"—the pastor hesitated only an instant before adding—"son."

Dirk shoved away his feelings of guilt and uncertainty. "Good day, sir."

Life was hard, he rationalized as he walked beside Inga toward the front door of the parsonage. Folks did what they had to do to survive, to get along as best they could. He needed someone to care for his nieces, and Inga was the logical person. He hadn't lied to her about his reasons for proposing. He hadn't professed feelings that weren't true. He'd told her why he wanted to marry her and what the terms of their marriage would be. She was going into it with eyes open. She was intelligent, just as her father had said, and she knew what she was doing.

Besides, the state of their marriage was no one's business but their own. He had nothing to feel guilty about.

So why, when he looked down at her as he bid her farewell, did he still feel that irritating sense of guilt?

~Eleven

Invitations were hastily written and dispersed to members of the community, Inga's wishes for a quiet family affair ignored. In deference to the groom's recent bereavement, Bernadotte agreed there should be no dancing at the reception. Still, she fussed over a hundred different details for Inga's wedding, and she had all of her daughters working throughout the evening and way into the night, preparing food and cleaning and pressing clothes for everyone in the family.

As they worked, Thea and Gunda tittered and teased Inga about how the handsome Mr. Bridger had swept their very sensible sister off her feet. Astrid and Kirsten swore no woman, not even Inga, could have resisted him. They weren't far wrong. Inga had fallen helplessly in love with Dirk almost from the first moment they'd met.

But her sisters also waxed eloquent about how Inga had made Dirk fall in love with her—and *that* she knew was a lie. Rather than compound the falsehood with words or risk her sisters seeing the truth, Inga remained silent, averting her eyes, and allowed them to think her the shy bride.

In her heart, she knew women married every day for reasons of convenience. There was no shame in what she was doing. Love was a bonus rather than a necessity for marriage.

But still she had her tattered pride—sin or not—to consider. She didn't want others to know the real reason Dirk had proposed. Not now. Not yet. Soon they would guess the truth. She couldn't expect Dirk to pretend a passion he didn't feel. Eventually, others would recognize that theirs was not a love match.

Strangely enough, during that wakeful hour before dawn, when the house was completely quiet and still, Inga realized she *felt* like a bride who was loved. She was filled with nervous anticipation. She even allowed herself a few moments of fantasy, imagining Dirk standing beside her in his dark suit as her father joined them in holy matrimony.

His hair would be mussed by his fingers, as usual, and his tie would likely be knotted improperly. He would smell of soap and water. His jaw would be clean-shaven, but there would be that ever-present shadow of a beard beneath his skin. He would stand straight and tall, towering over everyone else in the room. As he promised to love and to cherish her, she would look into his brown eyes and believe it was true. And when they were pronounced husband and wife, he would kiss her.

What would it feel like, that kiss? Would there be a particular taste to his mouth? Would his kiss feel hard or would it be tender?

I'm not askin' you to ... well ... to share my bed.

What would it be like to share his bed? She had only a nebulous understanding of what that meant. A woman didn't have children unless she lay with her husband. It was something married women whispered about. Why?

As if summoned by Inga's thoughts, Bernadotte appeared in the doorway, a lamp in her hand. Light spilled into the bedroom, illuminating Inga's bed. She sat up.

"Mamma?"

Bernadotte put a finger to her lips as she glanced toward Thea, who was buried beneath her quilts. "I thought you might be awake," she whispered. "I could not sleep on the morning of my wedding. Come with me, Inga. We must talk, you and I."

Inga tossed aside the blankets and rose from the bed. She slid her bare feet into her house slippers, then grabbed her dressing robe and put it on as she followed after her mamma.

They went to the kitchen where the stove burned hot, chasing away the cold. Inga sat in a chair by the table while Bernadotte poured coffee into cups. After her mother had taken her own seat, the two women spent several moments in silence, looking at each other while sipping the hot drinks they had both sweetened with cream and sugar.

Finally, Inga couldn't stand the quiet any longer. "Why did you bring me down here, Mamma?"

Bernadotte wore a gentle smile, but it was tinged with sadness. "You are the first of my daughters to marry and leave home. I am having a difficult time adjusting."

"Oh, Mamma."

"I pray this union will make you happy, Inga. You never showed an interest in suitors before now."

It was more like suitors had had no interest in her, Inga thought.

Bernadotte touched the back of Inga's hand. "Marriage is a sacred union, *dotter,* and the joining of a man and woman in marriage is meant to be a beautiful thing." She pulled her hand away and gazed down at her cup. "You must not expect too much at first, but it need not be unpleasant. I know you will feel shy and embarrassed. That is only natural, and even as it should be for a maiden. But you must not deny him, for it is his right as your husband."

For a moment, Inga was confused. She didn't know what her mamma was talking about. Then it dawned on her. "What ...

what really happens, Mamma?" she whispered, her stomach fluttering with nervousness.

Bernadotte didn't look up. "A husband enjoys . . . touching his wife. In bed. The . . . the act of marriage is intimate, and many women are embarrassed or frightened. But I have found . . . well . . . Oh dear." She drew a quick breath, then took another sip of coffee.

Inga had never seen her mother blush before. Bernadotte Linberg seemed always to be calm, serene, and collected.

"Inga, what I am trying to say is that your wedding night may not be perfect. But given time, you may find yourself anticipating . . . even desiring . . . your husband's attentions. If he is gentle and patient and loves you, he will learn to please you." At last she looked up and met her daughter's gaze. "And even if that never happens, it is this very intimacy that gives a woman her greatest blessing. Children. Do you understand?"

No, she didn't understand. Her mother's words had left her bewildered and curious at the same time. But she nodded anyway, certain she would learn nothing more even if she inquired.

Bernadotte let out a deep sigh of relief. "Thank goodness," she whispered as she reached for something on the chair next to her. Then she held the white bundle toward Inga. "This is for you, my dear. It was your grandmamma's for her wedding night, and she gave it to me for my wedding night. Now it goes to my eldest daughter for her wedding night. When your husband sees you in it, may he say, like Solomon, 'Behold, thou art fair, my love; behold, thou art fair.'"

I'm not askin' you to . . . well . . . to share my bed.

"Oh, Mamma." Inga's voice cracked as she fought the tears welling up in her eyes.

She should refuse to take the gown. She wouldn't need it. She would never understand the obscure references her mother had made. She would never know if she thought her husband's attentions or his touch were pleasant or not.

Because Dirk didn't want to touch her. Because he didn't find her fair as King Solomon had found his bride.

Never had Inga felt more plain and unattractive than she did at that precise moment.

———

"Miss Inga's always gonna live with us, huh, Uncle Dirk? She's never gonna go back to town to live. Right?"

He looked at Martha, who was sitting to his right on the seat of the sleigh. "Yeah. She's going to come to stay."

"She's gonna be Aunt Inga now. Isn't that right?"

"Yeah, that's right."

"I love Miss Inga!" Suzanne piped up from his other side.

He glanced at his younger niece. Her eyes sparkled with merriment, and her cheeks and nose were the color of ripe cherries. He didn't know when she'd ever looked this adorable.

He'd done the right thing, asking Inga to marry him. Both the girls were as pleased as punch. As for Dirk himself . . . well, he hadn't spent much time worrying about his own feelings. A man did what he had to do. It was as simple as that. And he didn't reckon he would mind having Inga Linberg in his house again.

He remembered the many kindnesses she had shown his mother. He remembered the frigid mornings she had brought hot coffee to him when he was working in the barn. He remembered the fragrant odors of supper cooking. He remembered the children's laughter as Inga told them stories at bedtime.

No, he didn't reckon he would mind having her there again.

The parsonage came into view, and his stomach muscles tightened in a flash of jitters. This was it. He was taking a wife.

Unconsummated or not, it would still be a marriage, and marriage was one more link in the chain that kept him shackled to a life he'd never wanted.

He set his jaw, irritated with himself. There was no point wanting things he could never have. He'd be better off to accept the hand fate—or was it God?—had dealt him.

If you clutch that bitterness to your chest so hard, son, there'll come a time when you won't be able to let it go, even if you want to.

Ma had been right. Only he didn't know how to let it go.

———

From the window of her parents' bedroom, Inga watched the sleigh pull up to the house. Her heart skittered and her pulse pounded. He was here. He had come. She hadn't realized until this moment that she'd been afraid he would change his mind. But he was here, and in a short while, she would be his wife. In name only, perhaps, but his wife nonetheless.

Mrs. Dirk Bridger.

"I wish it was me," Gunda said as she stepped up beside Inga. "You are so lucky. He is the most handsome man in all of Uppsala. Of course, if he had asked me, I would have made him marry me proper. I would have made myself a new bridal gown for my wedding instead of wearing something out of fashion like Mamma's dress. Everyone would have brought gifts to the receptions we'd have had after church when the banns were read, and all of our friends would have gathered for the tug of the birch tree. And we certainly would have had music and dancing."

Inga nodded absently.

"You and Mr. Bridger did not even exchange gifts," Gunda continued. "Not so much as a silk handkerchief or a pair of gloves."

"It is not the same in America," Inga whispered as she watched Dirk lift first Martha and then Suzanne from the sleigh.

That wasn't true, of course. The Linberg sisters had attended a wedding in Uppsala three months before. They had toasted the bride and groom with Swedish vodka and partaken of coffee and cake at the various receptions. They had watched young men cut down a large birch tree and haul it to the bride's home where it was sawn into pieces, some to be used for furniture in the couple's new home. They had listened as their pappa conducted the marriage ceremony, seen the bride blush, watched as the groom sealed their vows with a kiss.

"You didn't even have reading of the banns." Gunda clucked her tongue. "It isn't right."

Thea took Gunda by the arm and pulled her away from the window, scolding softly, "Why should Inga wait three weeks so the banns can be read? She is in love. And Mr. Bridger just lost his mother. It would not be seemly to celebrate in the usual way. Of course Inga would want to marry quietly and go with her husband." She paused a moment, then added, "It is what I would do if Karl was here and the circumstances were the same."

Inga turned around and met Thea's gaze. Usually her sister was wrapped up in her own concerns. Inga was grateful for her understanding. Perhaps it was because Thea would soon go to New York City to marry the man she loved, the man who was going to travel across an ocean to make her his wife. If only Dirk loved Inga even half as much as Karl loved Thea.

Inga forced a smile, trying to hide the pain that suddenly pierced her heart. She was greedy, she decided. She had never expected to marry at all. Now that she had fallen in love, now that she was about to wed, she wanted more. She wanted his love, too.

Her mother appeared in the doorway, the white bridal veil draped over her arms. "It is time," Bernadotte said as she entered the bedroom. She stopped in front of Inga, then leaned forward and kissed her daughter's cheek. "All the guests are here, and your groom has arrived. Are you ready?"

Inga nodded.

"You look beautiful." Her mamma set the crown of artificial white flowers on Inga's head, then smoothed the sheer, floor-length veil until it fell gently over her shoulders and her back.

Inga glanced down at the black silk wedding gown that had been her mother's before her. The dress had been taken in everywhere except for the hem, which had had to be let out. A new white lace collar had been added, this a gift from Gunda.

Beautiful? Oh, how she longed for Dirk to think so.

—

As he'd done countless times already, Dirk yanked at his collar with his forefinger, trying to loosen it so he could swallow comfortably. The parlor of the parsonage buzzed with the soft conversations of the guests, most of them strangers to him. Occasionally someone spoke to him or patted his back in congratulation. They all received the same response—a tense smile and an abrupt nod.

When the room suddenly stilled, he knew Inga had arrived. He turned and saw her, standing in the parlor doorway, surrounded by her mother and sisters. But when his eyes met with hers, he forgot the others.

She was lovely, as every bride should be. Pale and fragile. Flaxen wisps of hair curled across her forehead and around her temples, only a shade darker than the gossamer lace of the veil cascading around her shoulders. He could read the anxiety in her ice blue eyes, see it in the slight tremble of her lips.

I swear I'll be good to you, he promised her silently.

She came toward him, gliding across the floor, tall and willowy. When she reached him, he turned, Inga standing to his left, and together they faced her father.

The pastor cleared his throat, then began, "'In the Name of the Father, and of the Son, and of the Holy Ghost.'"

"Amen," everyone said.

"'Dearly Beloved: Forasmuch as Marriage is a holy estate, ordained of God, and to be held in honor by all, it becometh those who enter therein to weigh with reverent minds, what the Word of God teacheth concerning it. The Lord God said: It is not good that the man should be alone; I will make him an help meet for him . . .'"

A help meet. Wasn't that what Dirk had asked Inga to be? Wasn't that what she had been to him for several weeks? He glanced sideways at her. She was staring at her father, listening intently, her expression solemn.

"'. . . The Apostle Paul, speaking by the Holy Spirit, saith: Husbands, love your wives, even as Christ also loved the Church, and gave himself for it . . .'"

She deserved to be loved. She deserved better than he had offered her. But he'd offered all he had to give.

"'Into this holy estate this Man and this Woman come now to be united. If any one, therefore, can show just cause why they may not be lawfully joined together, let him now speak, or else forever hold his peace . . .'"

Was he doing the right thing? Was this marriage fair to her? Shouldn't he have tried to find someone else to work for him rather than asking Inga to give up her freedom?

"'Dirk Bridger, Wilt thou have this Woman to thy wedded wife, to live together after God's ordinance in the holy estate of

Matrimony? Wilt thou love her, comfort her, honor and keep her in sickness and in health, and, forsaking all others, keep thee only unto her, so long as ye both shall live?'"

He drew a deep breath. "I will."

Inga heard the deep timbre of his voice, and her gaze was drawn to him. One month before, he had stood in this parlor and asked her father for help. In the brief weeks since, she had lived in his home, had watched him lovingly care for his mother and his nieces. She knew the goodness of his heart. He would comfort and honor her. He would care for her in sickness and in health.

But would he ever love her as he had just sworn?

"'Inga Linberg, Wilt thou have this Man to thy wedded husband, to live together after God's ordinance in the holy estate of Matrimony? Wilt thou love him, comfort him, honor and keep him in sickness and in health, and, forsaking all others, keep thee only unto him, so long as ye both shall live?'"

"I will."

Her pappa took hold of her right hand and placed it into Dirk's right hand. At the touch, her heart began to race, and light-headedness overtook her.

Olaf looked at Dirk. "Repeat after me. I, Dirk ..."

"I, Dirk ..."

"Take thee, Inga ..."

"Take thee, Inga ..."

"To my wedded wife ..."

"To my wedded wife ..."

She fought unwanted tears as she listened to his vows. And when it was her turn to repeat them, her voice was so soft, Dirk had to lean toward her in order to hear. She wondered if he would guess how desperately she meant each word, not certain if she wished he would or not.

Her pappa blessed the wedding ring, then gave it to Dirk. As her groom then slipped it onto the third finger of Inga's left hand, he said, "Receive this Ring as a token of wedded love and troth."

Inga stared down at the simple gold band. *Wedded love.* If only ...

"'Forasmuch as Dirk and Inga have consented together in holy wedlock, and have declared the same before God and in the presence of this company, I pronounce them Man and Wife: In the Name of the Father and of the Son and of the Holy Ghost, Amen. What God hath joined together, let not man put asunder.'"

As her father then began his closing prayer, Inga opened her eyes and observed her husband.

My husband.

It was done. She was married. She was his wife, and she wanted to remain his wife forever. She wanted to lie beside him in his bed. She wanted to love him in all seasons, to love him in every possible way. She wanted to raise his nieces and to bear his children.

He had told her she would have her freedom one day, but she knew she would never want it. She was bound to him in a way she had never imagined possible. A way he would probably not understand.

What God hath joined together, let not man put asunder, her pappa had said, and to those words, she added her own silent prayer: *Father God, let him love me.*

Olaf's hands clasped Dirk's and Inga's. "'The Lord bless thee and keep thee. The Lord make his face shine upon thee, and be gracious unto thee. The Lord lift up his countenance upon thee, and give thee peace.'"

And everyone said, "Amen."

For the briefest of moments, Inga's gaze held her husband's, and she thought he might kiss her. Then the solemnity of the ceremony was over. The guests pressed forward, joyous voices filling the room. She was kissed and hugged by everyone except Dirk, and she let her tears spill over, hoping no one would guess how truly bittersweet they were.

~Twelve

It began to snow as the Bridger sleigh, carrying the newly-weds and the groom's nieces, pulled away from the parsonage, accompanied by shouts of good wishes from friends and family.

"Oh, isn't it pretty?" Astrid said to Thea who was standing by her side on the porch. "What a perfect way for it to end, riding off into a gentle snow like that."

For some reason, Thea didn't feel like agreeing. Ever since Pappa had begun the ceremony, her mood had grown darker and darker.

It wasn't right for Inga to be the first to wed. True, Inga was the oldest, but Thea was the prettiest. It had always been Thea who had the suitors sipping coffee in the parlor in Jönköping. Even after she'd made it clear she'd given her heart to Karl Gustav, the other boys had still come calling. And she, of course, had been flattered and had flirted right back with them. It would have been rude to do otherwise.

Besides, it had been harmless, for she never would have truly betrayed Karl.

Karl Gustav had owned Thea's heart since she was a girl of fourteen. That her pappa opposed the match when they'd declared their intention to marry only added to the romance of their young and desperate love, only made their furtive kisses more exciting.

She gave her head a tiny shake as she turned and went inside. There was no reason to be jealous of Inga. Dirk Bridger could not possibly love her the way Karl loved Thea. Karl was leaving behind family and country for her. Now *that* was love.

Of course, she'd never doubted he would do so. No other girl in Jönköping could have convinced him to stay in Sweden and forget Thea, for Thea, as everyone always said, was unforgettable. When she went to New York City to be with Karl, her sisters and all the other girls in Uppsala, Iowa, would be pea green with envy.

The Dolk twins came to stand on either side of her, one bringing her punch, the other bringing her cake. She smiled at them and batted her pretty blue eyes and giggled when they vied for her attention. She did so enjoy being the center of attention. Pappa had scolded her more than once for her actions, telling her she was vain and that vanity was a sin. But how could that be so? Thea had not made herself beautiful. She had been born that way, and she could do nothing to hide it.

Yes, she'd been silly to waste even a moment of jealousy on Inga. Poor Inga would never inspire young men to acts of passion the way Thea did, and Dirk Bridger, although quite handsome, was much too old—almost thirty!—to have ever caught Thea's attention.

She decided to enjoy the remainder of the celebration. In only two months she would be far away from this place and these people. She would have a husband of her own, a husband who loved her more than any woman had ever been loved before.

Which was just as it should be.

They rode in silence for a quarter of an hour before either bride or groom said a solitary word. Dirk was the first to speak.

"Sorry we had to leave so early." He slapped the reins against the backsides of the horses. "The milking won't wait. Not even for a wedding."

"It is all right," she whispered. "I did not mind leaving."

She looked behind her at the backseat of the sleigh. Cuddled up beneath several blankets and a large fur, Suzanne slept, her head cradled in her sister's lap. Martha looked ready to nod off, too. Inga understood. She felt exhausted, worn out by a day filled with warring emotions.

Dirk glanced at the lead gray sky. "Looks like the old year is gonna end with another good snowstorm."

"It would seem so."

"Ma always sat up to watch the new year come in. She said she liked to think ahead to what it might bring." He paused a moment, then added, "Sure wish she could've lived to see another one."

We could sit up together and watch, Inga thought, but she hadn't the courage to say it aloud. Perhaps, if Dirk really thought of her as his wife . . .

Tears burned the backs of her eyes and her throat, much to her dismay. It seemed all she had done for the last twenty-four hours was cry, and she was tired of it. No one had forced her to marry Dirk Bridger. She'd wanted to marry him. She'd wanted to be with him.

She swallowed hard, then drew a deep breath and said, "This new year will be a good one. You will see."

The rest of their trip home passed in silence, accompanied only by the *whish* of the runners gliding over the road. Snow continued to fall, large, wet flakes that drifted and cartwheeled toward earth, landing on the noses and eyelashes of the sleigh's occupants.

When they arrived at the farm, Dirk put away the horses while Inga ushered the children into the house. The moment she stepped into the large kitchen, she knew she was home. She smiled in earnest as a glimmer of hope lightened her heart.

The mood stayed with her as she prepared the family's supper. It stayed with her as she put away her things in the same bedroom she had vacated less than a week before. It stayed with her as she tucked the children into their bed and told them a bedtime story. It stayed with her right up until the moment Dirk announced he was going to retire for the night.

They were in the living room. A fire blazed in the fireplace, chasing the chill from the room. Inga was working on a new quilt, as much to give her hands something to do as for the enjoyment she usually took in her craft. Dirk had been standing at the window for a long while, staring out at the blackness that disguised the whirling snowstorm.

"I reckon I'll turn in," he said as he turned around.

She glanced up, her heart suddenly pounding like a bass drum. Her mouth and throat were dry, and her chest felt tight, almost painfully so.

Dirk took a step toward her. "Reckon I ought to thank you again for what you've done."

She shook her head, unable to speak.

"The girls were happy today. They're glad to have you back."

Inga laid her quilting piece on top of the basket. "I am glad to be back as well." She rose from the chair and faced her husband.

Dirk watched the firelight play over her hair, turning it from pale blond to red-gold. She had changed out of her wedding dress and was wearing an earth-toned blouse and skirt. He suspected he'd seen them several times in the past, but if so, he hadn't noticed before how the color infused her complexion with a golden glow. Nor had he remembered that the shape of her mouth—pink and moist and slightly parted—was somewhat like a bow on a Christmas package.

The silence of the house reminded him they were alone except for two sleeping children. She was his wife. Perhaps . . .

But he'd promised her an annulment one day, and he'd promised himself freedom down the road. If he took her innocence, both of those promises would be broken.

He wondered then if Inga knew the bitter taste of unrealized dreams. What had she wanted and lost before settling for a loveless marriage? What if . . .

But what-ifs were the same things as hopes and dreams, and he was better off not to entertain them. It wouldn't be fair to either one of them. He didn't want Inga to be hurt because of anything he did or said, and he didn't want to fool himself into thinking things were different than they were.

Raking his fingers through his hair, he turned his back to her. "The storm's getting worse. I'd better check on the livestock one last time. You don't have to wait up for—"

"Would you mind if I came with you?"

He glanced over his shoulder.

"I would like to be of help," she added.

He shrugged. Wasn't that why he'd asked her to marry him? So he'd have help with the farm? "Sure. If you want. Get your coat."

A few minutes later, they went out into the storm and walked side by side toward the barn, leaning into the wind as blowing snow stung their cheeks. The temperature had plunged since milking time. Dirk suspected it had fallen well below zero. He thought of the book he'd once read about the Sandwich Islands and wondered briefly what it might be like to spend New Year's Eve on the sands of a South Sea island instead of on a dairy farm in a blizzard.

The wondering of a fool, he chided himself.

When they stepped inside the barn and he closed the door behind them, the sounds of the storm became muffled. The barn seemed warm, at least at first. Dirk lit the lantern that hung near the tack room, turning the flame up high. Then he walked toward the nearest stall.

He muttered an expletive when he saw Flower moving in restless circles. The cow had chosen this night to give birth.

"Is something wrong?" Inga asked.

"No."

Inga came to stand beside him. She looked first at the Jersey, then at Dirk, a question in her eyes.

Leaning his arms on the top rail, he said, "She's going into labor."

"What must we do?"

He glanced over at his bride, thinking, *Good thing this wasn't supposed to be a real wedding night.* Then, he answered, "Nothing, if we're lucky."

He didn't bother to add that he was seldom lucky.

—

The laboring Jersey lay down in the straw with a plaintive *blat.*

"She's gonna get serious now," Dirk said as he entered the stall and knelt beside the cow, running his hand over her swollen side.

Inga stared down at man and beast and wondered at the gentleness Dirk displayed for an animal he professed to despise. "How long will it take?"

"Maybe another hour. Could be less. Could be more."

Flower's breathing grew heavier. She lifted her head and nipped at her side, then flopped back down with a groan.

"Easy, girl," Dirk whispered. "How come you always choose the coldest night of the year to do this? Stupid cow."

Inga watched with a sense of anticipation and apprehension. She had never witnessed a birthing, neither animal or human. Her mother wouldn't have allowed it. "Have you been through this many times before?" she asked Dirk.

"Many times. Cows, horses, litters of pups. It goes with farming and ranching. A few years ago, I worked on a horse-racing farm in Kentucky. Got to be present for the delivery of more than a dozen Thoroughbred foals that spring." Dirk sat back on his heels, his palms resting on his thighs. "The horse is a breathtaking creature. Especially the Thoroughbred. They're like a great work of art, the way they're formed. Of everything I've ever done, I enjoyed that work the most. Feeding them. Training them. Riding them."

She knew what he said was true. She could see it for herself in his expression, in the faraway look in his eyes. "Was that where you were when your brother was killed? Kentucky?"

His brows drew together in a frown. "No. I'd moved on by then. I was riding range in Montana." He shook his head and chuckled humorlessly, then muttered, "More blasted cows."

"But if you loved the horses so much, why didn't you stay in Kentucky?"

He met her gaze. "Because it was time to move on. I wanted my chance to see the world, to see it all, more than I wanted anything else. I didn't want to put down roots. I wanted to roam." One corner of his mouth lifted in a sardonic smile. "I think I've bored you with that story once before."

"You did not bore me," she protested softly.

"What about you? Tell me about where you came from?"

"Sweden?"

"No. Well, yes. Tell me about your hometown."

"Jönköping?"

"Uh-huh."

Inga brushed stray wisps of hair away from her face as her thoughts traveled across an ocean. "It is a pretty place in the south of Sweden. The town sits near a large lake called Vättern. There is much industry in Jönköping—the match factory, which is quite famous, a big paper mill, carpentry shops, machine factory, and the breweries. And churches. There are many churches. The hills around the lake are green and beautiful. Some of them are covered in orchards. Sometimes in winter the lake freezes over, but not always."

"You must miss it."

She didn't miss it when she was with him. "I was glad to come to America," she whispered. "You see, I wanted an adventure, too. Like you." Dirk was her adventure, though he did not know it.

Flower grunted, acted as if she might try to rise, then fell back again.

"I think the calf's coming." Dirk leaned forward for a better look. "Yeah, this is it."

Inga forgot everything else as she watched the cow slowly but steadily push her calf into the world, aided by Dirk's careful ministrations. It was an amazing thing, watching a new life begin. She forgot to be embarrassed or frightened or whatever it was her mother would have expected her to be. She could only be awed by the miracle of it.

As if giving birth were nothing at all, Flower raised up from her side and started to lick her offspring clean.

A short while later, Dirk said, "Watch." His voice was low and soothing.

The calf, a female, slick and dark, legs poking out like matchsticks, attempted to rise. She fell down with a thud. Flower nudged her calf gently with her muzzle. Again the newborn struggled to her feet. This time she managed to take a step before toppling over.

Dirk chuckled. "You'll get it right yet, little one."

"She will stand so soon?"

"Yeah. Amazing, isn't it?"

"*Ja.*"

In silence, they continued to watch until the calf not only stood and stayed upright but began to nurse as well. Then Dirk let himself out of the stall. As he shut the gate, he yawned. "I wonder what time it is?"

"It is midnight," she answered after checking her watch.

"New Year's." He met her gaze. "Guess Ma'd be glad we saw it in, like she always did." He stepped toward Inga.

The barn seemed suddenly warm, close, and intimate. Inga forgot the calf. Forgot the miracle of new birth. Forgot what Dirk had said to her. Everything was forgotten except his sudden nearness and the way being with him made her heart race. "*Ja.*" The word came out on a sigh.

He frowned, as if puzzled by her one-word response. "Come on. You look beat."

She didn't feel the least bit tired.

He took her by the arm and propelled her toward the barn door. But when he stopped to put out the lantern, he glanced her way once more. His frown deepened into a scowl.

Unconsciously, she swayed toward him.

"Happy New Year, Mrs. Bridger," he said, his voice low and gruff. Then he took her by the shoulders, and she knew he was about to kiss her.

Inga tipped her head back, waited for him to lean down to her, knew their mouths would fit together perfectly.

But instead of kissing her on the lips, he dropped a light peck on her forehead before turning away and extinguishing the lantern.

His rejection couldn't have been any more clear.

Saturday, January 1, 1898
Uppsala, Iowa

Dearest Beth,

I write to you with remarkable news. Yesterday, I was
married to Mr. Dirk Bridger. It was all very sudden. We
were married in the parsonage with family and friends in
attendance. We wanted to marry quietly as Mr. Bridger
lost his mother only a week ago.

I will not pretend to you, my dear friend, that this was
a love match on my husband's part. While I have confessed my deep feelings for him to you in an earlier letter,
his feelings for me are mostly gratitude for what help I
can give him with the children. It would have been impossible for him to manage without someone to help him.
Martha tries very hard, but she has yet to have her sixth
birthday. And little Suzanne? She is full of vinegar, as her
grandmamma called it.

So now this farm is my home and not simply my place
of employment. I am not certain I quite believe it myself,
although I am here and I am wearing the wedding band
he placed on my finger himself. I keep a secret hope in my
heart that one day Dirk will feel more for me than gratitude or friendship, but I will be happy even if it is never
more than what it is today.

I hope you are doing well. I have nearly finished the
quilt I am making for the newest member of the Steele
family, and I will send it to you soon so you will have it
before your confinement commences.

And speaking of my quilts, you will never believe what
has happened. Many in Uppsala have taken great interest
in my particular kind of quilting. Mrs. Dolk at the general

store has offered some for sale, and already I have earned nearly fifteen dollars. Can you imagine? It seems a fortune. Next she says she is going to send some quilts to her sister who runs a general store in Des Moines. She is certain I will soon not be able to keep up with the demand.

When Mrs. Dolk first suggested I sell my quilts, I thought it a foolish idea. But now it seems there is much I want to do for Dirk and the children, and the money would be a blessing.

I will close and hope to post this letter soon. Winter has arrived in the county with wailing winds and much snow, so I do not know when I will next be able to get to town to mail this letter or the one I have written to Mary.

Do write to me soon.

With affection,

Inga Bridger

~Thirteen

The frigid temperature held Iowa in its unforgiving grip throughout January. The Bridgers lost two milk cows and one newborn calf to the cold. A series of blinding snowstorms shut down all transportation for over a week. What milk the family was unable to use themselves went to waste.

Night after night, Inga watched her new husband sitting at the kitchen table, staring at his logbooks and ledgers, his forehead creased with concern. She longed to comfort him, but the invisible wall he'd erected between them on their wedding night stood strong and invincible. Without words, he'd made it perfectly clear he didn't want the succor of a wife.

In the wintery month that followed their wedding, their separate roles in the household became well defined. Inga cooked and cleaned and looked after the children. In the evenings, she worked on her quilts, sometimes on the ones she hoped to sell, sometimes on those she was making for Martha and Suzanne. Dirk took care of the livestock and the milking. He chopped cord after cord of wood for the stove and fireplace. He spent the better part of every day in the barn and his evenings with his ledgers.

Inga no longer helped him with the milking, because Dirk had told her he didn't need her help now. Several more cows were dry, he'd explained, awaiting the births of their calves. Besides, he'd added, he didn't mind working alone.

She hadn't let him see how this latest rejection wounded her. What right had she to do so? She had entered this marriage knowing he only wanted a housekeeper, knowing he didn't really want a wife.

There were moments in her days when she knew contentment, perhaps even some satisfaction. Usually they were times spent with the children. Martha and Suzanne could still make her laugh. They were generous with their love, and Inga soaked it up and returned it twofold. Sometimes, she looked at them and the longing for a baby of her own would overwhelm her, sting her eyes with unshed tears.

But she never let Dirk see anything but smiles. She never uttered a negative word in his presence. Perhaps it was her pride again. She hadn't wanted others to know she'd married for less than love. Now she didn't want her husband to know she was less than satisfied with the bargain she had made. She'd thought being with him would be enough. She'd discovered it wasn't. She wanted more. So very much more.

With the arrival of February came a respite from the storms. The gray clouds that had covered the heavens for many weeks drifted away, leaving behind a sky so blue it hurt the eyes to look at it. It was on one such day that Inga's sisters came for a visit.

"Mamma wouldn't have let us come sooner," Thea told her as Inga collected their coats, "even if weather had permitted. She said newlyweds need time alone."

Inga nodded, but thought to herself, *I am too much alone.*

She was glad her parents hadn't come with her sisters. She was certain her mamma would have seen through her veneer of pretended happiness.

"We've brought money from Mrs. Dolk. She has sold two more of your quilts." Thea glanced behind her at their younger sisters, then looked at Inga and in a hushed voice asked, "Is it wonderful, Inga? Is it wonderful to be married? Do you feel different now? Older?"

She felt the threat of tears and turned quickly away. *"Ja,"* she whispered. "It is wonderful."

Thea's hand alighted on her shoulder as she leaned forward, bringing her mouth close to Inga's ear. "I must go to New York City soon. Karl arrives in four weeks. I must be there to meet him. You have not forgotten? You will help me with the train fare to New York?"

"I have not forgotten." She made a quick decision. "You may keep the money from Mrs. Dolk."

"Thank you. I will never forget." Thea's fingers tightened. "There is something else. I cannot ask Mamma about it. You know. About what it is like, a man and a woman together. You must tell me, Inga."

"Oh, Thea. I cannot."

"But who else am I to ask?"

Fortunately—or perhaps not—Dirk chose that precise moment to come inside after putting the Linberg horses in the barn. For an instant, his gaze met with hers, and the longing to be near him, to lie in his arms, to be held and kissed and loved, to be desired, to experience for herself the mystery of the marriage bed, was too great to bear. Inga was ashamed, ashamed that she was so undesirable. Never had she resented being what she was—tall, thin, ordinary, or even worse, plain—as much as she did now.

⟶

For his part, Dirk was glad the Linberg sisters had come a visiting. While these gay, giggling girls were present, he could temporarily forget not only his financial worries but his confusion about his wife. More and more often in the weeks since their wedding, he'd found himself wanting to undo his promise of a celibate union. He'd found himself looking at Inga and wondering why he'd never before noticed the pretty shape of her ears or how the subtle lemon verbena fragrance she wore seemed so right with the color of her hair or how enticing the curve of her gracefully long neck was. That's why he'd spent so many aimless hours in the barn, cold and alone. Not because he still had chores to do, but because he was avoiding Inga.

Avoiding her because she wasn't like the women who had peppered his past. Intimacy with her would change everything—his plans for the future, her plans for the future. He knew, at some deep level, that it would change him inside, too. Change him in some indefinable but very permanent way.

And he wasn't ready for that change, whatever it might be.

⁓

The house seemed too quiet, too empty to Inga after her four boisterous sisters left. Secretly, she had been both delighted and tortured by Dirk's participation in the visit. He had remained in the house the entire time they were there. Inga had seen his smile, listened to his laughter, and wondered why he didn't smile and laugh when it was just the two of them. Somewhat bitterly, she'd been forced to acknowledge that *she* was not the cause for it now. No, it was her pretty, merry sisters who'd brought cheer back into this house.

Now, hours later, the memory of those smiles, the echo of that laughter replayed in her mind as she stared into the fire. *Why, God?* she thought angrily. *Why didn't you make me more like Gunda or Kirsten? Why did you make me like I am?* Self-pity brought tears to her eyes, and the tears only increased her anger.

She rose from her chair and wordlessly headed for the stairs. Her silence mattered to no one, for she was alone, as was usually the case. The girls were long since asleep, and Dirk was in the barn—again.

When she entered her bedroom, she caught a glimpse of her reflection in the mirror. Slowly, she walked toward it, the bitter taste of self-pity growing stronger on her tongue. She stopped and stared at her image, hating what she saw, hating what she was becoming—a bitter old maid. Only no one else knew she was an undesirable old maid. Except Dirk. He knew.

No one will ever want you, you fool. Not Dirk. Not anyone.

Her vision blurred as tears welled in her eyes, then trickled down her cheeks, unchecked.

She remembered thinking, the day Dirk had proposed, that she would have been wiser to refuse him, but she'd held onto a fragile hope that he would learn to love her, given time. What a fool she'd been. He scarcely knew she was alive. She was like a piece of furniture, simply a part of the house.

You are nothing but a bitter, unloved, homely old maid.

"Inga?"

She thought she'd imagined his voice. She'd imagined it so often in the past. She even heard him in her dreams.

"Inga, what's wrong?" His blurry image appeared behind her in the mirror.

She tried to swallow the lump in her throat.

"Tell me."

"I wish I was pretty like Thea and the others," she answered, then was blinded by more tears, appalled that she'd confessed her thoughts aloud.

"What?" He placed his hands on her shoulders and leaned in closer to her.

"I am so very plain," she whispered. She squeezed her eyes shut, feeling miserable and hating herself for it.

"Plain? But you're wrong." His fingers tightened gently. "Open your eyes, Inga. Look at me."

She shook her head, not sure if she hated herself more for her own self-pity or for revealing that self-pity to Dirk.

"Inga, look at me." He spoke more sharply this time.

See what she'd done? Now she'd made him angry.

"Inga . . ."

She opened her eyes and met his gaze in the mirror.

"Now look at yourself," he commanded.

She obeyed.

As she watched, he pulled the pins from her hair and let it cascade down her back. He ran his fingers through the fallen tresses, lifting it and loosing it again, letting it rain over her shoulders.

"It's like satin," he said, a note of surprise in his voice. He leaned closer and took a deep breath. "And it smells like lemons. Clean. Fresh. Like you."

Inga forgot to breathe.

His hands slipped to her jaw, framing her face and forcing her to look straight into the mirror. "Look at your eyes. They're the color of a robin's eggs. Or maybe the powdery blue of a late summer sky. Did you know, whenever you look at Martha and Suzanne, that anybody on God's green earth can see how much you care for 'em?"

Her eyes had always seemed too pale to her, too colorless.

"And your mouth. I remember thinking it's like a bow on a Christmas package. When you smile, the goodness in your heart is there for all to see."

Like a bow? Her mouth?

His left hand slid backward, looping her hair behind her ear. "Such pretty ears. Like seashells."

She gasped when he leaned closer and nibbled the tender lobe.

"Pink. Sweet."

There was a strange *whooshing* sound in her head, leaving her dizzy and making it difficult for her to hear what he was saying.

Dirk's other hand traced the curve of her neck. "Such an elegant throat," he whispered as he met her gaze in the mirror once again. "Have you ever seen a swan gliding across a lake? Elegant, like you."

If he brushed his lips against her neck, she would faint dead away.

"You're not plain, Inga."

But you don't want me either.

His eyes seemed to darken, and she had the feeling he'd read her thoughts. A shiver ran along her spine. She longed to turn around, to face him, but she had neither the strength nor the courage.

He cleared his throat, removed his hands, stepped back from her. She followed his movements in the mirror, still unable to speak for lack of breath.

"You're not plain, Inga," he said again, his voice deep and husky. "Don't ever think it." Then he turned and left the room, closing the door behind him.

With a sigh, Inga sagged against the mirror, glad for the cool feel of the glass against her skin. Little by little, her tilting, careening world began to right itself.

She straightened, stepped back from the mirror, stared once again at her reflection. She still saw the same person she'd always seen in the looking glass. She wasn't pretty like her sisters and would never be so. Yet she knew Dirk hadn't said anything out of pity or mere kindness. He had been telling her what he truly thought.

As the import of his words washed over her, she realized Dirk wanted her in the way a husband was supposed to want a wife.

She turned toward the door.

But if he did, why had he walked away? Why had he left her alone once again?

Her gaze shifted to the bureau on the opposite side of the room. Then, as if drawn there by an invisible cord, she went to it and opened the center drawer. There, lying where she'd placed it over a month before, was the white nightgown her mother had given Inga on the morning of her wedding. With trembling fingers, she lifted it from the drawer and clutched it close.

Could she do this? she wondered. Could she really do this?

⌒

Dirk lay on his bed, an arm thrown over his eyes to shut out the moonlight streaming through his window. But it didn't matter whether his room was brightened by moonlight or was cloaked in darkness. He wouldn't be falling asleep anytime soon. Not while images of Inga still flitted through his mind. Not while the fragrance of her cologne still lingered in his nostrils.

What had he been thinking? Why had he stopped at her bedroom door? Why hadn't he ignored what he'd seen, gone on to his room, and left well enough alone?

He knew the answer to his silent questions. He'd been stopped by her tears. Only when his ma died had Dirk seen Inga cry. In all the weeks since then, she'd seemed content with their living arrangements, with her life on the Bridger farm. Seeing her with tears streaking her cheeks had undone him. He would have tried anything to make her smile again. Inga deserved to be happy, and he knew he was the reason she wasn't.

He heard his door open. Expecting one of the children, he moved his arm and opened his eyes just as the door closed again.

Like an apparition, she stepped into the moonlight. It washed over her pale hair and white nightgown, making her seem more a dream than reality.

"Dirk?" she whispered.

"What are you doing here, Inga?"

"Do not send me away." She moved to the side of his bed. "Please."

"You shouldn't—"

"Why?"

"You know why."

"No one need ever know."

His throat was so tight it nearly strangled him. "When you marry again—"

"I do not care. Kiss me, Dirk. Please."

When he heard the break in her voice, the last of his arguments vanished. He was powerless to send her away.

~ Fourteen

What have I done?

Clad once again in his long underwear and socks, Dirk sat on the edge of the bed, his elbows resting on his thighs while he cradled his head in his hands. It was five o'clock in the morning, and he'd been awake for hours. Behind him, he could hear Inga's soft, steady breathing.

She'd been lovely, perfect, wonderful in every way. Too wonderful.

Their marriage was to have been a temporary situation. Just until the girls were old enough to take care of themselves. Now . . . last night . . .

Dirk hadn't wanted a real marriage. He'd wanted to be able to leave one day without guilt. He was so tired of feeling guilty! He'd wanted to shuck the heavy chains of responsibility that bound him to this miserable farm, to his brother's life instead of his own. Once the girls were old enough, he'd wanted to walk away without a backward glance and live the way he'd always planned on living. He could have done that if he'd been able to give Inga an annulment, but now . . .

She decided this for herself, he argued silently.

Inga had understood the bargain they made. She'd agreed this was a temporary marriage. She'd known there was no love between them. So what was he worried about? She'd said she wouldn't be sorry because of it.

She was innocent. She didn't know. You did.

Quickly, he rose from the bed and finished dressing, then went downstairs where he stoked the kitchen stove and put coffee on to boil.

They would have to talk about this, about what had happened last night. It had changed things, as he'd known it would, and they were going to have to come to terms with those changes. Maybe it would be better if she returned to her father's house now. Maybe she should get that annulment right away. Only how would he manage without her? His situation, his need for help with the children and with the household chores, hadn't changed because they'd shared a bed.

He should have had more self-control, he chided himself. He never should have let last night happen.

He frowned. Did it have to make such a big difference? There had been no guilt when he'd left Clara's horse farm in Kentucky. There'd been no remorse when he'd ridden away from the small town in Montana where Pearl lived and worked.

Suddenly it was clear to him why this time, this woman, was different from before. Because he could learn to care for her too much. Care for her as he'd never cared for another woman. Because caring for her—for his wife—would tie him down in a way he didn't want to be tied down, a way he *refused* to be tied down.

"Mmm. I smell coffee."

He turned toward the kitchen doorway, and there Inga stood. Her wheat-colored hair, becomingly disheveled, fell loose over her shoulders. Her eyes looked sleepy, dreamy. Her mouth was bowed in a tentative smile.

"It'll be ready in a minute or two," he told her.

"I did not hear you get up." A blush pinkened her cheeks. "I slept very soundly."

The urge to cross the room and take her into his arms, to kiss her until she was breathless, was nearly too strong to resist. "Look, we need to talk about last night," he snapped.

Her eyes widened. Her smile vanished.

"It was a stupid thing for us to do. It's my fault. I'm willing to take the blame 'cause I know you didn't . . . well, you didn't know what you were gettin' yourself into."

"You are wrong. I—"

"Inga, you're sweet, and I know you care a lot for Martha and Suzanne. But if we live like this—" He waved his hand toward the upstairs bedroom. "If we live like man and wife, there'll be no way for you to get an annulment when I leave. You'd be a divorced woman or else one whose husband's walked out on her. Think what that would mean for you. The gossip would be ugly. I don't . . . I don't want you to have t'go through that on account of me."

"I am willing to take that chance," she whispered.

He raked his fingers through his hair, feeling frustrated, angry, and confused. "You don't know what you're sayin'. And don't think I'll change my mind about leaving when the girls are older, 'cause I won't."

Inga was as pale as a ghost. "Of course you won't."

An even worse thought hit him. What if she got pregnant?

He turned his back and stared at the coffeepot as if it would provide answers. It didn't.

"Dirk?"

He heard the catch in her voice and felt about an inch high. He was a selfish lout. He'd said all the right words to sound like he was worried about her, but he was only thinking about himself.

Inga waited as long as she could, her hands clenched at her sides. Finally, she said, "Dirk, please look at me."

She could tell he didn't want to, but eventually he complied.

"I am not a fool, Dirk Bridger," she said, sounding more calm than she felt. "I understand it was not your intention for us ... that we ... be truly wed. But we are, so there is no sin involved. You worry about what the gossips will say eight or ten years from now when you go your own way, but I tell you they will talk no matter what happens between us now."

Tell him you love him, her heart said.

But she couldn't. Pride wouldn't let her. Pride was almost all she had to hang onto. Telling him she loved him, especially now, would not make things better, but it might possibly make them worse.

She stiffened her spine, lifted her chin. "I want to live as your wife."

"You don't understand—"

"I understand more than you think I do."

"What if you were to get pregnant?"

First surprise shot through her, followed by a warm sense of wonder she never could have described. "Pregnant?" she echoed softly.

"Yes. What would we do then?"

This time it was Inga who turned away. She walked to the window and looked out at the snow-covered barnyard, waning moonlight silvering the frosty scene. *Pregnant?* To have Dirk's baby. To hold his child in her arms.

She heard the scrape of the kitchen chair against the floor, heard Dirk's deep sigh of weariness.

"That's all I'd need," he said. "I'd never get away."

The brief moment of joy was snatched from her.

Swallowing the lump in her throat, she faced him once again. "Could it happen so ... quickly?"

"Not usually." He shrugged, then raked his hair again. "Never happened that way before ..."

She knew he continued talking, but she couldn't seem to hear him. *Never happened before?* Hattie had said Dirk might have been in love once, but it hadn't occurred to Inga that he might have been ... intimate ... with a woman who was not his wife. Fornication was a sin. The Bible was clear on that. Only the marriage bed was undefiled. But Dirk didn't believe in the God she knew. Would he go to another woman again? Would he commit adultery in the years ahead?

She felt both angry and sick at heart as she took a step toward him. "Dirk, what will happen if we don't ... if I don't share your bed?"

His eyes rounded in surprise.

"Will you ... will you find another to lie with?"

"Look—"

"Will you?"

He muttered an oath, then rose from the chair. He grabbed a mug off the counter and filled it with coffee.

More softly, she asked, "If it is a baby you fear, is there not some way to ... to prevent it?" It hurt to ask. Her throat hurt. Her head hurt. Her heart hurt.

He stilled as he braced his hands on the counter, his head hanging forward.

She placed her hand on his shoulder. "Is there?"

"Inga," he answered, "this isn't fair to you. Not any of it. I never should've asked you to marry me."

"But you did, and we *are* married. There must be—"

He spun around. His expression was harsh as he grabbed her and pulled her to him. "Yes, blast it, there are ways to prevent havin' a baby." He kissed her hard, then set her back from him, strode to the door, grabbed his coat, and headed outside into the frigid darkness that awaited him there.

—

"Is this better?" Martha asked, holding up two small squares of fabric.

Inga inspected the stitches. "That is very good, Martha. You will soon have a beautiful quilt."

"Really?" The girl beamed.

"Really."

"I wanna make a quilt, too," Suzanne stated loudly.

Inga turned toward the younger child. "But, *prinsessa,* you are making a quilt. If you did not help your sister choose which fabric to use, she would never get it finished."

"Isn't Uncle Dirk ever gonna come in?" Martha asked with a sigh. "I wanna show him what I've done."

"He is very busy." Inga ignored the pinched feeling in her heart.

"Too busy to come in for breakfast?"

"*Ja.*"

"Aunt Inga?"

"*Ja?*"

"How come you're so sad today?"

She shook her head, a sudden lump in her throat prohibiting her from answering.

"Because I wasn't very nice to her this mornin'," Dirk said.

Inga gasped as she turned toward the doorway to the kitchen. She hadn't heard him come inside.

He met her gaze. "Sometimes married folks argue, and sometimes they make each other sad. I'm right sorry I made your Aunt Inga sad. She doesn't deserve to be."

She feared she would cry again.

Dirk looked at the children. "Last Sunday after church, I promised Mr. Hansen I'd go have a look at his mare again this week. Reckon today's a good day. Want to go along?"

"Yes!" they both answered, their quilting project quickly forgotten as they jumped to their feet.

His glance returned to Inga. "And you?" he asked. "Want to join us?"

She nodded, afraid to hope what all this might mean.

Without breaking his gaze from hers, he said, "Martha, you and Suzanne run get on some warm clothes. It's plenty cold out there."

He waited until the children had thundered up the stairs before he took a couple more steps into the parlor.

"Inga, I've been doing a lot of thinkin' while I was out in the barn. I guess I wasn't being too realistic, thinkin' we could go back to the way things were before last night. You were right about the way folks'll talk, down the road a piece. I'm sorry about that, too. You don't deserve that, 'cause you've been nothin' but kind to me and the girls. It wasn't fair of me, getting you into this. I never should've proposed marriage in the first place. But I did, and here we are."

She rose from her chair. "*Ja,* here we are."

His eyes darkened. "The truth is, I don't reckon I could live here in the same house with you and not . . . and not want you with me."

She shivered—with understanding, with joy.

"I don't know how the girls and I'd manage, but I'd understand if you wanted to leave. You'd probably save yourself a load of grief later on. The longer you stay, the worse the talk'll be when I go. Do you want to leave now?"

She shook her head.

"Then I think"—his voice was low and husky—"we ought live like man and wife as long as you're here. If you're still willing."

She swallowed, then nodded.

He frowned. "You're doing this 'cause you want to?"

"*Ja*, because I want to."

"You know what you're givin' up?"

"I know."

He took another step toward her. "I don't reckon I understand you, Inga. You could've had a family of your own."

It was simple to Inga. She loved Dirk. *He* was her family.

He reached for her arm.

"We're ready, Uncle Dirk!" Martha shouted from the top of the stairs.

He cleared his throat, and his hand fell away without touching Inga. "Guess we'd best be on our way."

———

"Well, what do you think?" Erik Hansen asked as he leaned on the top rail of the stall.

Dirk straightened, then patted the pregnant mare's side. "She looks fine to me, Hansen. I'd say you worry too much."

"I paid a handsome price for this mare. I would hate to lose her or her foal."

"I don't think that's gonna happen. She seems plenty healthy." He opened the gate and stepped out of the stall. "Like I said, you worry too much."

"Mrs. Hansen says that is what I do best." The giantlike Swede barked a laugh. Then he clapped Dirk on the back with one of his large hands. "And all this is over a horse. When it is the missus . . ." He paused and grinned. "The doctor, he has said I am worse than an old woman."

"He's probably right."

"And when are you going to do some worrying of your own, my friend?" Erik winked.

Dirk frowned in return.

"We are hoping for a boy this time," Hansen continued, unfazed by the look Dirk had given him. "After four daughters, it is time we had a son."

"I didn't know your wife was expectin' again."

"Four months gone, she is, and happy now that the worst of the sickness is over. You will find out soon enough what I am talking about. The women, they are all the same when the babies start coming."

Dirk didn't much care for this topic of conversation. It was hitting too close to home. But how could he tell Erik that the *last* thing he wanted was for his wife to be pregnant? That a pregnancy would be nothing short of catastrophe for a husband who had no intention of staying married?

"Come. We will get us some coffee and warm up before you start your drive back to your farm."

Dirk nodded, and the two men headed for the rambling farmhouse.

Erik Hansen, a man in his late thirties, owned more land than anyone else in the area. He raised corn and wheat and hogs. He was probably one of the wealthiest men in the state and, without a doubt, was the wealthiest in the county. But he was not the sort to flaunt his good fortune and prosperous circumstances, and Dirk had always liked him because of it.

Erik was also one of the few men whom he felt he could call a real friend. Many, if not most, of the Swedish immigrants kept to their own community, but not so with Erik Hansen. He was a gregarious, friendly sort who reached out to everyone, and because of a mutual interest in Thoroughbred racehorses, a special bond had formed between Erik and Dirk right from their first meeting.

Perhaps this friendship was why Dirk was feeling so uncomfortable now. He was afraid Erik might start asking the wrong questions, and he didn't want to have to lie to him.

They found the two women in the kitchen, sitting at the table. From upstairs came giggles and laughter—six girls, counting the Bridger two, having a grand time.

"Josephine, my love," Erik said as he strode across the room, "you will be glad to know the mare is doing well." He planted a kiss on her cheek.

"I told you it was so before you made Mr. Bridger come to see her," his wife replied with a smile.

"That you did."

Inga watched the interplay between the Hansens, then turned her eyes toward Dirk, who was also watching the couple. A wave of pure, unadulterated envy washed over her. How she would love it if he would look at her the way Erik looked at Josephine! Then she was immediately ashamed. She had so much, and yet she always wanted more.

First pride. Now envy. What had happened to Pappa's sensible daughter?

Dirk's gaze swung to meet hers. Her heart thumped. He hadn't rejected her. Why wasn't she satisfied? Why wasn't that enough?

"I have you to blame for Mr. Hansen's latest obsession, Mr. Bridger," Josephine said to Dirk, interrupting Inga's thoughts.

Dirk looked away and smiled at the other woman. "I doubt that."

Josephine rose from the table and went to the cupboard. "Once he had the name of that Thoroughbred farm in Kentucky, he never stopped talking about going there and buying some horses until he had done it. Now all I hear about is that mare and her foal." She filled two mugs with coffee. "Except when he is talking about the yearling and the races that colt will one day win."

"I'm hoping Dirk will help me with the training when the time comes." Erik poured cream into one cup, followed by several spoonfuls of sugar. Then, leaning against the counter, he blew into the cup to cool the beverage while holding out the other mug toward Dirk.

"I'll be glad to help," Dirk answered. "You know that."

"*Ja,* I know." Erik looked at Inga. "Your husband should have a stable full of horses of his own. He is quite an expert."

Dirk shook his head. "I'm no expert, and there's no room in the Bridger barn for anything as useless as a racehorse would be. What we need is a new team of workhorses." He glanced at Inga. "Speaking of the barn, we'd better get a move on. It'll be milking time 'fore we get home."

—

"I wanna story," Suzanne demanded as Inga tucked the blankets tightly around her.

"Tell us another one from Sweden," Martha chimed in.

"All right. Just one." Inga sat on the edge of the bed. "This is the story about the little, little old lady. Once upon a time, there was a little, little old lady who lived in a little, little cottage. And in this cottage she had a little, little table. She also had a little, little barn. And in that barn she had a little, little cow. She also had a little, little milk pail."

The children giggled softly.

"One day she went to the little, little barn and milked the little, little cow into the little, little milk pail. Then she took the little, little milk pail with the little, little milk and went into the little, little cottage and placed it on the little, little table."

"That's like Uncle Dirk," Martha said. "Only he's not little, little. Uncle Dirk's tall."

Inga smiled as she continued with the story. "She also had a little, little cat that said 'Meow.' And when the little, little old lady went to get a little, little plate to filter the little, little milk, the little, little cat jumped up onto the little, little table and finished all the milk."

"The little, little milk!" Suzanne exclaimed.

Inga nodded, then frowned dramatically. "But then the old lady cried, 'Shoo!' And the cat ran away to the forest and never returned again." She kissed Suzanne's forehead and said, "The end." Then she stood, leaned over, and kissed Martha's forehead, too.

"It should be so easy t'get rid of those pesky cats," Dirk said from the doorway.

Inga looked up, his presence causing her heart to quicken, as was always the case.

"Didja hear the story, Uncle Dirk?" Martha asked.

He walked into the bedroom, crossing to stand beside the bed. "The little, little story?"

Both girls giggled.

"Yeah, I heard. Aunt Inga's a good storyteller, don't you think?"

"Uh-huh," they answered in unison.

"It was not my story," Inga demurred. "It is a children's story from Sweden."

Dirk kissed the girls as Inga had done moments before, then straightened and turned. "But you tell the little, little story very, very well." He grinned.

Her heart flip-flopped and her stomach felt all fluttery. A silly overreaction to something so simple as a smile, yet it was the way she always reacted to him.

He turned down the lamp, plunging the bedroom into darkness. Then he took hold of Inga's arm and said, "Good night, girls. Sleep tight."

"Don't let the bedbugs bite," Martha responded, then giggled again.

Inga didn't feel like laughing. She felt utterly breathless as her husband drew her out of the children's bedroom and along the shadowed hallway to his own.

Moonlight filtering through the window and a lamp on the dresser, turned low, revealed her white nightgown lying across the foot of the bed. She knew Dirk had put it there. He hadn't changed his mind, as she'd feared he might.

"Inga," he said, his tone serious. "How much do you understand about procreation?"

Heat rushed up her neck and into her cheeks. "Only a little," she answered. "Mostly what I have guessed."

"There are things you need to know." He closed the door behind him. "I don't want more misunderstandings between us." He proceeded then to explain things she had not known before—had never even guessed—including the steps he would take to prevent a child of their union.

She told herself she wouldn't mind. She loved Dirk, and for now, he wanted to be with her. It would have to be enough. Only now she thought of the day he would leave her, and secretly wished she would have his child with her when that day came.

Was that such a terrible thing to want?

Fifteen

Late February treated Iowa to a glimpse of springtime, turning the top layer of snow on the roads to slush and melting it from the barren tree branches. The sun shone bright yellow in a cloudless blue sky, a welcome treat after more weeks of gray and gloom.

Although Dirk told Inga the respite from winter would be temporary, she was nonetheless buoyed by the change in the weather. It seemed a reflection of the hope and happiness that grew a little stronger in her heart with each passing day.

It was on one such balmy Wednesday that Inga drove the sleigh out to the Hansen farm and asked Erik if he would help her with a surprise for Dirk's birthday in March. After obtaining his promise of help and some needed information, she went into Uppsala and stopped at the general store, where she purchased supplies and left three more quilts with Mrs. Dolk. Inga herself was surprised when the proprietress paid her for several more recent sales. She could scarcely believe the good bounty coming her way.

Her spirits soaring, she decided to surprise her parents and sisters with a weekday visit. But her entrance into the parsonage's parlor wasn't noticed at first.

"But, Olaf, we cannot simply do nothing. Think what might become of her." Her mamma hid her face against his shoulder and sobbed.

Pappa, looking strangely helpless, patted his wife's back. "Do not cry. We will find her." Then he spied his eldest daughter, standing in the doorway. "Look, here is Inga."

"What is wrong, Pappa?" she asked, alarmed by the tearful scene.

"It is Thea. She has run away. She has gone to join Karl in New York City."

She dropped her gaze to the floor, afraid he would see her guilt in her eyes. "Oh."

"Why would she do this?" Mamma lamented as she crossed to where Inga stood and embraced her. "Why would she run away from her home?"

"Because she loves Karl," Inga replied softly, "and she was afraid Pappa would not let them marry if she told you Karl was coming. That is all she has wanted for a long time. To be with Karl." When she lifted her gaze, she saw that it was too late to hide the truth of her collaboration from her pappa.

"You knew she was going to do this, *dotter?*"

"*Ja,* Pappa. I did not know when, but I knew she would go."

"And you did not tell me?"

"I could not. I promised Thea."

"Is this how you honor your pappa and your mamma? By deceiving us?"

"*Nej,* Pappa," she whispered, "but it is how I keep my word to my sister. Thea loves Karl, and she wants to be his wife. He will take good care of her."

"He is a *boy!*" her pappa shouted. "How can he take care of her?"

Inga shook her head. "He is a man, Pappa."

"Thea thinks only of herself. She doesn't know what it means to be a wife."

"Then she will learn. She will grow up. She will have to."

"Did you think of the danger she could be in before you gave her your promise?" her father demanded, accusation making his voice harsh. "Didn't it occur to you she could fall into the hands of evil men? A young girl, traveling alone. What if something were to happen to Karl before he arrived in America? Did you think of that? Thea would be alone in New York without family or friends." He pierced her with his gaze. "*Nej,* I can see by your face that you didn't think of such things."

"Thea will be all right," Inga insisted. "God will look out for her. I am sure of it."

Olaf paced the length of the parlor, his hands clasped behind his back. "I do not know what has come over you, Inga. You and your sisters." He stopped and glared at her. "You have forgotten the way you were raised."

"We have not forgotten, but we are no longer children either."

Her pappa threw up his hands in surrender. "You have broken your mamma's heart, that is what you have done. Wait until you have children of your own. Then you will understand." With that, he strode out of the room.

Children of my own. She would never understand, if that was what it took.

She gave her head a tiny shake, driving off the depressing thought, then took her mother by the arm and led her to the sofa. "Sit down, Mamma, and I will tell you what I know of Thea's plans." Carefully, she detailed everything she knew about Karl's trip to America, the promise of factory work he'd received before leaving Sweden, and Thea's plans to meet him upon his arrival.

When Inga was finished, Bernadotte nodded sadly and said, "I should have guessed she would do this. Thea was always swept up in her own grand dreams. She has never been sensible like you."

I am not so very sensible, Mamma, she thought.

"Your sister thinks too much of her own appearance and her own comforts and too little of the feelings of others. I fear it will not go well for her, so far from home." Bernadotte sighed. "Thea is spoiled and vain. She doesn't know that life is often hard."

"Karl loves her, Mamma. Of that I am sure. He knows her faults and loves her despite them. Such love is rare, I think. She is blessed to have found such a man."

Her mother turned a questioning gaze on Inga. "And you, *dotter?*"

"Me?"

"Are you blessed?"

She thought of the many nights she had lain in her husband's embrace. Did he love her with his heart? She could not be sure. Sometimes, she thought so. Other times . . .

"Inga, are you happy?"

She forced a smile. *"Ja,* I am blessed, too, Mamma. I am happy."

"Married nearly two months already. It does not seem possible." Bernadotte dabbed at her eyes with a handkerchief before asking, "Have you been sick in the mornings?"

Inga drew back in surprise. The past few mornings had been wretched. Cooking breakfast had been agony. "How did you know?"

"Oh, Inga." Her mamma gave her a tight hug. "I am so delighted. This will soften your pappa's heart and make him forget his anger."

She was confused, and her face must have shown it.

Bernadotte took hold of both her hands. "Don't you realize what it means?"

Inga shook her head.

"Your monthly flow, it is late? *Ja?*"

She thought about it, then nodded. *"Ja,* a little. Perhaps a week or two."

Her mamma squeezed Inga's hands. "My darling *dotter,* you are going to have a baby."

"A baby?" She shook her head again. That was impossible. Dirk didn't want a baby. He had told her how he would prevent it. How could this be?

Suddenly she was flooded with such exquisite joy she could scarcely contain it.

"Your pappa cannot stay angry now," Bernadotte repeated, grinning all the while. "To think. I am going to be a grandmamma."

"You mustn't tell anyone yet," Inga said hastily. "Not even Pappa. Not yet."

"But, Inga—"

"No one, Mamma. I want … I want to keep it a surprise. I … I want to wait to tell Dirk on his birthday." In truth, she wanted to keep it a secret so she might enjoy it a little while longer. She wanted to savor it before she had to tell her husband that what he'd wanted most to avoid had come to pass.

There was a chance, she told herself, that when he knew she was carrying his child, he might come to love her. Perhaps then he would want to stay with her forever. She knew it was only a slim possibility, but she clung to it tenaciously.

An hour later, she set off for home, the melody in her heart singing along with the runners on the sleigh.

A baby. A baby of her own. Dirk's baby to love and cherish, to nurture and watch grow. A child who would love her in return. A son with his father's dark hair and eyes. A boy who would grow tall and strong and become a man of integrity, like his father before him.

Thank you, Father God. Thank you for this miracle. It must be of you for Dirk has done everything a man can do in order to avoid creating a child. But you had a different plan it seems, and I am grateful, my Savior, for the blessing you have poured out upon your handmaiden. Thank you for bringing me to America and to Iowa. Thank you for sending Dirk to see Pappa. Thank you for my new family, for my husband and my children and the baby who grows within even now. My heart sings with joy, O God. Let all that I do please you, my Lord.

She smiled, thinking that Dirk would have to recognize God's hand in all of this. He would realize they were meant to be together and that they were meant to have a family. At last he would realize he loved her.

Yes, it would be perfect to tell him on his birthday. It would be one more surprise. Wasn't a birthday the perfect day for surprises?

———

With every *clackity-clackity-clackity* of the wheels on the tracks, Thea grew a little more frightened, a little more unsure of herself. The woman seated next to her had a sour odor that made Thea's stomach roll, and the man seated directly across from her was drooling as he slept, his head resting on the seat back.

Thea was sure it would be better when she was in New York, better when she was with Karl again. Tomorrow she would meet the steamship that was bringing her bridegroom to America. Soon after they would be married. Then everything would be perfect, just as it was meant to be for the two of them.

Mrs. Karl Gustav . . . Fru Gustav . . . Thea Gustav . . .

In a pouch, secured beneath her bodice and tied around her waist, was the last of the money Inga had given her, along with the address of a reputable rooming house for unmarried young women. Thea hadn't asked Inga how she had obtained such an address. She'd simply trusted that her eldest sibling would be able to solve her problems, as had been so often the case throughout her life.

She felt a sudden pang of missing her older sister, and she wished Inga hadn't married Dirk Bridger. She wished she'd been free to accompany Thea to New York City. She didn't doubt she would have been able to convince Inga to do it. Inga might be the levelheaded, sensible one of the Reverend Linberg's five daughters, but she was also the most sentimental and soft-hearted when it came to members of her family. Thea had always known how to use those traits to get what she wanted from Inga.

But maybe it was for the best Inga was in Uppsala. She would be able to calm their pappa. By now he would have found Thea's note. By now he would be furious because of her disobedience. Inga would be able to convince Pappa to forgive Thea.

Although, when she thought about it, there was nothing for him to forgive. This was *his* fault. If he'd let her marry Karl while they were still in Jönköping, she wouldn't have had to run away. She could have had a Swedish wedding with all the trappings, just as she deserved.

The woman beside her snorted and coughed, then spit into a rag of a handkerchief. Thea wrinkled her nose in dismay and looked the other way.

This was not the romantic adventure she had envisioned, but everything would be all right once she was with Karl. Once they were married, her life would be perfect.

His wife grew prettier every day, Dirk thought at supper that night. There was a special softness about her expression. He couldn't help wondering if he was the cause, at least in part, of the pretty glow in her eyes, the gentle sweep of her smile.

It surprised him that he wanted to be responsible for it, but he realized he did. He liked thinking he might make her happy.

"Tell me what you did in town today," he said as he scooped more potatoes onto his plate. "You must've spent a long time at your parents'."

Her gaze flicked to him, then away. "*Ja,* I was there for some time. All is in turmoil. Thea has run off to New York to marry Karl Gustav. He is a boy ... I mean, a *man* she knew in Jönköping. Pappa thought they were too young to wed. He is very angry."

"Hmm." Dirk had a hard time imagining the minister angry. Stern, perhaps, but not angry.

"*Ja,* and with me, too."

"Why you?"

"Because I helped her. I gave her some of my quilt money to pay for her train fare." A becoming blush painted Inga's cheeks. "Thea loves Karl. She belongs with him. He will be good to her. When she asked for my help, I could not deny her."

He chuckled softly. "It seems you're more of a romantic than your pa thinks you are."

She looked up, and in that instant, he saw the depth of her emotions, the largeness of her heart. The knowledge hit him like a fist in the belly, leaving the breath knocked out of him. It scared him, the sheer power of her love for others.

She smiled as he continued to stare. He remembered thinking—on the day he'd hired her to work as his housekeeper— that the last thing he'd needed was a bona fide saint living in his house. But it wasn't that Inga was a saint. It was simply that she cared about others. Deeply, truly cared. She loved openly and freely. She'd loved his mother. She loved Martha and Suzanne.

She might even love him.

He supposed he'd already known, at some deep level, that it could happen. What he didn't know was how he felt about it. He had loved his parents and his brother, but they had died, leaving him bound to a life and a place he didn't want. If Inga were to love him, would her love do the same?

But how could it, he argued with himself, as long as he didn't love her in return?

He thought of the sweetness of their union and wondered if he could avoid more entanglements to his heart. He'd made it clear to her in countless ways that he had no intention of staying. But leaving her, he realized now, might not be so easy. He had fallen into a tender trap. He knew desire often faded over time. Would his dreams fade, too?

Or would it be too late by then to matter?

———

Thursday, February 24, 1898
Uppsala, Iowa

Dear Mrs. Keene,

I am writing because I hope to purchase a Thoroughbred filly as a gift for my husband on his birthday. I obtained your address from Erik Hansen who purchased some horses from you last year. I do not have a great deal of money and so cannot expect to choose from the best of your stables, but I am hoping we might come to some arrangement for an animal of sound breeding, preferably a filly. Mr. Hansen assured me that you were fair in all your dealings with him and that I might expect you to be the same with me.

Would you be so kind as to write to me if you have any foals for sale and detail what you might be asking for them? I would be most grateful to you for a quick reply as time is short before my husband's birthday.

Yours most sincerely,

Mrs. Dirk Bridger

Inga smiled to herself as she sealed the envelope. Surely she would be able to buy a good horse with what she'd saved from the sale of her quilts. She had offered the money to Dirk to help with the expenses of the dairy farm, but he'd refused to accept any of it, telling her the money was hers to do with as she pleased.

It would seem she was not the only one who was subject to the sin of pride.

Her smile broadened. Wouldn't he be surprised when he saw that she had purchased a Thoroughbred filly with the money he'd rejected? In a few years, they could breed the mare with Hansen's young stallion, and that would be the start of the Bridger Thoroughbred stables.

She saw their rosy, perfect future in her mind. Martha and Suzanne would marry men who wanted to be dairy farmers. Dirk and Inga, meanwhile, would buy land nearby, so they could visit their little grandnieces and nephews when they started to arrive.

Instead of dairy cattle, she and Dirk would raise horses on their new farm. Dirk and his sons—for she anticipated many children, many sons—would become famous for their stock. They would go to the racetracks in New York and Kentucky and wherever else they were, and the Bridger horses would win race after race after race.

Dirk would be happy and content and forget his dreams of traveling the world. He would love her, and they would grow old together, surrounded by their adoring children.

Surely that was the way it would be.

~Sixteen

Shivering inside her coat, Thea paced anxiously, waiting for her first glimpse of Karl. She was tired and irritable. She hadn't been sleeping well at the rooming house. The bed was lumpy and uncomfortable. The walls were paper-thin, allowing her to hear nearly every word that was said in the rooms on either side of hers. To be honest, she had been terrified every night she'd been forced to stay there, afraid someone would break into her room and accost her. She'd spent most nights staring at the door and holding her breath.

To make matters worse, she was hungry. As soon as she learned Karl's ship had arrived, she'd spent the last of the money Inga had given her on the pretty new frock she wore. She hadn't thought ahead to the lengthy wait she would have to endure while Karl and the other passengers from the various steamships were processed through the federal immigration building on Ellis Island. She kept telling herself not to worry. Karl would be with her soon. Then he would buy her something to eat before they went to be married.

Married. Married to Karl. She wondered if Pappa was terribly angry with her. And Mamma? Mamma would still be crying. Of course, her younger sisters would all be envious. They would understand what a wonderful thing Thea had done, running away to join the man she loved.

It was like a fairy tale, her elopement. Or it would be soon. Exciting and romantic, as it should be. Two lovers, separated by an ocean, desperate to be together, defying their families, willing to do anything in order to reach the other. She sighed, forgetting the nightmarish train ride to New York City and the horrible rooming house where she'd stayed since.

Then she saw him, his sun gold hair making him stand out from those around him.

"Karl!" She waved her arm frantically. "Karl, I am here!"

He heard her. His entire face beamed with a smile as he moved through the crowd. Finally, he broke free of the other immigrants and ran to her. Suddenly she was in his arms and he was spinning her around and around. Then he kissed her, still holding her off the ground.

"I was afraid you wouldn't be here," he whispered when their lips parted.

"Nothing could have kept me away."

"I am glad. Oh, Thea, I am glad."

"Put me down," she demanded. "Now look at me. Do you like my wedding dress? Is it pretty?"

He obediently perused her attire, then said, "Any dress would look pretty on you, Thea, and you know it."

"But I want you to say it. Oh, Karl, I can't believe you are truly here and we are to be married."

"It is true." He kissed her again. "Now, show me this city which is to be our home."

—

Iowa's respite from winter didn't continue for long. The month of March began with a blast of icy wind hurtling down from the north.

And with it came disaster.

The family had retired early for a change, and Dirk was just drifting off to sleep—Inga lying nestled in the circle of his arms, her head on his shoulder—when the pounding started on the front door.

"What the—?" he muttered.

Huskily, Inga asked, "Is something wrong?"

"I don't know, but somebody's sure raisin' a racket for some reason." He tossed aside the blankets and reached for his trousers. A few moments later, he hurried down the stairs, shouting, "I'm coming. Hold your horses."

He yanked open the door. Sven Gerhard stood on the front porch. One look at his face confirmed this was no late night social call.

"What is it, Sven? What's wrong?"

"There's been an accident. We need your help."

"Come inside."

"A sleigh full of young people went off the bridge." Sven glanced toward the stairs where Inga was standing, wrapped in her dressing gown, her hair tumbling over her shoulders. Lowering his voice, he continued, "They were returning from Thunder Creek when it happened. The sleigh broke through the railings and landed half in the water, half on the bank. We've found four of the passengers. Orbert Finster is bringing them here, yours being the closest place. He should be right behind me. I came ahead to ask your help. There are still two missing. Vilhelm Dolk and"—his voice lowered further— "Gunda Linberg."

Dirk glanced toward his wife, hoping she hadn't heard. Judging by her expression, he guessed she hadn't.

"Tilford Starr and Klas Hallström are still out there look- ing, but if we don't find them soon . . ." Sven let his voice trail into silence, his meaning clear.

"I'll get my boots and be right with you." Dirk headed toward the stairs, brusquely adding, "Inga, make some coffee. Lots of it. And get out some blankets. They'll be needed."

He took the steps three at a time. He didn't have to be told every second counted. The warming spell they'd enjoyed a week ago had started breaking up the ice that had covered the river since December. Anyone falling into the frigid water would have a hard time making their way toward shore due to the bobbing obstacles, and that was only if the shock of the cold river didn't make them pass out and drown almost immediately.

Just as Dirk headed down the stairs again, the front door opened and those who'd been rescued spilled into the house. He recognized Vilhelm's twin brother, Valdemar, by the old scar on his right cheek, but the other young man was a stranger to him. He glanced at the two girls who were clinging to each other and crying, their teeth chattering. He didn't recognize either of them.

But apparently Inga did. "Julia?" he heard her say from the kitchen doorway.

The girl, perhaps fifteen or sixteen years of age, broke away and hurled herself at Inga. "Oh, Mrs. Bridger, we could not find them. We could not find either of them. It was so terrible. I was so afraid, and when we could not find them—"

Inga gathered the girl in her arms. "Hush, Julia. The men will find your friends. I am sure they will. It will be all right. You will see."

"But I heard *Herr* Hallström say Gunda and Vilhelm could not survive in this cold."

"Gunda?" She glanced over Julia's head toward Dirk. "Gunda is out there?"

He nodded.

She paled.

Gruffly, he said, "I'll find her, Inga."

As if his promise was all she'd needed to renew her strength, she stiffened her back and gave him a brief nod. Then she turned and ushered the four survivors into the kitchen where they could warm themselves by the stove.

"Come on, Sven," Dirk said to his neighbor. "Time's a-wastin'."

They rode in the sleigh that had carried Valdemar, Julia, and the two others to the Bridger farm. The driver, Orbert Finster, pushed the team as fast as he dared. Luckily, the moon was nearly full, providing enough light for Orbert to make out the road ahead.

"We happened upon them just minutes after the accident," Sven said in a loud voice. "We were on our way back from the Hadrian farm. Found the Dolk boy hanging onto the side of the bridge where they went over. The other three had managed to cling to the sleigh. It was a miracle we were able to get them out."

It would be an even greater miracle if the other two were still alive, Dirk thought grimly.

———

Inga made another pot of coffee for the shivering young people in her kitchen. They had all changed into the dry clothing Inga had found for them. They didn't speak, but the silence said more than words. None of them believed Gunda and Vilhelm would be found alive.

But Inga had to believe. Dirk had said he would find Gunda, and she had to believe God would help him keep his promise. She couldn't bear the alternative.

When she heard the knock at the front door, she ran to it, her heart pounding crazily, fear and hope warring in her chest. She yanked open the door.

"Pappa!" Relief flooded her. "You've come."

"Is she here?" Olaf demanded angrily. He swept into the house. "Is it not bad enough her sister has run away to New York City? Now Gunda thinks she can stay out with that Dolk boy into the night and worry her mamma sick. Did you encourage her like you did Thea?"

Her heart sank. His words were like darts, wounding her, but she ignored the pain for now. "You don't know."

"Don't know what?"

"There has been an accident, Pappa."

"An accident?" The pastor's anger vanished in an instant. "What sort of accident?"

Inga glanced toward the kitchen. "The sleigh they were in slid into the river. The other young people, they are by the stove to get warm. But ..." She swallowed the sting of hot tears, then looked at her pappa again. "But Gunda and Vilhelm Dolk are not among them. Dirk and several other men are out looking for them now."

"Dear God," Olaf breathed, clasping his hands in front of his chest and bowing his head. His lips moved as he prayed silently.

When he opened his eyes again, his gaze meeting hers, she said, "Dirk will find Gunda, Pappa. I know he will."

His expression was sad. "I wronged you, Inga. I am sorry."

"It does not matter."

"*Ja,* it matters, *dotter.* Will you forgive me?"

"Thea's leaving has hurt you, and so have I. I understand, Pappa. There is nothing to forgive."

Olaf turned, walked to the sofa, and sank onto it. Staring into the fire, he asked, "Did I make a mistake, bringing my family to America?"

"*Nej.* It was not a mistake."

He looked up. "I wonder."

⌒

"Gunda! Vilhelm!"

Moving along the bank of the river was slow going. Dirk held the torch aloft as he stumbled through the deep snow. His exposed skin ached with the cold. If either of those kids were alive ...

Behind him, Sven shouted their names again. "Gunda! Vilhelm!"

Dirk saw the faint flicker of two more torches moving along the opposite bank. He heard the other men's shouts and wondered if they felt the same sense of despair he did.

"Gunda! Vilhelm!"

They couldn't possibly feel the same. It wasn't their sister-in-law out there, and only he had the image of Inga's eyes etched in his mind, beseeching him not to let her down, not to fail.

He stopped suddenly. Had he heard something? "Gunda!"

"Here." The voice was faint. "H–here I am."

He looked behind him at Sven, then shouted, "Gunda!"

"Help m–me."

Adrenaline surged as he pushed through the snow and underbrush, stumbling in his haste. "Keep talking, Gunda."

"O–over here. I'm over h–here."

Suddenly he saw her, lying on the bank between two tall trees. "There she is, Sven. I've found her."

What happened next, no one would ever know for sure. One minute Dirk was rushing along the snow-covered bank of the river. The next minute his feet went out from under him and he was in the water, sinking fast.

The cold was unbelievable. He fought his way toward the surface, gasping for air when he broke through. He caught a glimpse of Sven's torch, flailed his arms as he tried to haul himself in that direction. His coat and boots acted like anchors, and he felt his strength rapidly draining from him.

Inga.

Something hit him from behind. Pain exploded in his head, and he sank into a watery darkness.

"There is someone coming," Olaf announced from the front entry. "I can see torches."

Inga checked the mantel clock. An hour ago, Valdemar Dolk had taken the Bridger sleigh into Uppsala, carrying the other young folk home to their parents, along with the news about his brother and Gunda Linberg. He had promised to send the doctor back to the Bridger farm to be on hand for Vilhelm and Gunda. Inga expected Bjorn and Sonja Dolk and her own mamma to accompany Dr. Swenson, but this could not be them arriving so soon. Even if Valdemar had pushed the team of horses to the peak of their endurance, he would have made Uppsala no sooner than a quarter of an hour before.

"Dirk," she whispered as she rose from her chair near the fire and hurried to join her father in the entry hall. To Olaf, she said, "They have found them, or else Dirk would not have returned." She reached for her coat. "She will be all right. You will see, Pappa."

"I want you to stay inside," he replied.

"But—"

"Listen to me." He put one hand on her shoulder. "Do not argue. You must wait inside."

"Gunda will be all right. We have prayed for her safety. She will be well."

Olaf's skin was ashen. "We cannot know she is all right. That is up to God. Please, wait inside."

Fear shivered up her spine as she realized he was equally afraid. "All right, Pappa. I will wait here."

He slipped his arms into the sleeves of his coat, then opened the door and stepped outside, closing the door firmly behind him. She heard him hail the driver. Waning moonlight followed him as he approached the sleigh that had come to a halt not far from the porch.

Please let Gunda be all right. And Vilhelm, too.

Blankets. They would need more blankets.

She rushed to get them, then hurried back to the front door just as it opened and Olaf carried Gunda into the house. Her sister lay utterly still in his arms.

"Pappa?" she whispered, lifting her gaze to meet his.

"She is alive," he answered.

Inga had only a moment to feel relief before two more men—their clothing stiff and frozen—entered the house, carrying another man between them. Her view was partially blocked, but she assumed it must be Vilhelm. Then she recognized the coat.

Dirk!

She thought she had cried his name aloud, but no sound came out, terror having temporarily stolen her voice.

"Put him on the floor near the fire," Olaf commanded. "Get him out of those wet things."

She wasn't sure how she got there. She couldn't remember moving. But there she was, kneeling beside Dirk's eerily still body. She laid her fingers against his icy cold cheek.

"He almost drowned," Sven Gerhard said.

He looked as if he *had* drowned.

Inga leaned forward, put her ear near his nose, waited to feel his warm breath on her lobe. It was there. Barely.

"Dirk? Can you hear me?"

No reply. Not so much as the flicker of an eyelid.

She took one of his cold hands between hers and began to rub. "You are going to be all right. Wake up, Dirk. Look at me. You are going to be all right."

She heard the murmur of men's voices from behind her, but she couldn't make out what they were saying. Didn't care what they were saying as she began to remove her husband's damp and ice-covered clothing.

"Wake up. Look at me, *kära du*. You must look at me."

I cannot lose him, God. He is my world. He is my everything. Do not take his life. Take me instead. Take anything I have. Anything! But do not take Dirk. Please save him. I will never ask for anything else if only you will spare his life. Please, oh please, spare his life.

When the last of his clothes had been tossed into a heap, she wrapped Dirk in several blankets, then resumed rubbing his hands and arms, feet and legs, attempting to bring warmth back to his limbs. Her father tried once to tell her to rest, to let him tend to her husband, but Inga refused his help. Dirk needed her, she insisted, and nothing would take her from his side. When he opened his eyes, she was going to be there. She was going to be the first person he saw.

In a voice so low only Dirk—if he were conscious—could have heard, she told him she loved him. She told him he was going to be a pappa. She commanded him to live. "We need you to live, Dirk," she whispered, unaware of the tears streaking her cheeks. "Martha and Suzanne and the baby and me. We need you to live. Do not leave us this way. Not now. Not this way. On my word, I will never hold you to me or to this farm, but do not die. Just do not die."

Dear Father, I will never ask for another thing if only you will spare him. I will not ask that he learn to love me. I will not ask that he forget his dreams and choose to stay with us. I will let him live the life he chooses without complaint. I swear it. Dear God, I swear it.

Gentle hands held her shoulders. Her mamma's voice said, "Inga, come with me."

She glanced up, surprised to find she wasn't imagining it. Her mamma was there. So was Dr. Swenson.

"Come, Inga. Let the doctor tend to your husband."

"But I—"

"Come with me, dearest. You are exhausted."

"He cannot die." Her throat hurt. "He cannot die. Do not let him die."

"No. Of course not. Shh." Bernadotte pulled her close in a tight embrace. "Of course not."

"I love him so very much."

"Of course you do."

But her mamma didn't understand. Couldn't possibly understand. "I wanted too much," she confessed. "I wanted too much."

"What are you saying, darling? You are distraught. Come and lie down. You will feel better soon."

Let him live, God, and I promise not to want for more than what I have. I promise.

—

The apartment that was to be Mr. and Mrs. Karl Gustav's home was a cold-water, third-story walk-up with two rooms. For furniture, there were two leather-seated ladder-back chairs, a small table with one uneven leg, and an even lumpier looking mattress than the one Thea had slept on at the rooming house. But they had been searching for hours, and this was the best they had found for the price they could pay.

Perhaps the place wouldn't have seemed so dismal to Thea if her wedding hadn't also been a disappointment. They had taken their vows in front of a dour-faced justice of the peace who, obviously, couldn't have cared less about the young couple before him. There had been no gifts, no food, no music and dancing. There had been no one there to bless them and wish them well. No friends. No family. Just Thea and Karl.

Why had it seemed so romantic when she had imagined it all in her mind? Instead of romantic, it had felt rushed and shoddy and a little bit shameful.

Still, she reminded herself, she was married to Karl. That was all she had thought about for more than a year. He was going to make her happy.

After their landlady left, clutching the first week's rent in her filthy hands, Karl shut the door and turned toward his bride. "We will find something better as soon as I am working at the factory."

She nodded.

"I love you, Thea."

Tears filled her eyes. "I love you, Karl."

He moved toward her. "Are you afraid?"

"*Nej*," she lied, while trying not to cry.

—

Vilhelm's body was found the next morning, five miles downriver from the place of the accident. No one had expected to find him alive after a night in the subfreezing weather, but his death still came as a shock to his family and friends.

Gunda—bright, flirtatious, pretty Gunda—suffered from severe frostbite in her left leg. Dr. Swenson insisted Reverend and Mrs. Linberg take their daughter immediately to a surgeon he knew in Minneapolis, for he suspected amputation was the only course open if they were to save her life.

Dirk continued to lie unconscious in his bed. *Pneumonia,* the doctor had said as he'd listened to his patient's labored breathing two days after the accident. One look at the doctor's face had told Inga he didn't expect her husband to survive.

But she swore she would prove him wrong. She wouldn't let Dirk die. No matter what it took, no matter what she had to do, Dirk Bridger was going to live.

With Sven Gerhard's help, Inga managed to keep the cows fed and milked. Frida Gerhard, Sven's wife, kept an eye on the children, and women from the Prärieblomman Lutheran

Church brought food dishes out to the farm. Inga ate little and slept even less. Hour by hour, day after day, she sat beside her husband's bed and willed him to live, for she would accept nothing less.

Miraculously, she didn't have to.

On the fifth day after the accident, Dirk opened his eyes and met her worried gaze. Her heart nearly stopped as she leaned forward, clutching his left hand between both of hers. Tears welled in her eyes, and a lump formed in her throat.

"Gunda?" he whispered after a long while.

Inga nodded. "She will be okay. Do not worry."

He sighed as his eyes drifted closed. "Good."

He slept again, but it was a different sleep, a more restful sleep. Inga could hear and feel the difference.

With a prayer of thanksgiving in her heart, she lay down beside him on the bed, closed her eyes, and slept in peace.

Dirk was going to live.

~Seventeen

Dirk was a lousy patient.

Inga was an unyielding nurse.

"Look at you," he groused. "You're workin' your fingers to the bone. It's time I was outta bed and doing my part." He threw aside the covers.

Inga pulled them back to his waist. "You will do no such thing, Dirk Bridger. The doctor said you must stay in bed another week, and that is exactly what you will do."

He scowled at her.

She scowled right back, hands on her hips, her chin thrust forward.

"Your pa was right. You're darn stubborn."

"Pappa would never say such a thing."

"That you're stubborn? Well, he—"

"*Nej*, the other word. Pappa does not use coarse language."

"Coarse? You call that coarse?" Dirk groaned in frustration. "This is why men don't want t'get married. Women like you drive 'em crazy."

"A woman who would want to marry a man like you is already crazy," she retorted. She grabbed his empty lunch tray from the bed stand and marched out of the room.

For such a slender slip of a thing, she was mighty formidable. Stubborn woman.

His anger vanished, and he laughed out loud.

Then he sighed as he sank against the pillows at his back. The truth was, he *didn't* have the strength to get out of bed yet, and he knew it. Just arguing with her had left him drained and weary. But he'd meant what he'd said about Inga. She looked near sick herself. She constantly insisted she was getting plenty of help from their neighbors and the women of the church. Still, Dirk knew she was doing far too much. Weariness shadowed her eyes, and her cheeks had a drawn, hollow appearance.

He glanced toward the window where sunlight filtered through the curtains. March winds rattled the panes of glass and whistled around the corners of the house. It was still cold outside, but spring was coming fast. He had a couple of cows due to calf by the end of March. He needed to be up and about before that happened, because he sure couldn't count on them calving in the middle of the day when Sven might be there. There was equipment to be repaired before the first hay crop could be harvested. While June seemed a long way off, Dirk knew it really wasn't. Time had a way of running out, like flour through a sieve.

He heard the thunder of children's footsteps moments before Martha and Suzanne scampered into his bedroom.

"You awake?" Martha asked, even though she could see he was sitting up in bed.

He grinned. "I'm awake."

"Good. Look what we brought you." She handed him a piece of paper upon which was written, *Get well, Uncle Dirk.* The writing was Martha's. The squiggly lines below it were obviously the work of Suzanne.

"Thanks," he said. "I intend to."

"Saturday's your birthday. You gonna be up for your birthday?"

"Why? You plannin' a party or somethin'?"

Martha's eyes widened. "How'd you hear about it?" She glared at her sister. "Did you tell?"

Suzanne shook her head.

"Betcha did."

Before the littlest one could burst into tears, Dirk said, "No one told me anything. I guessed." Actually, he hadn't known until Martha gave it away, but he was smart enough not to say so. "Let's keep this between us. Okay?"

"Okay." Martha wagged a finger at Suzanne. "You don't tell. Okay?"

"'kay."

"You promise?"

"I promise, Martha." Suzanne looked at her uncle and shook her head. "I won't tell."

Dirk suspected she didn't have a clue what she wasn't supposed to be telling.

Inga's voice drifted up the stairs. "Martha? Are you and Suzanne upstairs?"

"They're with me," Dirk called back.

Her footsteps were much slower than the children's had been. He could see her in his mind, one hand on the rail, the other resting on her thigh as she climbed the stairs for what felt like the hundredth time that day.

A short while later, she paused in the doorway. "I told you to only stay a moment," she gently chided the girls.

"We're sorry," Martha replied.

Dirk patted his niece on the head while looking at Inga. "No, don't be sorry. I liked havin' the company."

"But Dr. Swenson said you must rest," his wife insisted.

He was sorry he'd argued with her. She had enough problems without him causing her more.

"You must sleep, Dirk. Please."

He remembered thinking her name just before the river swallowed him. He'd been about to die, and his last thought had been of Inga. Strange. He couldn't remember what life on this farm had been like without her.

"Come along, girls." Inga motioned to them. "Downstairs now."

"But—"

"Now, Martha."

"Oh, all right," his eldest niece grumbled.

Dirk watched them go, all the while wondering, *What would it be like without her?*

He didn't think he wanted to know.

———

"Thank you, Mr. Hansen," Inga called as her husband's friend mounted his saddle horse.

"You get some rest, now," Erik called to her.

She nodded, thinking he sounded like Dirk, then stepped inside the house and closed the door. She looked at the letters Erik had brought from town, along with another casserole and a pie from his wife. One letter was from her mamma. She recognized the pretty handwriting. The other envelope didn't say who it was from. She hoped it was a reply from that woman in Kentucky.

Inga sat down at the kitchen table and opened her mamma's letter first.

Dear Inga and family,

I hope this letter finds Dirk well on the road to recovery. Dr. Swenson sent us word that our prayers were answered and he has awakened. We thank God daily for it. As you probably have heard, Dr. Nessle found it necessary to amputate Gunda's left leg below the knee. He feared for a time she might also lose toes from her right foot, or worse, the foot itself, but it seems now that such will not be necessary. We are very grateful she is alive. We could so easily have lost her as the Dolks lost Vilhelm.

Gunda's spirits are sometimes good and sometimes very low. Her pappa spends many hours in prayer for her. We hope to return to Uppsala by the end of the month, but we have sent for Astrid and Kirsten to join us here in Minneapolis so that we might all be together until Gunda is able to travel. I wish you were with us, too.

Has there been any word from Thea? Please write to us soon in care of the hotel.

Love, Mamma

"Poor Gunda," Inga whispered as she wiped tears from her eyes. "Poor Mamma."

She opened the second letter.

My dear friend, it began.

Her eyes scanned to the bottom of the paper. "Mary!" she whispered in surprise.

It is sorry I am not to have written all of these months, even though I was thankful for the letters I received from you and Beth. It is only now I find myself able to write about what happened after you left for Iowa.

Seamus died in a coal mining accident in West Virginia before he knew I was in America. His son, Keary, was born before his time had come, and I feared I would lose him, too. But he is doing well now and is the brightest, most handsome babe you have ever seen.

We are living on the Lower East Side with the Dougals, a nice Irish family, and I recently found employment with a fine gentleman and his wife who have a grand house on Madison Avenue. I am beginning, at last, to feel there is hope for our future. For so very long, I had lost heart.

I will write again soon.

Yours very truly,

Mary Emeline Malone

Inga laid the letter on the table. "Oh, Mary. So this is why I have not heard from you before now."

She placed the palm of her hand on her flat stomach as her gaze lifted toward the ceiling. Mary had lost Seamus before her baby was born, before he had even known he would be a father. The same could so easily have happened to Inga. Dirk had nearly died in that river, then again from pneumonia.

"How did Mary bear it?" she whispered. "I would have wanted to die, too."

She had a sudden, urgent need to be near Dirk. She refolded both letters, returned them to their envelopes, and stuffed them in the pocket of her apron. Then she hurried upstairs. She found him sleeping. She tiptoed into the room and stared down at him, watching the steady rise and fall of his chest. It had been difficult to make him follow the doctor's orders. She would rather have to milk a dozen more cows than argue with him one more time about it.

And *he* called *her* stubborn!

She thought again of Mary and Seamus and little fatherless Keary, felt a tightness in her heart, wished she could lie in Dirk's arms and pour out her feelings to him. But she had made God a promise. She had sworn an oath that she would never again want for more, never ask for more than what she had, if he would spare Dirk's life.

She turned away, walked to the window where she looked outside. The winter's accumulation of snow, no longer a pristine white, was melting fast. The barnyard and driveway, as well as the road to town, had become a thick, sucking mixture of mud and muck. Everything within view appeared dismal, shoddy, bleak. A pewter sky, gunmetal gray clouds hiding the sun, only made things seem more bleak.

Weariness overwhelmed her, and she sank onto a nearby chair.

She hadn't time to sit idle. Sven would be here soon to help with the milking. Then the girls would need their supper. Tomorrow she would need to do laundry, for she hadn't done it on Monday, as was her custom.

She gave her head a shake, feeling ashamed of herself. She had no right to complain. No right at all.

She was about to rise from the chair when she saw a carriage turning into the drive off the main road. She didn't recognize the vehicle and couldn't imagine what would bring someone out to call so late in the day. She certainly hoped it wasn't another woman from church bringing a casserole.

With a sigh, she went to greet her latest caller.

The coach pulled up to the front of the house just as Inga opened the door and stepped onto the porch. Now that the vehicle was closer, she realized this was no neighbor come calling. The black-and-green carriage was much too fine to belong to anyone around here. The team of matching black horses wore fancy ostrich plumes on the top of their harness, and the driver—a man of color—was dressed in red livery.

"Would this here be the Bridger farm?" he asked as he climbed down from his perch.

She nodded.

He opened the carriage door. "We be here, Miz Keene."

Mrs. Keene? From Kentucky?

The young woman who emerged was no less elegant than the transportation that had carried her here. She was clad in a gown of black moiré with a collar of sable and chinchilla furs. Unlike the muddied coach, which bore the evidence of long travel, she looked as if she'd just stepped out of her dressing room.

She glanced up, revealing a pretty, heart-shaped face and large brown eyes. When she saw Inga, she smiled what could only be described as a dazzling smile. "Mrs. Bridger?"

Inga nodded again.

"Thank goodness. I was afraid we'd become lost again. Jack and I have had the devil of a time finding you." Holding the hem of her traveling dress out of the mud, she approached the porch. Once safely on the first step, she said, "I am Clara Keene. You wrote to me about a horse for your husband's birthday."

"*Ja,*" Inga answered, "but I did not expect you to come in person."

Clara laughed. "I'm an impetuous woman, Mrs. Bridger. I simply had to see you for myself."

"See me? But I—"

"I've brought a filly which I believe your husband will approve of." She motioned behind her.

Inga hadn't noticed the bay-colored horse tied to the back of the carriage until then.

"This is Orient out of Emerald Seas by King Keene." There was pride in Clara's voice. "She's one of our finest two-year-olds."

Inga didn't have to know anything about horses to see that. Everything about the filly, from her intelligent eyes to her long, fine-boned legs, proclaimed her excellent breeding.

She returned her gaze to Clara. "I am afraid there has been a misunderstanding, Mrs. Keene. We could never afford such an animal. I . . . I only meant to inquire. I never thought—"

"May we go inside?" Clara interrupted. "I am desperately in need of something warm to drink. I do declare, the grayness of this day has seeped right into my very bones."

"Of course. I am sorry. I should not have kept you standing out here. Please, come in."

Clara glanced over her shoulder at the driver. "Jack, put the animals up in the barn. See that they're fed and get a good rubdown."

"Right away, Miz Keene."

Clara looked at Inga again. "I don't suppose you have servants' quarters? No, of course you don't. Well, you can send something out to Jack later. He can stay in the barn." She swept past Inga and entered the house. "My, my. I had no idea it would take us so long to get here from Des Moines. I declare, the train ride from Kentucky was dreadful, but I did so want to arrive before Dirk's birthday. Otherwise, I would have taken a rest in Des Moines before starting up this way."

There was little Inga could do except follow her inside.

Clara walked into the living room. She tossed her sable muff onto the sofa as her gaze swept over the small room. "How quaint."

It didn't sound like a compliment, and Inga swallowed the impulse to defend her home. "Won't you please sit down?"

"And you, Mrs. Bridger"—Clara turned to face her—"are not at all what I expected."

That didn't sound like a compliment either. "You wanted something warm to drink, Mrs. Keene. I will bring coffee." She walked quickly toward the kitchen.

"Oh, do let me join you," Clara said, following right on Inga's heels. "Now, you must tell me everything." Once in the kitchen, she settled onto a chair, reached up and unpinned her fur hat, then placed it on the table with one hand while patting her dark brown hair with her other hand. "First of all, how is Dirk?"

Someone in town must have told Clara about the accident, Inga thought as she walked to the stove. Still, it irritated her, the way the woman used his first name in such a familiar manner. Things must be done quite differently in Kentucky. *"Mr.* Bridger is much better. The doctor says he will fully recover. Thank you for asking." But she didn't want to thank her. She didn't like her. Was it money, beauty, or both that gave Clara her superior demeanor?

"Dirk's been ill?"

Inga turned, coffee cup in hand.

Clara rose from her chair. "May I see him?"

"Mrs. Keene, he is resting. Besides, I—"

"I wasn't simply your husband's employer for all those months, Mrs. Bridger. I was his . . . *friend*. Surely he told you, or you never would have written to me about the horse. Won't you at least tell him I'm here?"

A chill ran up Inga's spine. *His employer? His friend?*

"You needn't wake him if he's asleep."

A premonition warned her she should send Clara away, should send her packing back to Kentucky with her fine Thoroughbred filly and her coach and her liveried driver. But before she could follow her instincts, Martha raced into the kitchen, excitement glittering in her eyes.

"Aunt Inga, whose—" She stopped abruptly when she saw Clara. "Is that your carriage, all gussied up with feathers?"

Clara's smile never reached her eyes. "Indeed, it is."

"Uncle Dirk was wonderin' who it was when I told him about it."

"Your uncle is awake?" Clara asked, sudden sweetness in her voice.

"Yeah," Martha answered, "he's awake."

"Would you take me to him? My name is Mrs. Keene, and I've come a long ways to see how he is doing."

"Sure." Martha looked at her aunt. "That okay, Aunt Inga?"

She wanted to refuse, but all she seemed able to do was nod.

"Come with me," her niece told their visitor, then led the way out of the kitchen.

With reluctant footsteps and a wary heart, Inga followed after them.

—

Suzanne held up four fingers. "I was this many on my birthday. Remember? Aunt Inga baked me a cake. How many're you gonna be, Unca Dirk?"

Before he could answer, Martha hurried into the room. "The lady's come t'see you, Uncle Dirk."

"What lady?" he asked. But the words stuck in his throat when the widow Keene of King Meadows, Kentucky, stepped into the doorway.

After a long moment, she gave him one of her sultry smiles—a Clara Keene specialty. "Well, you needn't stare at me as if I were a ghost, Dirk."

"What're you doin' here?"

"I understand you've been ill, but have you no manners at all? You might at least say hello." She sashayed into the room. "After all, it's been a long time, and I've come a long way to see you, as I was telling your wife." She sat on the chair beside the bed as if it were her own. "What a pretty thing she is, too. Why, it's no wonder you married her. She must have simply made you forget yourself."

Dirk's gaze darted to the doorway where Inga now stood. Clara's sarcasm had been disguised in pretty words, but Inga had heard it as clearly as he had.

"I'd wondered what became of you, Dirk," Clara continued. "I was hoping you'd write, but you never did. It was like you'd dropped off the very ends of the earth." She touched the back of his hand. "But then, that was what you wanted to do, wasn't it? What a terrible thing for you, ending up here in little ol' Iowa. Whatever made you change your mind about seeing the world the way you always talked about?"

He looked at Clara. She was as beautiful as she'd ever been. Not that long ago, he'd thought she was the perfect kind of woman for him, but now he didn't know why he'd thought so.

"And these charming little angels are your nieces?" she continued, looking at Martha and Suzanne. "Aren't they just as cute as buttons?"

"What brought you here, Mrs. Keene?" he asked, ignoring her question about the girls.

Her brown eyes widened as she met his gaze again. *"Mrs. Keene, is it? Such formality between friends."* The look she gave him spoke volumes. *But we were more than friends, weren't we, Dirk? Remember . . .*

But strangely enough, he couldn't seem to remember much about those months he'd spent in Kentucky. Didn't want to remember them, actually.

Clara waved one of her dainty hands. "Well, if you must know, I am here because your dear wife wrote to me. She wanted to surprise you for your birthday." She rose from the chair. "But I'll tell you nothing more or the surprise will be ruined. You'll have to wait until Saturday. That *is* your birthday, isn't it? I did remember the date right?"

"Yeah, it's—"

"It has been three years, but I've never forgotten the day you left King Meadows. It was your birthday then, too." She leaned over and kissed his cheek. "Well, I'm tired, and I must ask your wife to show me to my room so I can freshen up before supper."

Clara was planning to stay here? Dirk's gaze darted once again toward Inga.

"I will put her in your mamma's old room," she told him softly, her voice devoid of expression. Then to Clara, she said, "Please come with me. Children, you come, too. Your uncle is supposed to be sleeping."

Inga stood beside the doorway until the others had all passed through the opening. Then, with only the briefest of glances in Dirk's direction, she went out and closed the door behind her.

He didn't understand. Inga had brought Clara here as a surprise? But that didn't make sense. Why would she do it? How did she know about Clara? He hadn't mentioned Clara's name when he'd talked about working in Kentucky. He was certain he hadn't.

With a groan, he leaned his head back on the pillow and closed his eyes. Why had Clara kissed his cheek? Why was she implicating with her words and her actions that there had been more between them than was true? Clara Keene was rich, beautiful, and ambitious. She had never wanted anything more from Dirk than he had from her. So why pretend otherwise now?

—

The why was quite simple: Clara was bored. And Clara Keene absolutely despised being bored.

Thus, when she'd received the letter from Mrs. Dirk Bridger, she'd decided a trip to see her former lover and to meet the woman who—it seemed—had made him forget his plans of world travel might be just the cure for that boredom.

Clara looked around the small bedroom on the ground floor of Dirk's home and wrinkled her nose. It was primitive to say the least, but she supposed she could make do for the duration of her stay.

It was a shame, really, to find Dirk living so humbly. She'd remembered all his wonderful plans, and she'd enjoyed entertaining thoughts of him in different parts of the world. Of all her gentlemen friends—and there had been more than a few in the years since Mr. Keene passed away—Dirk had been the most handsome and most amusing. Admittedly, she hadn't known how much she would miss him until he was gone or she might have tried harder to persuade him to stay another season.

And his wife! Inga Bridger was nothing like what Clara had expected. She wasn't beautiful, and she most definitely wasn't rich. A man like Dirk could have had his pick of women. Why had he settled for Inga?

If Clara thought about it, it was actually insulting. Dirk had never proposed marriage to her, not even in the heat of passion. In fact, he'd said he didn't want to ever marry. Neither did she, of course. She enjoyed her freedom too much. She had paid for that freedom with five miserable years as the wife of her much older but extremely wealthy husband. After his death, nothing could have induced her to give up control of her own finances—let alone how she lived—by marrying again. Still, it was nice to be asked.

Now, to find Dirk here with that woman as his wife . . . To think that he had asked *her* and not Clara . . . Yes, it was indeed insulting.

Clara settled onto the stool before the dressing table and stared at her reflection in the mirror. Then she smiled.

Perhaps her stay needn't be dreadful. It would be entertaining, if nothing more, to toy with Dirk's affections. Of course, things might take a little longer, given his illness—whatever the nature of that was—but Clara had all kinds of time. That was one of the benefits, and one of the curses, of the idle rich. Lots and lots of time.

———

"Oh, but I insist I be allowed to help, Mrs. Bridger," Clara said at supper that evening. She laughed and gave a self-deprecating shake of her head. "Of course, I don't cook a lick and I know even less about keeping a house. But I'm sure there must be something I can do."

Inga wanted her help about as much as she wanted a toothache.

"I know!" Clara's eyes widened as she clapped her hands in front of her chest. "I can look after Dirk for you while you go about milking your cows and caring for these sweet children and whatever else it is you do."

Uncharitable thoughts raced through Inga's mind. "Mrs. Keene, I—"

"Now, don't you tell me no, 'cause I simply must insist on doing something. What else are old friends for? Why, you're worn out, Mrs. Bridger. I haven't seen anybody look so wan and tired in a month of Sundays. If you don't take care o' yourself, you're going to make yourself sick. Just see if you don't."

Inga had developed a quick dislike for the Southern accent of her uninvited houseguest. She wished Clara would shut up.

"You just tell me what I need to do," the woman went on, oblivious to Inga's private thoughts.

Go home to Kentucky, Inga wished she could say. *That is what I need you to do.*

"I cannot believe how timely my arrival was. Why, without my help, who knows what would have happened to y'all."

"Mrs. Keene—"

"Isn't it time we called each other by our given names?" She leaned forward. "Do call me Clara. Please. I intend for us to be good friends."

Inga thought not. "Clara, about that filly. As you can see, we really cannot afford such a—"

"Goodness, is that what's on your mind, causing such a frown? You know, if you go on scowling like that it will cause the most dreadful wrinkles in your forehead. The last thing a man wants is a woman with wrinkles. Anyway, you just forget about that little ol' horse."

"But—"

Clara laughed. "It isn't like I need the money. All I care about now is that your husband makes a full recovery. I mean to do everything I can to see he does."

Inga was at a disadvantage with a woman like Clara Keene. She couldn't outtalk her, that was for certain. And for the first time since Dirk had truly made her his wife, Inga felt all her old insecurities raising their ugly heads. She was too tall. She was too thin. She was too plain. She couldn't hold a candle to the likes of Clara.

Why on earth would a man want a plain loaf of bread when he could have cake smothered in sugar frosting?

Why on earth would Dirk want Inga when it was so obvious he could have Clara Keene, just for the asking?

~Eighteen

The entire tenement building smelled of onions and boiled cabbage.

Thea stared out the window of her Lower East Side apartment, trying to ignore the horrible, constant odor. There wasn't much to see. Just the neighboring tenements, most of them filled with European immigrants. Beyond a sea of rooftops, she could see the Brooklyn Bridge. Out of view was the waterfront, steamships and ferries docked at the piers, people bustling in every direction. She hated it all.

It wasn't supposed to be like this.

She was crying again. She couldn't seem to help herself. She was lonely. Karl was gone from dawn until dusk, six days a week, working in that dreadful factory. He came home at night, exhausted and sweaty and invariably hungry. Poor Karl. He seemed always to have to eat something Thea had either half cooked or scorched.

It wasn't supposed to be like this.

She turned away from the window and sat in one of their two chairs. She wiped the tears from her cheeks with an already damp handkerchief.

She did love Karl. She really and truly did love him. She remembered how lonely and bereft she'd been all those terrible months they'd been separated. Now they were together. Now she was his wife. Everything should have been perfect.

But still she was unhappy. She was disillusioned. When she had fantasized about her marriage to Karl, she had imagined a beautiful home with pretty furniture and bric-a-brac and flowers in tall vases and lovely place settings on the table. She had pictured her devoted husband arriving home from work, looking handsome as always, with some special gift he'd purchased because he'd been thinking of her. She hadn't given any thought to who would do the cooking or any of the other housework. Not that Thea hadn't done her share when she was living at the parsonage, but it had been different with her mamma and five girls, all working together. As for gifts, her new husband was always quick to tell her, there was no money for anything beyond the essentials.

It wasn't supposed to be like this.

She hated New York City. She hadn't remembered it being so dirty and crowded. Here on the Lower East Side, she didn't even understand what most people were saying. She was an outsider, and she was alone much of the time.

She missed her mamma and pappa and her sisters. She'd thought she would never want anyone else once she had Karl, but she'd been wrong once again. She was homesick.

It wasn't supposed to be like this.

On the morning of Dirk's birthday, Inga dragged herself out of bed at the usual predawn hour, made the coffee, then went out to the barn. At Inga's insistence, Sven had stopped coming to help with the morning milking. She already felt obliged to their neighbors for so much, and now that Clara Keene was here to help with Dirk . . .

Inga gritted her teeth as she yanked open the barn door with more fervor than necessary.

How she detested that woman! And how intimidated she was by her. Countless times over the last three days she'd wanted to send Clara packing, but she hadn't had the courage. She'd heard Clara chattering on with Dirk about when he'd worked on her farm in Kentucky, and more importantly, she'd heard all that had been implied but not said.

He's my *husband!* she wanted to say. So why didn't she act like it? Why didn't she tell Clara that her assistance was not needed and she could go back to Kentucky and her precious horses? Dirk might have married Inga only to be his housekeeper and to look after the children, but he was *still* her husband.

Orient nickered from a nearby stall. Then the filly thrust her fine-boned head over the top rail and watched Inga's approach with large dark eyes.

Inga's anger faded into despair. "Oh, why did I ever write that letter?" She stroked the animal's velvety muzzle.

Dirk was going to love this horse. Many times, she'd imagined the look that would be in his eyes the first moment he saw Orient, and Inga had sworn to herself she would find some way to pay for the filly so it could be his. They could not simply accept the horse as a gift as Clara had insisted several times. They were not going to be beholden to her.

One of the cows mooed, reminding Inga of her duties. She gave Orient one last pat, then went to retrieve her stool and milk pail.

She should be grateful, she thought to herself. Dirk was much better. Dr. Swenson had said he could get out of bed today. He thought the danger was past and now it was simply a matter of Dirk's regaining his strength.

Last night, for the first time since the accident, Dirk had drawn Inga into the circle of his arms. That was how they'd drifted off to sleep. Listening to his steady breathing, Inga had found herself wishing he would make love to her. Then she'd scolded herself for it because she knew he wasn't well enough yet. But then she'd wondered, if he did make love to her, would he be thinking of Clara?

The cow she'd been milking moved restlessly, and Inga realized her hands had become idle while tears streaked her cheeks. Suddenly she was angry again. She loved Dirk. He was her husband. She was pregnant with his child.

What was she doing, standing by while Clara Keene toyed with their lives?

Well, she wasn't going to do it any longer. When she was done with the milking, she was going to march into the house and send that woman packing.

Dirk had had enough.

For three days, he'd put up with Clara's fawning attentions and unwelcome flirtations. Three days, and Inga didn't seem to care. Like leaving a sheep to the slaughter, Inga had left him to Clara's ministrations with scarcely a backward glance.

He'd had *more* than enough!

He was up and half-dressed before Clara arrived with a tray and two cups of coffee, as she had for the past three mornings. When she saw him standing near the window, wearing his trousers, she exclaimed, "Well, I do declare! Look at you. You're out of bed."

"What is it you want here, Clara?"

Her expression changed to bemusement. "Why, to see you well, of course. Whatever else?"

"No. I mean, what do you *really* want?"

She set the tray on the bedstand, then folded her hands in front of her waist and faced him again. Her look was solemn as she returned his gaze. Then, slowly, her mouth curved in a familiar come-hither smile.

Three years ago, that same kind of smile had set him ablaze. This morning he felt repulsed.

"I came because I wanted to see you, Dirk, to see how you were doing. I was curious." Her voice was low and husky. "I've stayed because I couldn't make myself leave." She closed the distance between them. "What happened to your dreams of seeing the world? Why did you come to this godforsaken place?"

"I had responsibilities." Even as he said it, he realized she would never understand. Clara had no responsibilities other than to herself and her own pleasure. She never thought of anyone else. He hadn't recognized the trait when he'd been with her years ago, perhaps because he'd been much the same, only interested in himself and what he wanted.

"When I learned where you were, I came at once. I brought you a horse as a surprise for your birthday. A filly I named Orient. Do you know why she's named that? Because you were there when the mare was bred, and the next day you left King Meadows. When the foal was born, I thought of you. I thought of you in the far-off Orient, like you'd always talked about. I wanted a constant reminder of what we'd shared."

She placed her hands on his bare chest and leaned into him, her head thrown back so she could look up into his face.

"You don't belong here, Dirk. You don't belong with Inga. Come away with me. I know how to make you happy. You can't be happy here. She isn't the woman for you. Anyone with eyes can guess the reason you married her. I have. So let her take care of those children and you come away with me." She pressed closer. "Remember what it was like. You and me."

He was about to push Clara away when he heard a strangled gasp from the doorway and looked in that direction. Wide-eyed, Inga stared at him. At them.

"Inga—" he began, but she whirled away and disappeared before he could say more.

Now he did shove Clara back from him.

"Inga!" he called as he headed after her.

Clara grabbed his arm. "Dirk, don't! Let her go. Stay with me."

He shook her off without breaking his stride.

A second later, he heard Inga's cry of alarm, then the unmistakable sounds of someone falling. "Inga!"

He couldn't reach her fast enough. His heart was pounding and his head was swimming. His chest felt as if it were about to burst.

She lay in a still heap at the bottom of the stairs. When he reached her, he dropped to his knees. "Inga," he said hoarsely. He leaned over her.

She opened her eyes, and he breathed a sigh of relief.

She started to sit up. He moved his hand to her back to help her. Then she gasped and grabbed at her abdomen.

"What—" he began.

She cried out in pain, then curled into a ball. That was when he saw the blood soaking her dress.

Fear iced through him as he scooped her into his arms and carried her up the stairs. "Hang on, Inga. Hang on."

—

Frida Gerhard laid her hand on Dirk's shoulder, stopping his pacing. "Mr. Bridger, you must sit down and rest. You are not well yet yourself, and you will do Inga no good this way."

"What's taking so long?" he asked, ignoring her advice.

"The doctor will let us know as soon as he is able."

"There was so much blood. So much."

Frida took his arm and guided him to the living room sofa. "Sit down, Mr. Bridger."

"It was my fault."

"No. It was an accident. You must not blame yourself."

"It was my fault."

"Hush, you must not say that."

It didn't matter if he said it or not. It was true. It was his fault. Because he'd never told Inga he loved her. Because he'd been too blind, too stupid, and too selfish to see it for himself. He'd fallen in love with his wife, and he'd never told her so. Now it might be too late.

"Mr. Bridger, I am going to take Martha and Suzanne home with me for the night," Frida offered gently.

He glanced toward the oversized chair where the girls were sitting, watching him with wide, frightened eyes. Then he nodded, the lump in his throat making it too difficult to speak.

"Sven will take care of the milking. You must not worry about anything."

He looked at his neighbor. What would he have done without the Gerhards? First Sven and Frida had helped out when he'd been hurt. Now they were doing even more because of Inga's fall. They'd gone beyond neighborliness. They'd been true friends to the Bridgers.

Frida squeezed his shoulder. "We are glad to help." She smiled sadly. "You've had much to bear. You and the children. But I'm sure Inga will be all right. You'll see."

He closed his eyes, remembering again the scarlet stain that had soaked Inga's skirts. How could she be all right, losing so much blood? And what was taking the doctor so long? Why didn't he tell Dirk anything?

"I'm going upstairs." He started to rise.

His neighbor gently pushed him back down. "The doctor asked you to wait here."

Frustrated and anxious, he raked his hands through his hair as he stared toward the living room doorway.

If only he'd sent Clara away when she'd first arrived, this wouldn't have happened. If only he'd made it clear sooner that she wasn't wanted or welcome. If only he'd told her he didn't want her bringing him coffee or sitting by his bed, talking about long ago. He didn't even know who that young man was, the one she'd kept talking about. It wasn't him. Not anymore.

Clara was gone now, of course. In a rare display of decency—or maybe it was only out of humiliation because she'd failed to entice him away—Clara had left the Bridger farm as soon as her driver returned from fetching the doctor. Without a word to anyone, she'd simply gotten into her fancy carriage and departed the Bridger farm. Dirk wouldn't have known at all if Martha hadn't seen her go.

But what did it matter? The damage had already been done, and it was his fault. He couldn't blame Clara, as much as he wanted to.

Why didn't the doctor come down and tell him what was wrong? How much longer was it going to take?

My fault.

He hid his face in his hands. If only he'd told Inga how he felt about her, she never would have misinterpreted that moment when she'd seen Dirk and Clara together. If she'd known he loved her, she wouldn't have run, wouldn't have tripped, wouldn't have fallen down the stairs.

The instant he heard Dr. Swenson clearing his throat, Dirk was on his feet. "How is she?" he demanded as he stepped toward the physician.

"Sit down, Mr. Bridger."

"I want to see her."

"Not yet." Like Frida Gerhard had done a short while before, the doctor placed his hand on Dirk's shoulder and gently forced him to be seated. "I have given her something to make her sleep. She won't awaken for quite some time."

There was a hollow feeling in the pit of Dirk's stomach.

Behind him, he heard Frida say, "Come, children. Let's go into the kitchen."

The doctor sank onto a chair opposite Dirk. He removed his glasses and cleaned the lenses with a white handkerchief. Only when the spectacles were back in place did he speak again. "Your wife suffered a severe hemorrhage. The next twenty-four hours will be critical. If she makes it through them, then I believe she will have a chance of returning to good health."

"Thank God," Dirk whispered, grabbing hold of the doctor's words of hope and forgetting the words of caution.

"I would like to bed down here so I might monitor her condition. If you could set up a cot in her room?"

"Of course."

"Mr. Bridger, you must have guessed the fall induced a miscarriage. It is my opinion that—"

"Miscarriage?" He straightened with a jolt. "She was *pregnant?*"

"You didn't know? Ah, well." Dr. Swenson shook his head. "It was early yet, of course. She was probably waiting until she was sure. She might not have realized it for herself. Young women often don't."

She'd been pregnant.

With his baby.

His baby.

He groaned as he hid his face in his hands.

"Mr. Bridger ... Dirk ... There is more."

More? He raised his head, met the doctor's gaze.

"There must have been serious internal tearing. It is why she hemorrhaged. Because of that, you see, it is unlikely she will be able to carry a child again."

It shouldn't hurt so much. He'd never wanted a wife and family. It shouldn't hurt so much.

"Are you sure?" he asked after a lengthy silence.

Dr. Swenson nodded. "Reasonably sure, yes."

"Does Inga know?"

"Not yet."

This time when he stood, no one tried to stop him. "I'm going up to sit with her. I want to be with her when she wakes up."

"She will sleep a long time. Through the night, most likely. Rest now while you are able, Mr. Bridger. You will need your strength."

"I'm going to sit with her." He glared at the doctor, a challenge in his eyes.

"Very well. I will pour myself some coffee."

Dirk climbed the stairs, his footsteps heavy and slow. He was tired, but he doubted it had anything to do with his own health and recovery. It had everything to do with the way he had failed Inga.

He opened the door to their bedroom. The curtains had been pulled, but the doctor had left a lamp burning on the bedside table. It was turned low, barely shedding any light. Inga lay on the far side of the bed, her slight form seeming even more slight beneath the quilt that covered her.

Dirk strode to the stool beside the bed, settled onto it, stared at his wife. She had always been fair-complexioned. Now her skin seemed translucent, as if she might fade away, vanish before his eyes. Her satiny hair lay limp against the pillow. Her bow-shaped mouth—usually pink and moist, always so sweet when he kissed her, always so ready to speak a word of praise or comfort—was a gray-blue color now.

She cared for him. He knew that. He'd always known that. Might she have loved him if he'd been the least bit lovable? He'd like another chance to prove to her he was worthy of her love. If only it wasn't too late.

"I'm sorry, Inga," he said after a long silence. "Sorry about everything. I'd make it up to you if I could. What a mess I've made of it. If you weren't so kind-hearted, you wouldn't—" The word choked off, silenced by an excruciating pain in his heart. Tears welled in his eyes.

He laid his forehead against the quilt—one of her beautiful quilts, made lovingly with her own hands—and did something he hadn't done since he was eight years old.

He wept.

~Nineteen

Inga, don't give up. You wouldn't let me. I'm not lettin' you do it either. Wake up, Inga. Come back to us. Martha and Suzanne and me, we all need you. Nothing else matters except you gettin' well."

You don't belong here, Dirk.

There was pain.

You can't be happy here.

Always so much pain. Like something clawing and white hot tearing at her insides.

Come away with me.

Why wouldn't it stop? Why wouldn't the pain go away?

Remember what it was like.

And why wouldn't that voice stop? Why did those words keep repeating? Over and over and over again.

"I cannot answer your question, Mr. Bridger, because I do not know. There is much we doctors have yet to understand. We can only wait and see. The bleeding has stopped, but if she does not wake up soon . . ."

"Aunt Inga? Suzanne and me, we've come t'see you. You gonna wake up now? You been asleep a long time . . . How come she doesn't wake up, Uncle Dirk?"

"I don't know, moppet. I don't know."

You don't belong here . . .

"I'll make it up to you, Inga. I don't know how, but I swear I will. Just don't die. I'll find a way to make you happy. You'll see."

You don't belong here, Dirk . . . Come away with me . . .
You don't belong here, Dirk . . . Come away with me . . .
You don't belong here, Dirk . . . Come away with me . . .
Come away with me . . .
Come away with me . . .

———

The sun hurt Inga's eyes. It spilled through the windows, warm and yellow, casting its brilliant glow throughout the bedroom and blinding her.

She couldn't believe she had overslept. Not so late the sun was up already.

She sat up and swung her legs over the side of the bed, then stood. The floor seemed to vanish beneath her feet. The world spun out of control and darkness surrounded her as she crumpled downward with a pitiful cry of alarm. She thought she heard someone shout, "Mr. Bridger!" but she couldn't be sure. The voice seemed to come from so far away.

It was Dirk who drew her back from the dark void into which she'd fallen. "Inga, what have you done?"

She recognized the warmth and strength of his arms as he lifted her into the safety of his embrace. She was disappointed when he lay her on the cool sheets and left her there. With enormous effort, she opened her eyes and looked at him.

He was leaning over her, his hands braced on the mattress. He was unshaven. A dark, unkempt beard hid much of his handsome face from view. She frowned. Why hadn't she noticed he was growing a beard? She wasn't sure she liked it. If he was growing it to hide the hollowness of his cheeks and the dark circles beneath his eyes, he had failed.

"You are unwell." Her words came out half whisper, half croak. "Why aren't you resting?"

He gave her a hint of a smile but didn't answer her question. Instead, he said, "Frida, would you send Sven for Dr. Swenson?"

"Of course."

Inga turned her head on the pillow—something it took great effort to do—and focused her gaze on her neighbor.

"It's good to have you back, Inga," the woman said softly.

Back? She didn't understand. Back from where? She looked at Dirk again.

"You don't remember what happened?"

She shook her head. *"Nej."*

A dark and worrisome expression passed over his eyes. "It doesn't matter for now."

"But what—"

"We can talk about it later." He touched her lightly on the shoulder, then took his hand away. "Do you think you could eat something?"

She didn't feel hungry, but he seemed to want it. "I suppose so."

His smile was more earnest this time. "Good."

"I will get it," Frida offered. "And then I will send Sven for the doctor."

"Dirk?"

"Hmm?"

"Have I been ill a long time?"

Again that shadow across his face. "Yeah, a long time."

"How long?"

He hesitated, then answered, "Almost two weeks."

She frowned. It was odd not to remember, to have two weeks of her life simply disappear. She grasped at memories. "You had pneumonia," she said.

"Yeah, but I'm okay now."

"You look tired." She paused, frowned again. "Did I have pneumonia, too?"

He shook his head.

"Why can I not remember?"

"I don't know, Inga."

She closed her eyes and sighed. "You would think I could remember." She felt herself being tugged toward sleep.

On the thin edge of unconsciousness, she thought she heard Dirk whisper, "And I wish I could forget."

That was a strange thing for him to say.

⎯

Dirk leaned on the corral fence and watched Orient trot around the muddy enclosure, shaking her head and flicking her tail, occasionally giving a little kick with her heels.

He was going to have to send the filly back to Kentucky, of course. He wasn't sure why Clara had left her behind. Probably because she'd been in such a hurry to get away from the farm. She'd just forgotten in her haste. Whatever the reason, Dirk wasn't about to let the horse stay. Orient could only be a reminder of what had happened to Inga—and he didn't need any more reminders of that.

He turned his back toward the corral and gazed at the house. Dr. Swenson's black buggy stood near the back door. The doctor had chased Dirk out of the bedroom over half an hour before while he examined Inga. Dirk's endless pacing in the kitchen had caused Frida Gerhard to send him outside.

Was Dr. Swenson telling Inga now that she'd lost her baby, that she would never be able to have a child of her own? Would she tell the kindly old physician what she had seen, why she had fallen down those stairs? Would she hate Dirk now? He'd deserve it if she did. It was all his fault. His own fault.

The kitchen door opened. "Dirk!" Frida waved to him. "The doctor says you should come in now."

His stomach felt hollow. His feet felt weighted. Guilt walked beside him as he moved across the barnyard.

—

No more babies.

Inga knew that's what the doctor had told her, but it didn't seem real.

No more babies.

She supposed she should cry. Dr. Swenson seemed to expect her to cry. Why didn't she?

Come away with me ... You can't be happy here ...

The memory of that moment had returned, and she was sorry it had. She remembered them, standing close together, Clara's hand on Dirk's bare chest. Clara—beautiful, rich, sensuous Clara Keene—and Dirk, so handsome, so strong. They'd looked perfect together.

Would Dirk have agreed to go with Clara if Inga hadn't happened upon them?

Nej, she answered herself. He wouldn't have gone. Dirk might be unhappy, but he would never turn his back on his responsibilities. He had promised to raise his nieces, and he would keep his word. He was a man of honor, Hattie Bridger had said, and it was true. No, Dirk wouldn't have deserted the children—or Inga—for Clara, no matter how much he might have wished he could. She knew he would leave one day, but it wouldn't be for Clara, and it wouldn't be by stealth.

So why had she run when she'd seen them together? Why had it hurt so much, like a knife plunging into her heart?

Probably because she believed Clara was right. Dirk didn't belong on this dairy farm and he didn't belong with her. He couldn't be happy here.

If I had not run, I would not have lost the baby.

The baby. Dirk's baby. She would have had his child when he went away. Now she would have nothing except memories.

No more babies. Not ever. She felt empty, hollow, useless.

Did Dirk know? Would he care?

As if summoned by her wondering, Dirk appeared in the bedroom doorway. He looked haggard, so worn and thin. He hadn't been eating right. Who was cooking for him and the children?

"How are you?" he asked as he approached the side of the bed.

"Better, I think." Her voice sounded raspy, unlike herself.

Dirk knelt beside the bed and took her hand in his. "I'm sorry, Inga. I've made a real mess of things."

"You need a shave."

"It was my fault. You could have died, and it would've been my fault."

She looked toward the window. "Let's not talk about it."

"All right. We won't for now." His hand tightened on hers. "But we'll have to eventually. There's a lot I have to tell you, Inga. I've made so many mistakes."

"I do not wish to talk about it now," she whispered, wishing she would cry. Crying would be preferable to this hollowness.

"Inga—"

"Frida said it is almost April. In Jönköping the first wild-flowers are out. The coltsfoot are showing their little yellow faces amidst the brown, dry grass. Soon they will be finding blue hepaticas in the birch tree groves. And nettles, too. Mamma always picked the sprouts of nettles for her nettle soup." She closed her eyes. "I wish Mamma was here."

"Me too."

"I would like to sleep."

"Sure. We'll talk later, Inga."

—

But they didn't talk later. Inga wouldn't let them. She retreated from him in the days that followed. She retreated from everyone, locking herself behind some invisible wall. Physically she improved much more quickly than the doctor had expected, but emotionally she shut herself off from the world.

Dirk recognized what she was doing. Probably because, in his own way, he'd done much the same thing in the past. Only he'd used bitterness as his wall of defense. Inga was using indifference and silence.

She resumed sewing. For hours on end, she sat in the bed, pillows at her back, and stitched on a quilt, this one made only with red and white bits of fabric. It wasn't like her usual quilts. There were no individual panels telling a story. Dirk hated the predominantly red quilt, although he couldn't say why.

The Linbergs returned from Minnesota, but even Inga's teasing, laughing, smiling sisters seemed unable to draw her back from that quiet place of refuge she'd found. She listened and watched and nodded, but she never actually participated. She was there, but she wasn't.

Dirk watched Inga and knew fear. He was helpless. There was nothing he could do, nothing anyone could do, but watch and wait and pray. And Dirk had never been much good at prayer.

—

Inga awakened with a start, a baby's cries echoing in her ears.

She glanced toward her left side. Dirk lay sleeping beside her, his profile kissed by the silvering light of the moon. Carefully, so as not to awaken him, Inga slid from beneath the covers. Her legs were weak and unsteady, but she managed to rise and stay upright. She reached for her robe, slipped her arms into the sleeves, then walked to the door of the bedroom.

The house was silent, cloaked in the stillness of night.

She went to the children's bedroom and walked in, stopping beside the bed. Martha's head was covered in a nightcap. Suzanne had lost her cap in her tossing and turning, and her red hair spilled over the pillowcase in a puddle of tangles and curls. Angelic and impish at the same time. Inga's heart ached as she looked at them. She loved them so very much.

But it had been a baby's cry she'd heard. Where had it come from?

She left the children's bedroom and went downstairs, wandering from one room to another. All was silent. All was as it should be.

She opened the kitchen door and gazed out at the barnyard. The snow was gone. She would have sworn she could see crocuses blooming beside the back steps. It had to be a trick of the moonlight. Winter couldn't possibly have ended while she slept.

She closed the door and leaned against it. She felt lost, alone, and afraid.

Terrified.

Walking as quickly as her legs would carry her, she returned to her upstairs bedroom. A glance at the bed proved she was not alone. Dirk was there, sleeping, one arm thrown over his forehead.

Then she saw the quilt, lying across a chair near the window. She crossed to it, stared at it. Scarlet. So very scarlet.

She had prayed and asked God for Dirk's life. She had sworn she would never want anything again if only he would spare Dirk, even if it meant losing him later to the things he wanted more. She had told God to take anything of hers but to let Dirk live, and she would never ask for another thing.

God had heard her request and taken her unborn child.

She picked up the red and white quilt, held it to her face, and began to weep. Her heart was torn and bleeding, like the scarlet of the quilt, and she couldn't stop weeping. She knelt on the floor, clutching the quilt, swaying forward and back as she mourned the baby she would never have. All the babies she would never have.

She wasn't sure when Dirk came to kneel beside her, when he took her into his arms and held her head against his chest, when he began to whisper words of comfort and remorse.

"We'll start over, Inga. You and me. We'll do things right this time."

She had wanted too much. Her destiny had been to stay at home with Pappa, to take care of him. She should have learned to be content with what she had, but she hadn't been. She'd wanted adventure. She'd wanted to be pretty. She'd wanted Dirk, and then she'd wanted his child. She'd wanted more, always more. She'd wanted too much.

Dirk stroked his hand over her hair. "When I asked you to marry me, it was for plenty of selfish reasons. I never thought about what it would cost you. You gave me more than I deserved. It's my fault, all your unhappiness. Nothin' I can do will ever give you back what you've lost, but I want you to know how sorry I am. How sorry I'll always be."

Dirk thought it was his fault, but he was wrong. Inga knew the fault was hers and hers alone.

"I've got no right to ask you to love me, Inga. I know I'll have to earn it."

She had loved him too much and now she had paid the price.

"What do you say? Can we start over? Can we make us into a real family, you, me, and the girls?"

She couldn't answer him. Fear of the future, of still wanting too much, kept her silent.

Sobs tore at her throat, and she was inconsolable, for she believed, deep in her wounded heart, that she had bargained one life for another.

And then she had found the price too high.

Monday, April 2, 1898
Uppsala, Iowa

Dear Mary,

It has been nearly a month since I received your letter with the sad news about Mr. Maguire. I am glad, however, to learn of the good health of your son. I know little Keary must be of comfort to you now.

There has been much heartache for my family this winter. Gunda was in an accident. The sleigh she was riding in went into the icy river. One of her friends drowned and she could easily have died as well, if not for my husband's rescue. As it was, her leg had to be amputated below the knee. Dirk caught pneumonia after all his hours in the cold and I feared I would lose him, but he has recovered.

As for me, I had a bad fall down the stairs. I was pregnant at the time, and our baby was lost. The doctor says there can be no more children.

I had not realized how difficult it would be to write those words. It is because I wanted so much more than I was meant to have. I was envious of others. I wanted to be beautiful like my sisters. I wanted to love and be loved like you with your Mr. Maguire and Beth with her Mr.

Steele. I wanted to have a family of my own. I was never satisfied with what I had. I wanted more. Too much more.

Mary, I am frightened, for I have lost the ability to pray. From the time I was a little girl, I always felt the nearness of God. I told Dirk once I could hear God's voice in the wind, hear it whispering in the trees. But now, all is changed. I can hear nothing. I feel lost and alone and I do not know what to do.

When we were coming to America, you were the truly brave one, Mary, the one who believed in making things happen. I admired that trait about you most of all. I wish my nature was more like yours. I believe it would see me through this time better than my own.

Your friend,

Inga Bridger

Twenty

Get off me, Sunset!" Dirk elbowed the animal in the ribs but got little response.

He was trying to replace a shoe the big workhorse had thrown earlier in the day. Only the palomino had decided now was a good time to rest and was leaning hard against Dirk's back.

"You'd make great glue," he muttered as he measured iron shoe against hoof.

He lowered Sunset's leg to the ground, then straightened and walked to the anvil. Soon, the *clang, clang, clang* of hammer striking iron filled the barn. When he paused to wipe a trickle of sweat from his brow, he heard children's laughter wafting to him on a balmy April breeze. He was irresistibly drawn toward the sound.

He walked toward the open rear door, pausing at the entrance, his gaze scanning the pastures behind the large barn. Jerseys dotted the smaller paddock to the right, nibbling at the new shoots of grass that were beginning to appear. The larger pasture to his left held no animals as yet. He wouldn't graze his livestock there until late May.

He saw Martha first, high in the branches of a tall maple tree near the drive. Then he saw Suzanne sitting on Kirsten Linberg's lap, the two of them on the lowest and thickest limb of the ancient tree. Beneath them, a blanket had been spread on the ground, and on it, in various positions, were three more of the Linberg sisters. Astrid lay flat on her back, her eyes closed against the bright sunshine of early afternoon. Gunda sat beside her, her back propped against a fence post and her skirts carefully spread out in front of her, no doubt to hide her missing limb. Inga was on her knees, her folded hands clenched in front of her waist as she stared anxiously upward.

"Martha, be careful," she called. "I think you should come down."

"Not yet, Aunt Inga. I've almost reached the nest."

"Martha, I really think—"

Gunda took hold of Inga's arm and said something, but Dirk couldn't hear what it was from this far away.

He leaned his shoulder against the doorjamb.

Of the two of them, Gunda had bounced back much more quickly than Inga. Even though she would never walk without the aid of crutches, Gunda had remembered how to laugh, how to have fun, how to enjoy life. Inga seemed to have forgotten all of that and more.

Dirk frowned. Maybe he'd made a mistake, not saying he loved her that night two weeks ago. She'd cried in his arms, and he'd felt her pain. He could have said he loved her then, but he'd wanted to show her first. He'd wanted to prove it to her. Words didn't always mean a whole lot, and he'd wanted his actions to speak for him.

But his wife couldn't hear or see the love he felt, because even though she was up and about now, even though she had resumed caring for the children and cooking for the family, even though she was physically present, Dirk knew she was emotionally absent. Especially with him.

He thought back across the months since Inga had first entered their lives. He thought of her gentle ways, the sweetness of her smiles, the expectancy with which she used to greet each new day. She'd loved his mother in those short weeks before Hattie's death. She'd loved his nieces from the moment they'd all first met. He'd thought she might love him, at least a little. She hadn't been afraid to face life then. She'd had a sweet, abiding faith that she'd shared with others in her many acts of kindness. But now . . .

"Unca Dirk! Look at me!"

He glanced away from his wife and waved at Suzanne.

"Me too!" Martha shouted.

He obediently did so, waving to her as he had her sister. Then he pushed off from the door and started across the uneven ground, eating up the distance with long strides. As he drew near, his gaze returned to the blanket and those upon it.

Gunda smiled, a mischievous twinkle in her eyes. "Did you come to climb the tree, *bror?*" She had stopped calling him Mr. Bridger upon her return from Minneapolis and now used the more affectionate Swedish term for brother. "Martha is having trouble reaching that bird's nest."

"Make her come down, Dirk," Inga said softly. "It is too dangerous. She is much too high."

The fear in her voice nearly broke his heart. "All right. I'll get her."

He walked to the tree, grabbed the nearest branch, and hiked himself up.

"Sit with us, Unca Dirk," Suzanne said when he glanced her way.

"Sorry, pumpkin. I'm after your sister." Then he resumed his climb.

He heard Martha's giggles and looked up through the thick web of branches, new buds just beginning to make their springtime appearance. She was straddling a narrow tree limb, mischief twinkling in her eyes.

"What're you doin', Uncle Dirk?"

"What does it look like? I'm climbing a tree."

She snorted in disbelief. "Grown-ups don't climb trees. They're too old."

He paused and glared at her with all the indignation he could muster. *"Old?"*

She giggled again.

He quickened the pace of his ascent, accepting the six-year-old's unspoken challenge. In a matter of moments, he'd reached her. "Who're you sayin' is old, moppet?"

"Well . . . you never used to climb trees."

He grinned. "Well . . . neither did you."

"Look." She pointed to a sparse limb over her right shoulder. "Can you reach the nest?"

"I think we're gonna have to leave it there."

"But I wanted to show it to Suzanne."

"I know, but you've got your Aunt Inga mighty worried, being up so high and all. Besides, if you take the nest, when the birds come back, where're they gonna lay their eggs? There won't be any baby birds chirpin' out here in the tree. I'd miss the sound." He motioned for her to slide backward. "Come on. Let's not make Aunt Inga worry any longer."

With a sigh, Martha began inching her way backward along the branch. When she reached him, she said, "Aunt Inga worries a lot, doesn't she?"

"Yeah." He glanced toward the ground. "Yeah, she does."

"She used to be happier."

"I know."

Martha touched his shoulder, drawing his gaze to her. "What can we do t'make her happy again? She always did stuff to make Grandma happy, even when Grandma was so sick. You think Aunt Inga'd like it if Suzanne and me made her some yellow daffodils like we did Grandma?"

"She might," he answered. "But right now what would make her happiest is for me to get you outta this tree."

"Okay. I'm comin'."

What can *we do to make Inga happy again?* Dirk wondered as he and Martha descended through the branches of the old maple tree. There had to be something, and he had to find what it was.

—

Thea tossed a shawl over her shoulders and left the third-floor apartment, unable to bear being shut in for another moment, unable to bear the noise and the stench that was omnipresent.

The baby in the apartment across the hall had been squalling for over an hour. It was a skinny, sickly thing, that poor baby, and Thea suspected it would not live to see the end of its first year.

On the second floor, in the apartment directly below hers, a man and woman were arguing in a foreign language at the top of their lungs. Thea knew what would happen next. Before long the man would hit his wife—sometimes once, sometimes many times—and then things would fall quiet. Tomorrow, the woman would sport a bruise on her cheek or a black eye. Or she might have an arm in a sling or walk with a limp.

Thea released a sigh of relief as her feet touched the ground floor. A moment later she stepped outside into the fading light of early evening. She paused, looking up and down the street. Karl should be home soon. She was eager to see him, although she doubted he would believe it. She knew she didn't act like it.

She pulled her shawl more tightly about her shoulders as she thought, *Poor Karl.*

Six weeks married, and she could already see something defeated in his ice blue eyes. It was mostly her fault, too. No, it was *entirely* her fault. She knew it, but she couldn't seem to help it. She complained bitterly to him about everything. Every day he returned home from work to a poorly cooked dinner and a miserable, cramped apartment and a wife who nagged him about everything that was wrong. She blamed him, even when she knew he wasn't to blame. He had not forced her to come to New York and marry him. She had come willingly.

Others were happy. Others who were no better off than she and Karl. She saw them every day, on the streets, in the marketplace, on the stairway of her own tenement building. Why couldn't she be like them?

"I want to go home," she whispered as she started walking in the direction of the waterfront.

It was the first time she had voiced those words aloud, but she had thought it often in recent days. In Uppsala, the farmland would be turning green and the trees would be beginning to bud. The crocus would already be in bloom, their yellow heads bobbing in the spring breeze. Gunda and Astrid and Kirsten would be holding court with all the handsome young men in the area, and the parsonage would ring with laughter.

Inga would be there to answer Thea's questions. Inga, who had always been so giving, so willing to share. Thea had never realized before how often she'd depended upon her older sister to solve her problems or give her advice, how often Inga had rescued Thea from her own mistakes.

Still lost in thought, Thea reached South Street and turned left. The congested piers and ferry slips were bustling with activity, despite the hour. It seemed always to be so. She longed for quiet and wide empty spaces. She longed for the parsonage and her family. She longed to be the prettiest girl in town and to be spoiled and pampered. She even missed her pappa's disapproving glances.

Down past the James slip, where the ferry that carried passengers up the East River to Long Island City in Queens County was docked, past Pier 32, where the Long Island Railroad kept its car floats filled with freight boxcars, past the Catherine Street Ferryhouse, where Thea and Karl sometimes took the ferry to downtown Brooklyn, she saw the familiar sungold hair of her husband's head. Tall and slim, he walked with long strides. His shirt sleeves were rolled up above his elbows. He carried his jacket, still necessary in the crisp morning hours when he left for work, over his right shoulder.

Something tightened in her chest at the sight of him, and she felt like crying—something she did far too much of these days. She knew it was true, because she saw her puffy eyes in that tiny cracked mirror in their bedroom every morning.

He saw her then, raised his arm and waved at her, even smiled.

She swallowed the lump in her throat. She had loved him so very much for so very long. She had run away from her family to be with him, to become his bride. This had been what she'd wanted. To just be with him. She should have been happy. She should be making him happy.

But all she wanted now was to go home.

—

Inga held her breath, fear squeezing her chest, as she watched uncle and niece climbing down the tree. It was a familiar feeling, this fear. Every time one of the children or Dirk was out of her sight, she was terrified some calamity would befall them. She was afraid disaster would strike, and she would be helpless to save them. She loved them all, and simply by loving them, she feared she tempted misfortune's arrival.

"Inga," Gunda said softly, "they are all right."

She looked at her sister. "I know."

"In fact, when I am better, I think I will climb that tree myself."

"Oh, Gunda, you—"

"Do you think I couldn't?"

She remembered Gunda when she'd been about Martha's age. Gunda had been such a tomboy, always leading her younger sisters into mischief. Occasionally, she'd roped her older sisters into trouble as well. Later, as she'd developed into a pretty young woman, she'd taken her mischief-making in a new direction, flirting outrageously with all the young men of Jönköping and, once in America, of Uppsala. She had never been as flirtatious as Thea, but she had been bad enough.

Gunda touched Inga's forearm. "I lost my leg, Inga, not my life."

Inga swallowed the lump in her throat.

More softly, Gunda continued, "You lost something, too, but it must not cause you to stop living."

She closed her eyes.

"Pappa's worried about you. And Mamma. You haven't been to church or—"

Inga looked at Gunda, protesting, "I am still not well enough to go into town. I . . . I haven't the strength yet."

"Oh, Inga," her sister whispered, her expression filled with sadness. "It is more than a month since you fell down the stairs. It is time you put it behind you."

Inga wished she could be angry about Gunda's attempt at interference, but she couldn't summon that emotion. It seemed the only thing she could feel anymore was fear, trepidation, a sense of loss and foreboding. If she could, she would lock her family up in the house and never let any of them out of her sight.

"Look, Aunt Inga." Martha ran over to her and plopped down on the blanket. "I got a wildflower."

"Me, too! Me, too!" Suzanne's pudgy little legs carried her rapidly to Inga, her hands clutching a small purple flower.

When she reached her aunt, she thrust the flower close to Inga's nose. "Smell."

She smiled even as her heart ached. "Lovely, Suzanne. Yours, too, Martha."

"Uncle Dirk found 'em on the other side of the tree there," Martha said as she glanced behind her.

Inga lifted her gaze to Dirk, standing not far away. He'd been so attentive since her accident. She knew he felt responsible for what had happened. He'd said her fall down the stairs was his fault. But he had no way of knowing it was she who was being punished, she who had been greedy and wanted more, wanted too much.

Still wanted too much.

He smiled at her, and it took her breath away, the way it always did, the way it always had. Then he held out another cluster of flowers. "For you," he said.

She felt like crying again.

Dirk knelt on the grass beside the blanket, waiting for her to take the small bouquet from his hands.

"Thank you," she whispered as she accepted the flowers.

His grin broadened as their fingers touched. "You look mighty pretty today. Doesn't she, Gunda?"

"*Ja,* she looks very pretty," Gunda answered, a note of surprise in her voice.

Inga blushed as she looked at the flowers in her hands.

"You know, Gunda, your sister doesn't think she's pretty," he continued. "I guess it's 'cause she's different from the rest of her sisters. Different, but just as pretty."

"Stop it, Dirk," Inga ordered softly.

"Nah, I don't think I will stop it. I think it'd do you good t'hear how pretty you are on a more regular basis." He leaned closer. "I think I'll tell you at least once a day, no matter who else is around."

She met his gaze and felt a flash of unabashed happiness. It lasted only an instant before she wondered again when it would be taken from her. Then the fear returned and the moment was gone.

"Well," he said as he rose to his feet, "guess I'd best get back to my horse shoein'. You girls have a good time with your visiting." He glanced toward Gunda. "Give a holler when you're ready to go, and I'll help you to your buggy."

They were all silent while they watched Dirk walk away.

Then, with an exaggerated sigh, Astrid said, "You are *so* blessed, Inga."

She felt a shiver run up her spine. "*Ja,* I am blessed."

But for how long? she wondered. *How long before something else happens?*

⸻

Dirk was thankful for the help his neighbors and the folks from town had given him in recent weeks. Strange, other than Erik Hansen, Dirk hadn't thought he had any friends in Iowa. Not that long ago he'd thought himself alone against the world. Now he'd discovered he had an abundance of friends.

Still, he wasn't sorry to see an end to the casseroles and pies the women of the Prärieblomman Lutheran Church had prepared to keep the Bridgers from starving. He had to admit, as he and the girls sat down to supper that night, he was glad Inga had resumed cooking. Her skills in the kitchen were far superior to anyone else's.

"Mmm. Something smells mighty good," he said as he slid his chair up close to the table. "Doesn't it, girls?"

"Sure does," Martha replied.

"Uh-huh," Suzanne echoed.

Inga demurred. "It is just *hasselbackspotatis* and an oven omelette. Nothing special."

He opened his mouth to tell her everything she did was special but thought better of it. He would just foul up. He wasn't a man of many words. Never had been. Right now, he wished he were.

What could he say to tell her how much she had changed him? How did he explain the difference in the way he felt every morning, the new lightness in his heart? It wasn't so very long ago he'd hated everything about this farm, but now it was different. *He* was different. It wasn't that things had suddenly gotten easier for the Bridgers. It wasn't that he'd suddenly discovered a fondness for cows or early-morning milking or mucking out smelly stalls. It wasn't that there was any more money or they were any less in debt.

He guessed it was just love for Inga, pure and simple, that had changed him.

But words wouldn't be enough to convince her, even if he could find the right ones. Inga was hurting, down deep inside, and she needed a lot more than hearing that he loved her. He didn't want her to think he said those words out of guilt. She needed to see the changes in him. She needed to know those changes were real.

Inga needed to discover all this for herself, and she needed to believe it in her heart.

He wished his ma were still alive, he thought with a sharp pang. Hattie Bridger had been one of the wisest women he'd known, and he sure could've used some advice from her right now. She would've been able to tell him how to help things along between him and Inga. She would have known how to reach through Inga's hurt and pain and fear.

Hattie Bridger had known all along that Dirk and Inga were supposed to be married. His ma had known he was going to fall in love. That's what she'd been trying to tell him, right before she died.

He cleared his throat as Inga set the last of the food dishes on the table, then took her seat opposite him. "You know, I was thinking that maybe we oughta take a trip down to Des Moines, once you're feelin' up to it. Just the two of us."

"Des Moines? Why?"

"Well, I'd like to get a look at some of the new farming and milking equipment I've been hearin' about, and maybe you could buy yourself some quilting fabric." Actually, the idea had just occurred to him, but now that it had, he thought it a good one. "Or maybe you'd like a new dress," he added.

She lifted the platter of roasted potatoes, basted in butter and coated with grated cheese and bread crumbs, and held it toward him, her pale blue eyes looking wary and uncertain. "Who would take care of the farm and the milking while we were gone?"

"I reckon we could impose on the Gerhards again. Sven must feel like the cows are his, and Frida never seems to mind lookin' after the children."

She glanced down at her plate. "We owe them too much already. Besides, there is no money to be spent on a new dress or fabric."

"Erik Hansen would help out, too, if I asked him. You let me worry about what we can or can't afford."

"What if something happened to one of the girls while we were away?"

"We'll only be gone overnight. What could happen?"

"Anything." Her voice was tinged with panic, as if a hundred different calamities had occurred to her. "I do not think we should leave them behind. I do not think we should go. Any of us. We belong here."

He reached across the table and grabbed hold of her hand, forcing her to look at him. "Nothing's gonna happen to Martha and Suzanne. Or to you and me. I swear it to you."

"You cannot swear it," she whispered. "You tempt God to say so."

He stared at her for a moment, then firmly replied, "That's nonsense, and you know it." He realized he sounded angry.

Maybe he was angry.

He released her hand, then picked up his fork and stabbed a bite of omelet. "As soon as Dr. Swenson says it's okay for you to travel, we're goin' to Des Moines. Just the two of us. And that settles it."

Watching her husband, Inga remembered something Gunda had said earlier today. *You lost something, too, but it must not cause you to stop living.* But how did she keep herself from it? she wondered.

She lowered her gaze to her plate, her appetite forgotten.

Dirk couldn't know how much she longed to go with him to Des Moines, to spend all those hours alone with him. She wanted to be happy and carefree. She despised the fearful, timid person she'd become, but she didn't know how to overcome it.

"Uncle Dirk?" Martha asked softly, intruding on the strained silence that had gripped the room.

"Hmm?"

"Suzanne and me. We like to stay at Mrs. Gerhard's. We won't come to no trouble. We promise." The child looked at Inga. "Honest we won't."

Inga sighed, her heart tight in her chest. "All right then." She glanced toward Dirk. "For a couple of days. If Frida and Sven do not mind."

He smiled again, and she breathed easier.

Perhaps nothing untoward would happen. Perhaps it would be all right.

Twenty-one

A unt Inga!"

At the sound of Martha's cry, Inga's heart nearly stopped beating.

"Come see what Uncle Dirk's done!"

Relief flooded her. She drew a deep breath as she set aside the rolling pin. Then she turned toward the back door where Martha was standing.

The child's red hair curled in wild abandon around her face. It didn't look like it had seen a brush in a month of Sundays, even though Inga had braided it that morning. Martha's cheeks were rosy, and her eyes twinkled with excitement. "Come see! Hurry!"

"What is it?" Inga wiped her floury hands on her apron as she walked across the kitchen.

Martha grabbed hold of Inga's arm and pulled her outside. "You'll see."

The sun glowed warm in a cloudless sky. The air smelled sweet with the green scents of springtime. A litter of kittens scampered near the barn, chasing after shadows, while their mother slept, stretched out in the sunshine.

Inga felt her spirits lift as she followed Martha across the barnyard and down the drive.

"Look!" Martha pointed with one outstretched arm.

Inga saw Dirk then, standing near the maple tree where she and her sisters had sat only a few days before. From the thick lower limb of the tree, Dirk had hung a swing made with sturdy ropes and a wooden seat. He was pushing Suzanne in the swing now, and she was giggling merrily.

"Wait until you see how high I can go," Martha said. "Come on."

When Dirk saw them approaching, he smiled. Strangely enough, it made her remember the man who'd had no time to play with his nieces, the man who hadn't even wanted to have Christmas. When had he changed? How had he found the time when there was all the same work to be done every day?

She followed Martha into the pasture and up to the tree. Dirk's gaze never left her the entire time. She felt an old familiar pleasure shiver up her spine.

"Your turn, Mrs. Bridger," he said, stopping the swing with his hands.

"*Nej,* it is for the children."

He winked at her. "I don't think they'd mind. Would you, girls?"

"No, we don't mind," Martha answered for both of them.

Dirk helped Suzanne to the ground, then pulled the swing backward. "Okay, ma'am. It's your turn."

"Really, Dirk, I have my baking to do and there is a basket of mending still to be . . ." She let her protest drift into silence. It might be fun, after all, and it was terribly hard to deny him when he looked at her that way.

His grin broadened. Her heart thumped.

"All right," she whispered. "But only for a moment." She moved into place.

With his hands on the ropes on either side of her, he drew back on the swing, causing her feet to leave the ground. Then he gave her a push. Her stomach seemed to somersault as she flew forward, and she let out a tiny squeal of surprise. He pushed her again, higher this time.

There had been a swing behind the parsonage in Jönköping. Inga and her sisters had spent many hours there during the brief summers. Come to think of it, when Thea was about Suzanne's age, she'd taken a spill and broken her arm.

Inga's grip tightened on the ropes, her temporary pleasure evaporating. "Stop!"

"What?"

"Stop!" She dragged her feet as the swing arced backward. Dirk's hands on her waist completed the job, bringing her to a complete halt. Immediately, she pulled away from him and jumped up from the wooden seat.

"Inga, what's wrong?"

"Nothing. I . . . I have work to do." Quickly, she walked toward the house.

He caught up with her before she'd reached the barn, falling into step at her side. "Inga, I'm worried about you."

"Worried?" She glanced at him, then away.

"Yeah, worried." He stopped her with a hand on her arm. "Let's talk about it."

"About what?" She felt cold.

"About the day you fell down the stairs. About you and me and Martha and Suzanne. About the way I feel about you. Inga, don't you know that I've come to—"

She stopped him with her hand over his lips. *"Nej!* Do not say it!" Her vehemence seemed to stun him.

He took a step backward. "Do you hate me so much?"

Tears sprang to her eyes. "I do not hate you, Dirk," she whispered.

"Then what? Why?"

She turned her back to him. "You would not understand."

"Try me."

She shook her head.

He swore beneath his breath.

She spun to face him. "This marriage of ours . . . It is difficult enough. One day you will go away and I will return to my pappa's house. That is what we agreed. Let us not make more of it than it is."

"Is it really so difficult, Inga? Our marriage, I mean. Aren't you just a little bit happy with me? Would it be so awful if you and I . . . if we stayed together, like this, a family? What if I don't *want* to go away?"

Something terrible was going to happen. She could feel it. "Do not do this. Please."

"Ah, Inga." He gathered her in his arms. He kissed her forehead, kissed her eyelids, kissed her lips. "You're like a breath of heaven."

"You should not say such a thing," she whispered. "It is sacrilege. Besides, you do not know what I really am."

"Give me a chance to prove myself. Give us a chance. I can be a better husband than you ever imagined."

She hid her face in the curve of his neck, mostly to avoid having him kiss her again. She enjoyed it too much, wanted it too much.

He rubbed his cheek against her hair. "I've missed holdin' you."

She felt the stirring of desire for her husband. It surprised her. She'd thought, now that she couldn't conceive, that she would no longer want to lie with him as a woman lies with a man. She was certain it was only one more condemning piece of evidence against her, one more reason she didn't deserve happiness.

"I want too much," she whispered.

"What?" He lifted her chin with his index finger, drawing her gaze to his.

She hadn't realized she'd spoken the words aloud and was taken aback by his question.

"What did you say?" he persisted.

She gave her head a tiny shake. "Nothing."

He pulled her close against him. "You're a stubborn woman, Inga Bridger."

"*Ja.*"

"But I can be even more stubborn. You'll see."

Dr. Swenson turned away. "You may get dressed, Mrs. Bridger. I'll let Mr. Bridger know that I've finished my examination. You get dressed, and then we will talk."

Inga breathed a sigh of relief as soon as the door closed behind him. It was beyond embarrassing, to be examined so intimately. It didn't matter that Dr. Swenson was old enough to be her father or that he was a trained physician simply looking after her good health. It was still humiliating.

She got up from the bed and hurriedly dressed before he could return. She was tidying her hair when a soft rap sounded at the door, then it opened, and the doctor and Dirk entered the bedroom.

Dirk's gaze immediately sought hers, the look questioning and hopeful at the same time.

Dr. Swenson removed his spectacles and cleaned the lenses. "I am pleased with Mrs. Bridger's progress," he said to Dirk. "Quite honestly, I am surprised by how quickly she has mended. In someone less strong, the results would have been much worse." He looked at Inga now. "You are fortunate, my dear."

Fortunate?

The doctor returned his glasses to the bridge of his nose. "You may resume the remainder of your normal, everyday household chores, but I would like you to lie down every afternoon for at least one hour, and you are not to be on your feet for more than an hour at any one time. Is that understood?"

Inga nodded.

"No lifting heavy milk pails or other farm chores." Dr. Swenson reached for his black leather bag. "But I see no reason why marital relations need be restricted any longer, as long as there is no pain or discomfort."

She blushed as her gaze dropped to the floor.

"We appreciate you coming out, Dr. Swenson, instead of making Inga take that long ride into town. I'm sure glad to hear she's doin' so well." Dirk's voice seemed to caress her from across the room. "I don't know what I'd do without her."

He'd married her to be his housekeeper. He'd proposed for reasons of convenience, of necessity, not out of love or affection. Yet, something in the way he spoke those words seemed to imply more.

More. She was still wanting more.

She hardened herself against the thoughts, against the feelings. With a neutral expression carefully in place, her voice dispassionate, she said, "I will walk out with you, Dr. Swenson."

Several hours later, twilight settled over the earth like a comfy blanket. The evening star twinkled a greeting as Dirk stepped out of the barn. A breeze, crisp but not cold, tugged at his clothes and ruffled his hair. It was a beautiful night.

He thought about asking Inga to take a stroll with him, then discarded the idea. She would only refuse.

How do I reach her? He'd been thinking the same question over and over again, ever since the doctor left.

He wasn't mistaken. Inga *did* care for him, but every time she realized it, she withdrew into some protective place. She was afraid to love him. He stopped still and looked up at the heavens as voices from the past played again in his memory.

What makes you so sure there even is a God, Miss Linberg?

Because I can hear my Lord's voice in the wind and see his love all around me.

He felt the breeze brushing against his face as he closed his eyes. He was strangely warmed by it. "Jesus, she needs help," he said softly, "and I don't know how to help her." More softly, "She always believed in you, and I reckon I'm just comin' around to believing myself. Only . . . we need help. The both of us." He opened his eyes, looked toward the house where soft lights glowed in the windows. "I love her. More than I thought possible. But I can't help her without you, God."

It surprised him, the sense of peace that came over him as he stood there. He didn't know when was the last time he'd felt this way. Maybe he never had.

He walked on. When he reached the back door, he opened it slowly, quietly, and looked inside. Inga was washing the last of the supper dishes. Martha was drying them.

His heart seemed to swell in his chest. He supposed he didn't deserve to be this fortunate. He'd resented all that his brother's children had represented when he'd come to look after them, and he'd married Inga for all the wrong reasons. Yet here he was, part of a family. Ma had been right. He had been looking happiness right in the face.

He opened the door farther. Inga glanced over her shoulder and saw him. For an instant, the corners of her mouth curved in a smile. Then it was gone.

Whatever's causing her to be so afraid, let me help drive it away, God. Let me love her the way she's meant to be loved.

Maybe a walk wasn't such a bad idea.

He stepped up to the counter. "It's a nice evening out. How 'bout a stroll, Mrs. Bridger?"

She gave her head a tiny shake.

"Come on. Whatever reason you're gonna use to refuse me will still be here when we get back. Mending and sewing and washing. Whatever. It'll be here." He lightly touched her elbow. "Walk with me, Inga."

He'd wasted a lot of time, all those weeks they were together as man and wife. He'd even fooled himself into believing desire was all he'd felt for her. But he knew better now, and he didn't want to waste any more time.

"Walk with me, Inga. Martha'll keep an eye on Suzanne. Won't you, Martha?"

"Sure, Uncle Dirk."

He held out his hand. Wordlessly, Inga stared at it for several moments, then dried her hands on her apron before placing her palm in his. Dirk grinned as he led her across the kitchen.

"Grab your shawl," he said when they reached the door. "I don't want you getting cold." He lowered his voice. "Unless you'll let me keep you warm."

A blush pinkened her cheeks, telling him she wasn't averse to the idea. Nonetheless, she took her shawl from the rack and wrapped it around her shoulders while Dirk opened the door. Then he tucked her hand into the crook of his arm, and the two of them walked across the barnyard and down the drive.

The evening sky had grown darker while Dirk was inside, and now hundreds of stars were blinking down at the earth. The scent of new-turned earth drifted to them on the breeze. A meadowlark trilled a good-night song.

"I have been in America one full year," Inga said, a note of surprise in her voice.

"I'm mighty glad you came."

There was a pause before she said, "As am I."

"Are you?" He paused, then asked, "Why?"

She seemed to be holding her breath.

"Maybe you're glad because of me?" he suggested.

"*Ja*, perhaps," she whispered.

He stopped, turned her toward him. He wished he could see her face, but a moonless night had arrived in earnest. "Inga, you know that Clara . . . that I didn't have any interest in her, don't you?"

Again, it seemed she held her breath. After an endless moment, she said, "You did once."

"I was different then." His hands tightened on her arms. "Everything was different then." He raised his voice slightly, needing her to know his words came from his heart. "I want you to listen good. There's something that's been stewin' in my mind for weeks now, and it's time I got it said."

He wanted to draw her close again. He wanted to hold her head against his chest and stroke his hand over her silky hair.

"A lot's happened since I asked you to marry me. Things aren't the same anymore. I guess I knew they wouldn't be, even back then."

He felt her stiffen slightly. He kept talking.

"When I first left Ohio, all puffed up with big ideas of where I was gonna go and what I was gonna do, I thought nothing would ever make me want to settle down. It's true, what you've been thinkin' about Clara and me. We were more than just friends. She was more than just my employer." He swallowed, hating to speak the words. "But there wasn't any love shared between us. I'm not proud of it, but it's the truth. I thought that's all I'd ever want from a woman." He paused, then softly added, "Until you."

Her gasp was nearly inaudible.

"Inga, I was angry and bitter when I came to the parsonage looking for help last December. It seemed nothin' in my life would go right or had ever gone right. I felt like I'd been forced to live my brother's life. Oh, sure, I knew I was fond of the girls, but I didn't cope good with 'em. Leastwise, I never felt like I did." Again, he added, "Until you."

It was hard, finding the words. His whole future—*their* whole future—rested on his ability to say the right thing.

He turned toward her, leaning his shoulder on the fence, staring at her shadowed profile. "When I asked you to marry me, it's true all I thought I wanted was somebody to look after the kids. It's true I didn't plan on stayin' when they were grown. But it's not true any longer."

"You hate this farm."

"I used to."

"You hate the cows."

He chuckled. "Guess that's still true."

"What about traveling the world? Your dreams—"

He drew her back into his embrace. "You gave me new dreams."

"But—"

"What I'm trying to say is, I love you. I don't want to go anywhere without you." He sealed the words with a kiss.

Inga's emotions tilted crazily, swinging from joy to terror. She'd never heard anything more wonderful than Dirk's profession of love. Still, she couldn't escape the fear that she was being punished for wanting more than she was meant to have.

Dirk released her mouth but kept his face close to her own. She could feel his warm breath on her skin as he said, "I want us to make this a real marriage."

Inga wanted it too, only—

"Till death do us part," he added.

"Nej!" she cried, pulling away from him. That was it! That was how she would be punished. By Dirk's own words, he'd foretold the future. Unless she acted quickly, that's what would happen. Death would separate them.

Holding her skirts out of the way, she ran toward the house, failing to hear him calling her name above the fearful beating of her heart.

Dirk pursued her. He would have followed her right up the stairs and into their bedroom, except he saw the alarmed expression on Martha's face when he entered the kitchen. So he pretended nothing was wrong, telling his niece her Aunt Inga was tired and had gone to bed. Then he suggested the children do the same. It took a while. He'd learned in recent weeks that bedtime was never uneventful, not with an inquisitive six-year-old and a willful four-year-old who often decided they weren't sleepy yet.

It was Inga who had shown him the importance of spending time with these children. It was Inga's influence that had taught him to treasure little moments, like reading a bedtime story or tucking the blankets snugly beneath Suzanne's and Martha's chins. He'd even learned to look forward to this time of the day.

But tonight, he wanted the ritual over so he could be with Inga. Most of all, he needed to understand what was causing her to run from him.

And he needed her to understand he had no intention of letting her run away. Not ever.

—

Inga stood at the window, staring at the star-studded heavens. If only she could pray . . .

Tears of frustration and fear ran down her cheeks. All her life she had wanted to be different than what she was. Others had looked at her and thought she was the perfect daughter for a minister, kind and thoughtful. Pappa had thought her the most intelligent of his daughters. Her sisters had said she was levelheaded. But she had known she was plain and ordinary. She'd pretended to be satisfied with what she was. She'd pretended to be content with what others expected her to be.

But God had known her heart. God had known she was filled with envy. She'd wanted to be like others. She'd wanted to have what others had. Look what had happened because she hadn't been satisfied with the life God gave her. See what had happened because she had a rebellious spirit, a greedy heart, stubborn pride.

"Inga . . ."

With a gasp, she whirled toward the door. She hadn't heard Dirk enter.

Take anything I have, she had prayed that day. *Anything.*

"Inga, can't you tell me what's wrong?"

Do not take his life, she had pleaded. *Take me instead. Take anything I have . . . I will never ask for anything else if only you will spare his life.*

He crossed the space that separated them. "Inga?"

"You must not love me, Dirk," she whispered. "It is my fault. My fault."

"What is your fault?" He cupped her chin, lifted her face toward him.

"The baby."

"It was an accident. You fell down the stairs."

She began to sob. "You . . . do not . . . understand."

"Don't cry." He kissed one tear-moistened cheek, then the other. "I can't bear to have you cry. I love you. Do you hear me? I love you. It doesn't matter if we can't have children. We've got Martha and Suzanne. We'll be a family, the four of us. It's enough. I love you."

"You must not say that." She hiccuped over another sob. "Something terrible will happen."

He drew her close, pressed her cheek against his collarbone, rested his chin on her head. "I don't understand," he said as he stroked one hand up and down her spine.

How could he? How could he possibly understand?

Let him love you, a small voice said.

"Inga . . ." He cupped her face between his hands, tilted her head back, brushed his lips across hers. "Whatever is wrong, we can face it together. No matter what."

"I should go home."

"You *are* home, Inga."

She looked at him, repeating, "You do not understand." Tears glittered in her eyes. "I do not belong here."

"Of course you belong." He tightened his arms around her. "I love you."

"You should not."

"Why shouldn't I? I'm your husband."

She bit her lower lip, and Dirk knew she was fighting for control of her tears.

"Inga, I promise you, things will be different now. Maybe I didn't say it right earlier. Maybe you think I'm still just looking for somebody to take care of the girls. But that's not true." He lowered his voice. "When I was drownin', my last thought was of you. That was the moment I knew I loved you and didn't want to be without you."

She lost control over her tears. They streaked down her cheeks, and in her eyes, he saw the devastation of her soul.

"What can I say to make it better?" he asked, his voice breaking. "To make you believe me."

"I cannot believe, Dirk. I want to but I cannot."

"Why?"

She pulled from his embrace, and once again gazed out the window. "If I do not leave, something much worse will happen."

"Something worse?" Frustration burned in his chest. "What're you talking about? You keep saying that, but I don't understand."

"I was never satisfied with what God made me. I did not want to be the sensible elder daughter, the one who was always with her pappa, out doing good works. I wanted to be pretty and sought after and . . . and desirable."

"You are!"

She continued as if he hadn't spoken. "Usually it did not matter. Usually I was happy. I liked helping Pappa, and I loved listening to God's voice when he spoke to my heart. But there was always that seed of dissatisfaction with who I was and what my future would be." She clenched her hands together. "When I . . . I married you, I stopped asking for guidance. I only wanted what I wanted. That's all I cared about."

"That's not true," he argued. "I saw how much you cared for Ma and the girls. And for me, too."

She looked into his eyes. "I told God to take anything of mine as long as he saved your life. It's my fault our child will never be born."

It took him a moment to understand the import of her words. When he did, he leaned closer. "You can't think that's how he answered your prayer?"

"I was not supposed to want so much. I was envious. I should have been content with what I was, with what I had."

He grabbed both of her hands, pulled her toward him. "Look at me, Inga." When she did, he continued, "I've never been a religious man. I was angry and bitter 'cause life didn't go the way I thought it should. I figured God didn't care much about me. But I was wrong. He cared. You showed me that. In a thousand different ways, you showed me that. I may not know much, but I know the Almighty doesn't take unborn babies because of a wife's desperate prayers for her husband. God doesn't punish us for wantin' things either. I don't believe it, and neither should you."

"If I do not leave, something worse will happen. I can feel it."

Dirk wrapped her in his arms, held her close against him, wondered what he could say to reach her. He should have realized her sorrow went deeper than mourning the loss of a baby. He thought of that scarlet quilt and knew it stood for much more than a miscarriage. It represented all the guilt she was carrying on her narrow shoulders.

She choked on a sob, then whispered, "I cannot pray."

"Then I'll pray for you, Inga." Gently, he guided her toward the bed. "You'll see. It's gonna be all right." With patient hands, he disrobed her, then slipped her nightgown over her head. "You'll see," he continued to croon as he helped her into bed, tucking the covers around her. "You'll see."

God, help me, 'cause I don't know what to do.

Twenty-two

Reverend Linberg steepled his fingers beneath his chin and closed his eyes. "I didn't know it was so bad with her. She seemed too quiet when I was last out to the farm, but I thought time would take care of it." He shook his head slowly, then nodded. "To be honest, Gunda tried to tell me. I guess I didn't listen."

Dirk sank onto the chair opposite Olaf. "I couldn't think of anything else to do except bring her here. Every day I feel her pulling a little more away from reality. She seems so fragile. She kept saying she wanted to come back to the parsonage." Despair washed over him. "Maybe she's right. Maybe this is where she ought to be. For a while. Until she's better."

Olaf shook his head slowly. "Oh, Inga. My sweet girl."

"I was planning a trip to Des Moines, once the doctor gave his okay for her to travel. I thought it might cheer her up. I think she'd even come to like the idea. But then, a couple days ago, she just seemed to . . ." He let his words trail off unfinished.

Silence filled the room, made it seem small and closed in. Hot. Stuffy. Airless.

Dirk bolted out of his chair and strode to the window. He opened it and took a deep breath of fresh air. Then, chagrined, he turned to face Inga's father again. "I love her, Reverend, but she's getting worse instead of better, and nothing I say seems to help."

"Where is she now?"

It was Bernadotte who answered from the doorway. "She's upstairs. In her old room."

"You heard?" the pastor asked his wife.

"*Ja*, I heard. I think you should go to her, Olaf. It is always you she's listened to best."

With a nod, Inga's father rose from his chair and left the room, an unusual weariness in his step, an uncustomary sag in his shoulders.

Dirk leaned against the windowsill, raking the fingers of both hands through his hair while staring at the floor. "I feel so helpless."

"*Ja*, it is often so. To be human is to feel helpless at times." Bernadotte crossed her husband's study and stood beside his desk. "But when we are helpless in ourselves, then we remember to look to the one whose help we need. When we are yoked with Christ, he will carry our burdens."

He met his mother-in-law's gaze. "That sounds like something Inga used to say."

"*Ja*." She smiled sadly.

"It's like she's there with me, but not really there. She's doing her chores, taking care of the girls. She cooks our meals and cleans the house and sews on her quilts. She does all that, but she's not really there." He paused, then asked, "Does that make sense?"

Again she replied, "*Ja*."

The curtains were drawn, and the room was shadowed. Inga sat on the edge of her bed, staring at the things around her without seeing them. She was tired. It was a weariness of the soul. She understood that, but she felt too far away—removed, remote—to try to change. It was as if she were watching herself from a great distance.

The door opened, and her pappa entered. She met his gaze, tried to smile at him.

"Dotter."

"Pappa."

He sat beside her on the bed and took hold of her hand. "Your husband tells me you wish to come back to the parsonage."

"I must come home, Pappa."

"Why?"

Why? The question repeated again and again in her mind, but she couldn't find the answer. She knew there was one. She knew that not to go home meant something horrible would happen, but she couldn't remember the reason. It seemed so long ago since she could grab hold of a thought and hang on to it.

"Inga, it is hard to lose a baby. I know. Your mamma lost three. Do you remember?"

Did she remember? She wasn't sure. She couldn't think clearly.

"You must not give up hope. God is merciful. He will meet you at the place of your need if you will but ask."

Where was that place? She didn't know.

"Inga, tell me what is troubling you."

"I must come home."

Olaf's grasp tightened. "Look at me."

It took a great deal of effort, but she managed to do as he'd commanded.

"Dirk has told me what you fear. How is it this has happened? How is it you can believe God waits in heaven for his children to err so he can smite them with disaster? You have served him, Inga. You know better. He is a God of love. He loves and cares for you."

Tears filled her eyes, blurring her vision. "I must come home."

He sighed. "Your place is with your husband."

"Please."

"Has Dirk been unkind to you, *dotter?* Has he ever mistreated you? Is there something you are not telling me?"

"I must come home." She let the tears fall. Hot tears, streaking her cheeks, burning her throat. "Please, Pappa, I must come home."

He placed his arm around her shoulders and hugged her to him. "All right, Inga. Do not cry. We will find a way through this valley. I promise you."

Astrid Linberg returned with Dirk to the farm, but while she was able to watch over the children, she could do nothing to stop the loneliness that filled every corner of the house now that Inga was gone.

"Will Aunt Inga come home soon?" Martha had asked upon Dirk's return from Uppsala.

But he hadn't had an answer then, nor did he have one now.

As he worked on a broken section of the fence near the barn, he kept remembering the distant look in Inga's eyes when he'd bid her good-bye this morning at the parsonage. He wondered if he'd done the right thing, leaving her there. He'd never had a chance to prove he loved her. He'd never known for sure if she might love him, too. He felt lost without her, but he hadn't known what else to do. She'd been retreating, one moment at a time, into some safe harbor within herself.

Sunset and Robber raised their heads, looking toward the road. Sunset nickered softly.

Maybe she's returned! Dirk thought.

He lowered the rail he'd been about to hammer into place and turned with hopeful expectation to see who was coming up the drive. Disappointment followed. It wasn't the pastor's carriage. The black surrey carried strangers—a man and a woman—up the drive. Dirk stepped away from the fence and watched as the driver pulled the horse to a halt.

"Good day to you," the man said. "This is the Bridger farm, isn't it?"

"Yeah, it is."

The man glanced at the woman beside him. "We're here, Allison. I told you I remembered the way." He disembarked from the buggy and approached Dirk, hand outstretched. "I'm Harvey Trent. You must be John's brother."

He nodded. "Dirk Bridger." He accepted the proffered hand.

With a quick glance, Dirk made note of the man's appearance. Harvey Trent was of average height with a full head of stone gray hair. He looked to be in his early forties. Judging by his fine attire, he was not a farmer by profession.

"It is a pleasure to meet you at last," Harvey said. "I'm sorry we were unable to advise you of our exact day of arrival, but travel can be unpredictable."

Dirk frowned.

Harvey saw the look on his face. He glanced over his shoulder, then forward again. "You were expecting us, weren't you? Hattie wrote and said any time in April would be fine."

"Ma died in December."

The man drew back. His voice lowered. "I am sorry, Mr. Bridger. Hattie was an admirable woman. My wife and I took a great liking to her on our last visit. Margaret was expecting Suzanne at the time."

Dirk didn't know what to say. He didn't know who this guy was or what sort of game he was playing. Or even if it was a game.

"Mr. Bridger, do you know who we are?" Harvey asked, apparently reading his mind.

"No, afraid not."

"My wife is Margaret's cousin, Allison. We wrote to your mother late last year that we were returning to America this spring and wanted to come for a visit. We've never met Suzanne, and Martha was just a toddler when we were here last." He paused, looking slightly flustered. "Your mother said nothing about being ill in her reply. We had no idea."

"Harvey," his wife called from the surrey, "is something wrong?"

Across time, the memory returned to Dirk, his ma's voice whispering in his mind. *Only family Margaret had in the world, other'n us, after her folks died. Nice lady, Allison Trent ... Margaret's cousin ... She and Mr. Trent will be comin' to see the girls ...*

Tarnation! He didn't need houseguests on top of everything else. But what was he to do? His ma had invited them. They were family to the girls and had come to see them. He didn't seem to have much choice.

"Why don't you bring your wife into the house, Mr. Trent, and we'll get acquainted? There oughta be coffee on the stove or I reckon I could make tea for your wife if that's what she'd prefer."

Harvey nodded. "Thank you. Coffee will be fine." He returned to the surrey and helped his wife to the ground.

She was a handsome woman, probably in her mid-thirties, short of stature and plump, though not unattractively so. She had dark red hair which was swept up on her head and capped with a bright blue bonnet that matched her traveling dress. Even from where Dirk stood, he could see Allison Trent's resemblance to Margaret.

Speaking softly to her, Harvey took Allison's arm and escorted her across the yard to Dirk. Once there, he performed the introductions. "My dear, this is John's brother, Dirk Bridger. Mr. Bridger, may I present my wife, Allison Trent."

"This is a pleasure, Mr. Bridger." Her voice was soft, and even more than her husband's, it spoke of privilege and culture. "I am dreadfully sorry to learn of your mother's untimely death. Please accept our sincerest condolences."

"Thanks." He motioned with his head. "Come inside."

He took the couple into the living room, then left them there while he went after the coffee. When he returned, he found Harvey standing near the window, staring out at the fields and pastures. Allison was seated on the sofa, running a hand over one of Inga's quilts.

She must have heard the rattle of the tray as Dirk entered the room. Looking up, she said, "This is exquisite, Mr. Bridger. Wherever did you find such a quilt?"

"My wife made it."

"Your wife? I got the impression from Margaret's letters, and your mother's too, that you were not married."

He felt a heaviness in his chest. "Inga and I wed at the end of last year."

"Oh, I see," she said, but there was a question in her eyes.

"My wife's been ill. She's staying with her parents in town."

Allison studied him, her expression thoughtful. After a moment, she glanced at her husband. "Harvey, do come join us, dear." She took it upon herself to do the pouring. When each of them was holding a cup, she said, "We have been wanting to come for another visit for a long time. You are aware we've been in Europe four and a half years?"

"I seem to recall Ma saying something about it."

"Diplomatic service," Harvey interjected. "But we have returned to our home in Pennsylvania. It's good to be back in our own country again."

Allison rested her cup on her knee, holding it with both hands. "We shall always regret not seeing Margaret and John before they died. Margaret and I were as close as sisters, I suppose because neither of us had brothers or sisters of our own." Her voice dropped to a whisper. "I took her death very hard. I loved her dearly."

Dirk understood what she was feeling. He'd loved his older brother, too. He'd never come to see John and Margaret after they moved to Iowa and started this farm, and for that he would always be sorry.

"Mr. Bridger?"

He looked up, saw the sadness in her green eyes.

"May we see the children now?"

"Sure. I'll get them. They're upstairs."

Dirk left the Trents in the living room and went to the stairway. He opened his mouth to holler for the girls, then decided against it, climbing the stairs instead. Before he reached their bedroom, he heard Astrid reading aloud, and he felt a sting of longing for his wife. Astrid sounded so much like Inga.

When he stepped into the open doorway, all three looked up.

"Someone downstairs t'see you two," he said to his nieces.

"Aunt Inga's come back?" Martha asked excitedly, jumping to her feet and smiling for the first time today.

He remembered feeling the same way not more than fifteen minutes ago when the Trents had arrived. Then, in his mind, he heard Inga say, *Nej, I have not returned.*

When would she be back? How long before she returned from that hiding place within herself to the people who loved and needed her most? And what if she never returned?

His throat ached as he answered the girl, "No, it's not Aunt Inga." He held out his hands. "It's your ma's cousins, Mr. and Mrs. Trent. Come on now. They're eager to meet you."

He recognized Martha's obvious disappointment because it mirrored his own. Fortunately, Suzanne was more curious about their visitors and had already forgotten her sister's question. The littlest one hurried to take his left hand. Martha came a little more slowly to take his right. Then the three of them descended the stairs together.

When they stepped through the doorway into the living room, Allison rose from the sofa. "Oh my," she said softly. "They're the image of Margaret."

Martha's grip tightened on Dirk's hand as the older woman approached them.

"You must be Martha." Allison leaned forward. "I am your mother's cousin, Mrs. Trent." She shifted. "And you are Suzanne. What a darling you are."

Suzanne was rarely shy, but this time she tucked herself behind her uncle, never letting go of his hand.

Allison cast a glance over her shoulder at her husband, and Harvey responded to it by crossing the room to stand at her side.

"Hello, young ladies," he said to the girls, bowing at the waist and giving them a wink.

"Hello," Martha muttered, unimpressed.

Suzanne remained silent, moving farther behind her uncle.

"Why don't we all sit down?" Dirk suggested.

"A wonderful suggestion." Allison held out her hand to Martha. "Come and sit with me. I have stories to share about your mother when she was a little girl, not much older than you."

Martha looked at her uncle, and he nodded. Then she did as her cousin requested.

Watching them, unease settled firmly around Dirk's heart.

—

Over a supper Allison Trent insisted on preparing, she and her husband entertained the family with stories of their travels in Europe and England, as well as Allison's tales of escapades with Margaret when she was a girl. Little by little, the children warmed to their newfound cousins. In truth, there seemed no reason not to like both Allison and Harvey. They were friendly and good-humored, and they seemed genuinely interested in everything about the girls. Still, Dirk was bothered by their visit and knew he wouldn't rest easy until they were gone.

The feeling stayed with him throughout that evening and the following day as he observed Martha and Suzanne showing the Trents their room and their toys, the swing and their favorite animals. The feeling dogged his heels while he went about his work. It lingered no matter what he did to dispel it.

When he went to the parsonage to see Inga two days after the Trents' arrival, he tried talking to her about Margaret's cousin, tried sorting out the reasons for his feelings. At one time, Inga would have been able to reassure him. At one time, she would have given him sage advice. But now she merely listened with a distant look in her eyes and said nothing in return. He wondered if she even heard him. She seemed to be drifting farther away from him, away from reality. She was getting worse since coming to the parsonage. Worse instead of better, and there seemed to be nothing he could do to stop her.

Dirk returned to the farm, his heart heavy with worry for Inga, the Trents almost forgotten.

It was a delightful evening, nearly two weeks after the Trents had first arrived at the Bridger farm. It was the kind of evening when the air was rich with the fragrance of spring. After the children were in bed, the adults sat in companionable silence on the porch, watching the sunset, Harvey smoking his pipe and Allison sipping tea.

Dirk was thinking about Inga, eager to visit her again the next morning. Yesterday she'd looked at him, and he'd felt like she'd actually seen him. Really seen him for the first time in weeks. It had given him hope, something to hang onto. He missed her. He loved her. He wanted her home.

Allison broke the silence. "It is tragic, the loss of a child."

Dirk was jerked abruptly from his thoughts.

"It is something a mother never forgets."

He didn't bother to answer. He hadn't discussed Inga or her illness with the Trents in all the time they'd been at the farm. He didn't intend to now.

"Astrid told us about her sister," Allison explained.

Dirk wished Astrid hadn't said anything, but he wasn't sure why. He'd stopped feeling uncomfortable with the Trents more than a week ago. He'd actually been enjoying their visit. The only thing that would have made it more enjoyable was if Inga had been there, too.

"Harvey and I had a little girl of our own," Allison continued, her voice soft. "She was born in Austria. Her name was Lisette." She looked up at the sky. "She died before her first birthday. It was pneumonia that took her from us. I wanted to die myself. So you see, I do understand."

Dirk thought about saying he was sorry, but before he could do so, Allison changed the subject.

"Margaret always talked about her brother-in-law, the adventurer. She told us about all the places you planned to explore in your travels. It must have been difficult for you, returning here to raise Martha and Suzanne with only your mother's help. It must not have seemed very exciting."

He shrugged, feeling that odd uneasiness returning.

Allison glanced at her husband.

"Dirk," Harvey said, "my wife and I have been talking things over and we think we could be of service to you." He sounded every bit the diplomat.

"Of service?" Dirk questioned.

"Yes. You see, the Trent family home near Philadelphia is large and has been empty for too many years. It is a perfect place for children."

He frowned. "I suppose you mean Martha and Suzanne."

"We know John and Margaret intended for their daughters to remain here with you and your mother." Harvey looked at Allison. "But now that Hattie is dead and your wife is ill—"

"The girls aren't goin' anywhere." Dirk rose from his chair, glowering for emphasis.

Harvey stood, too. "Hear me out." When Dirk said nothing, he continued, "I inherited a great deal of wealth from my father, and I've done well in my own career. We'd like to share our good fortune. It seems we shall have no more children of our own, but we would love Margaret and John's daughters like they were ours. We can give Martha and Suzanne a life few others enjoy. They would travel. They would go to the best schools. They would wear the finest clothes and know the best people. They would never know want of any kind."

Allison touched Dirk's arm. "You have been a wonderful uncle to them, Mr. Bridger, and it's clear they adore you. But we would love them, too."

"I'm sure you would love 'em," Dirk began, trying to keep his voice calm, "but this is their home. This is where John and Margaret wanted them to be."

Harvey stroked his chin thoughtfully. "There is more we are prepared to offer."

"Whatever it is won't change my mind."

"We would like to underwrite your expeditions."

"My expeditions?" His gaze moved from Harvey to Allison and back again.

"That's right. We'll provide whatever funds you need, for as long as you need. Enough for you and your wife. You'll be able to pursue the adventures you always wanted. Go around the world. Visit exotic places."

Dirk shook his head, disbelieving what he heard.

"And," Harvey went on, "if your wife's health does not allow her to accompany you, we will see she receives the best specialized medical care money can provide."

Allison rose from her chair. "At least think about it, Mr. Bridger." She looked at her husband. "I believe it is time we retired for the night."

"Do give it some thought," Harvey said. Then he took Allison's arm and the two of them went inside, leaving Dirk alone on the porch.

Oh, he would think about their incredible offer, all right. He'd think about it and little else.

⎯Twenty-three

Karl slept with his head resting against the wall of the passenger car. Fatigue etched his youthful face. Thea felt a twinge of guilt, although she refused to recognize why she would feel that way.

She was seated across from Karl, watching him as he slept and wondering what the future held in store. Even more, she wondered what she felt for Karl, the boy who had made her laugh, the young man who had introduced her to the pleasure of his kisses.

What had happened to those feelings? She was confused so much of the time. Nothing had gone as she'd imagined it would.

With a sigh, she turned her gaze out the window at the darkness.

They were going home. At last. They would arrive in Des Moines before dawn, and they should reach Uppsala before lunch. It would be good to be home. Karl had resisted for a while, but in the end, he had given in to her—as she'd been certain he would. She knew he loved her. Karl had always tried to give her whatever she wanted. She knew he wanted her to be happy. And she *would* be happy, once things were as they used to be.

Except—she was beginning to realize—things would never again be as they used to be. She was going home with a husband. She was a married woman now. When her sisters saw her, they wouldn't look at her the same way they had before. Neither would her parents. Her pappa would give her that stern look of his. His gaze would be filled with disappointment but with love, too. Mamma would cry, of that Thea could be certain, but they would be tears of joy for a daughter returned. And tears of joy for her new son-in-law, too. Thea's parents would welcome Karl into the family, into their home. They would forgive the young couple for eloping, but things still wouldn't be the same as before.

Thea leaned her forehead against the window. What had happened to all those romantic notions of hers? Why hadn't any of them come true?

You're acting like a child! Karl had actually yelled those words at her last week. Then he'd told her it was time she grew up and thought of someone besides herself.

She looked at him again, wanting to summon the outrage she'd felt at the time. Karl was only a year older. What gave him the right to talk to her like that? He wasn't her pappa!

She shivered involuntarily. Pappa would always love her, no matter what she did. But what about Karl? What if he stopped loving her? What if she *had* been acting like a child?

She closed her eyes, refusing to consider her own questions. She wasn't ready to look for the answers.

—

It was like emerging from a fog. Inga had been lost in a thick white cloud of confusion. But slowly it began to lift, and today she knew she would find her way out, once and for all. The world around her was returning to normal. The heaviness on her heart had lightened.

Inga had begun to hope again.

She was seated in her bedroom. Early morning sunlight spilled through the east window. In her hands was the first panel of a new quilt, the one she already thought of as her love story quilt. She vaguely remembered the last quilt she'd made, the red one that had represented so much sorrow and uncertainty, but that was a thing of the past. This quilt would represent her future. It would tell their story, hers and Dirk's. It would tell a story of a young woman who had thought herself unlovable and the man who had proven her wrong. A new quilt made from patterns of love.

She was ready to go home. She had been at the parsonage for less than two weeks, but suddenly it seemed an eternity. Today she would ask Dirk to take her home.

She smiled sadly, remembering she'd used those same words to ask Dirk to bring her to the parsonage. But home wasn't here. Home was with her husband.

A soft rap sounded at her door.

"Come in," she replied.

The door opened. "Good," her mamma said as she stepped into the room. "You are awake. Dirk is here."

Her heart skipped. "So early?" He came to see her every other day, always in the afternoons. Perhaps he'd guessed she wanted to go home. She set aside her sewing and rose from the chair. "Tell him I will come down straight away." She smiled. "I want to freshen up."

Bernadotte returned her smile. "He's in the parlor. Come down when you are ready." Then she backed out of the room, closing the door after her.

Inga hurried to the dressing table. She sat on the stool and looked at her reflection. Her stomach felt as if it were filled with butterflies.

She began to brush her hair. Then her hand stilled as she made another discovery. She wasn't afraid.

She stared harder at her reflection. She looked much the same. Perhaps a little thinner, but basically the same. Yet she didn't feel plain and ordinary. Dirk had told her she was pretty. She had thought he was being kind, but today she believed him.

She didn't know or understand what had brought about this change. She only knew it had happened.

By the grace of God, Pappa would have said if she asked him. She smiled. *"Ja.* By your grace, Father." She was going home. She was going home with the man who loved her. She dropped the hairbrush, rose from the dressing stool, and hurried from her bedroom, down the stairs, and into the parlor.

Dirk turned from the window when she entered. He was holding his hat in one hand. His dark hair was mussed and badly in need of trimming.

I must cut it when we get home, she thought.

"Morning, Inga."

There was so much she wanted to tell him, but suddenly she felt as shy as a new bride. *"Goddag,* Dirk."

"Your ma tells me you're feeling better."

"Ja."

"You're looking better, too. More like yourself."

Her heart skipped again. "Shall we sit down?" She motioned toward the sofa.

"The girls're hoping to see you again soon," he said after he'd followed her suggestion.

"I miss them." She'd missed *him* as well. "You are here early."

"Yeah. I've got a busy day ahead of me." He gave her a half smile and shook his head. "Wait until I tell you what happened last night."

She watched him, waiting as he'd instructed, but all the while she was thinking how very much she loved his face, his long straight nose, the strong cut of his jaw, the crinkles near the corners of his mouth and eyes.

"Margaret's cousin, the Trents . . . They had a surprise for me."

"A surprise?"

He chuckled. "Well, I guess maybe that's what folks call an understatement. Last night, the Trents told me they had this big house, and they wanted to take the girls to live with them in Philadelphia. Wanted to give them fancy schooling and take them to Europe and such."

Her eyes widened. A chill raced through her. She must have heard him wrong. "Take the girls?"

Again he shook his head in a gesture of disbelief. "That's not all. They offered to underwrite my expeditions. That's how Harvey Trent worded it. He promised to underwrite my expeditions around the world. Can you believe it?"

The butterflies in her stomach turned to stones. "They would do such a thing?" she asked softly. "Pay for you to go around the world?"

"Yeah, apparently they would."

Perhaps it was for the best she'd never told him she loved him. Perhaps it would make it easier to let him go. "When?" Her chest felt as if it had been crushed. She could scarcely breathe.

He met her gaze. "When what?"

"When will you go?"

He laughed, a short sound of surprise. "Go? I'm not goin' anywhere."

"But this is your chance, Dirk. Your dreams. All your plans. You have waited so long for them to come true. If you do not take it, the opportunity may never come again."

His gaze was harsh, the set of his jaw determined. There was no sign of laughter or surprise in his expression. "No, I don't reckon it will. But I'm still not goin'."

She looked down at her hands, clenched in her lap. "You hate the farm."

"Doggone it, Inga!"

Her gaze shot to his face. He'd never before sounded so angry when speaking to her.

Dirk got to his feet, then glared down at her. "I told you none of that mattered anymore."

She rose, too. "I said I would let you go when the time came. How can I hold you to me when I promised you I would not?" The question came out in a whisper.

"Things were different then. *I* was different. *You* were different." He took hold of her upper arms, his grip firm, unyielding. "I promised before God and man I'd love and keep you, and that's what I intend to do."

She wanted to hold him to the promise, too. But what if he should regret it later? Old fears, old insecurities, resurfaced to taunt her. How could she hold him to her when he was being offered the chance of a lifetime? She would be thinking only of herself, of her own wants and desires. If she held him to his promise, he would eventually resent her. Hadn't this been the bargain they had made? When it was time for him to go, she would release him?

"Are they good people?" she asked. "Would they love the children?"

"You're not even listenin' to me, are you?"

"I do not want to stand in your way," she whispered.

"Well, aren't you the noble one." Sarcasm dripped from every syllable. He slapped his hat onto his head. Then he leaned down, bringing his face close to hers. "I've been plenty patient, Inga. You were sick, not just your body but in your heart. I could see that, and I brought you here 'cause it seemed like that was the only way you were gonna get better. Well, you're better now. I can see it in your eyes." He drew back. "Now you're just actin' plain ... plain stubborn."

He spun around and strode to the parlor doorway. Reaching it, he stopped abruptly, stood perfectly still for a breathless moment. Then he turned slowly to face her again. His dark gaze seemed to bore straight into her soul.

"You do yourself some thinkin' about what it is you really want, Inga Bridger. I'll give you a day to do it in. I'll be back in the morning."

A moment later, the front door of the parsonage slammed behind him as he left.

—

Before he was a mile down the road, Dirk began to regret yelling at Inga the way he had. But hang it all! He'd been walking on eggshells for weeks now. He'd despaired as he'd watched Inga shrivel behind sorrow and uncertainty. He knew she'd been hurt by the loss of their baby. He knew it wasn't easy, accepting that she'd never have children of her own. But he loved her and he hoped she loved him. They had Martha and Suzanne. They had a place to call their own. Maybe life wasn't easy. Maybe it wasn't perfect, but it was a good life, all the same.

He hadn't been wrong to yell at her. She was being stubborn and foolish. Hadn't he told her he loved her? Hadn't he already told her she was what he wanted, her and the girls?

What about what Inga wants?

The thought gave him a moment's pause. Maybe she really didn't want to come back to the farm. Maybe she was using the Trents' offer as a convenient excuse.

But then he remembered the look in her eyes when she'd entered the pastor's front parlor. No, he refused to believe his wife didn't love him, and he was willing to do whatever he had to do to make her see it for herself.

Because the idea of a life without Inga was too awful to contemplate.

"Git up there!" he shouted at the team, slapping the reins. "We got us a long way to go today."

—

After Dirk left, Inga sank down on the sofa. She hugged herself, feeling chilled. For a long while, she stared at the cold hearth, her mind blank. Then the conversation began to replay itself in her head.

Well, aren't you the noble one.

She hadn't meant it to be a noble gesture. She'd sincerely wanted to give him what he'd always longed for. This was his chance. Probably his last chance.

You do yourself some thinkin' about what it is you really want, Inga Bridger. I'll give you a day to do it in. I'll be back in the morning.

She wanted him, but . . .

"Oh, my dear Lord!" her mother cried from the hallway. "Olaf, it is Thea and Karl! Thea!"

The entire household erupted with surprise and joy. Inga's younger sisters came running—Gunda on her crutches—from other points in the house. Their pappa emerged from his study; judging by his expression, all would be forgiven.

The prodigal daughter had come home.

There was hugging and kissing and crying and much confusion. And it wasn't until later—too much later, perhaps—that Inga realized Astrid was also there to participate in the family celebration.

—

Bernadotte soon went to work, preparing a feast to celebrate her daughter's return, while Olaf shut himself up in his study with his new son-in-law. Thea took the opportunity to draw her older sister outside where they could be alone.

"It is hard to believe all that's happened while I was away," she said to Inga as the two young women strolled beside a brook running behind the church and down toward the school. Songbirds serenaded them from spring green treetops. "You and Gunda . . . It is so tragic."

"Gunda is recovering beyond anyone's expectations," Inga said. "And I am well now, too."

Briefly, Thea wondered if Inga's last statement was true. Then she discarded the thought. It was Thea herself who needed attention. "Vilhelm always flirted with me, even when I told him I had given my heart to Karl. It is so sad. I will never see him again."

Inga said nothing.

They walked in silence for several more minutes. Thea had the feeling her sister's thoughts were far away, and it made her angry. Inga didn't seem to care that she was miserable and confused. Irritably, she snapped, "I wish you had warned me what marriage was really and truly like."

Inga looked surprised. "What do you mean?"

"I don't know." She kept her gaze locked on the path before her, feeling waspish.

Again Inga was silent.

"Oh, Inga, it isn't what I expected. Karl had no money to speak of when he got to America. We were married by a justice of the peace, and then we had to rent the most awful apartment. It was small and smelled bad. And the noise. There was always so much noise. Babies crying and husbands and wives fighting. Karl had to work all the time for the most pitiful wages. I hardly ever saw him, and he always came home from work so tired. We never had any fun. I thought marriage would be fun. He never brought me any presents or flowers or ... or anything!"

Thea stopped abruptly. Inga took one more step, then did the same, turning to face her sister.

"And the first night of our marriage ..." Thea felt heat rising in her cheeks. "The first night was horrid. You should have warned me."

Inga's eyes took on a dreamy, distant look. Somehow, Thea knew her sister was remembering something beautiful and special.

Thea wanted to tear her hair out in fury. She wanted to cry in despair. "Maybe Pappa was right. Maybe we were too young to wed. I just wanted to come home. Only now Karl is here, too, so even home won't be the same." She caught her breath. "I don't know if I want to be married."

"Oh, Thea." Inga hugged her, then took a step backward. Their gazes met again. "I am not certain you should be talking to me of this. I have not done so well with my own marriage." She paused, seemingly lost in thought. Then she said, "I know this much. You went to New York because you loved Karl. You married him because you loved him. He is your husband because you promised to always love him."

"But I don't *feel* the same about him as I did—"

"Falling in love is the easy part, Thea. It is quite different from *being* in love. If you are blessed, I suppose, you fall in love with your husband again a little bit every day. But most often, love is a choice, a decision to love no matter what the day brings. You are in love because you choose to be in love. You made a promise, a commitment, to love him."

Thea hadn't wanted a lecture. She'd wanted sympathy. "It's just all so different now. Karl isn't the same as he was in Sweden. He's so . . . so serious all the time."

"Being a husband *is* serious. Supporting a wife, taking care of children." Inga's expression changed. She looked . . . happy. "We cannot know what tomorrow will bring. We must not look for trouble. Have some faith in your husband, Thea. Karl is more man than you credit him to be, I think." Suddenly Inga turned toward the parsonage. "Dirk," she whispered.

Thea knew she'd been completely forgotten. "Inga—"

"I have to go." Inga started walking back along the path.

"Wait!"

Inga stopped and turned. "Do not be foolish, Thea. Do not throw Karl away. You may not have another chance to love him as he should be loved."

"I thought you would understand." Tears filled Thea's eyes.

"I do understand. More than you know." Inga turned again. "Now I have to go." She began to run. "I have to go home."

Thea wanted to stay angry. She wanted to shout at Inga and demand to be heard. But something happened. She caught a sudden, unflattering glimpse of herself—and she didn't like what she saw.

Maybe Karl was right. Maybe it *was* time she grew up . . .

Before it was too late.

— Twenty-four

We cannot know what tomorrow will bring. We must not look for
trouble. Have some faith in your husband . . .

Inga's advice to Thea replayed in her mind as Olaf's buggy,
driven by Karl, carried her home. And with those words, she
remembered the instant of revelation, the moment she'd understood what she had done to Dirk this morning, what she'd
been doing for far too long.

Dirk was more man than she'd given him credit for being.
She had thought him less able to commit to marriage than she
herself. Even less than young Karl to Thea. She had pushed
Dirk away because of her own fears. Earlier this morning, she'd
thought all that was behind her, but she'd let one moment of
doubt bring the fear roaring back. She'd let it control her once
again. She hadn't listened to what Dirk was telling her. He
loved her. He'd said he loved her, and she had pushed him
away because she was afraid to take hold of what had been
given to her.

"It doesn't appear anyone is here, Inga."

She looked with some surprise at her surroundings. She
was home. But Dirk and the children weren't there. The wagon
wasn't standing in its usual place beside the barn. Robber and
Sunset weren't in their paddock, grazing on new shoots of
grass. There was no laughter of children falling through open
windows to greet Inga upon her arrival.

She climbed out of the buggy. "Just leave my things on the porch, Karl. Then you can go back to the parsonage. I will wait for my family here." Her family, her husband, her children.

"Are you sure, Inga? Your pappa didn't seem to think you should be alone."

"I am sure."

"But it seems so—"

"This is my home, Karl," she interrupted gently. "I will be fine." She stared up at the house, feeling as if she hadn't seen it in years.

Karl carried her portmanteau and valise to the porch and set them there, then turned toward her. "I am going to follow your advice, Inga. *Tack.*"

"My advice was small." In truth, she couldn't remember what she had said to him during the drive to the farm.

"*Nej,* you have been of great help." He smiled. "We will be happy, Thea and I."

She returned the smile, took hold of his hand and squeezed. "*Ja,* I know you will. Now go home, Karl. Go back to your bride."

This time there was a bit of youthful cockiness in his grin. "Tell *Herr* Bridger I look forward to meeting him." Then he hurried to the buggy, sprang onto the seat, and lifted the reins. In a moment, he was on his way.

Inga waited until her pappa's buggy had turned onto the main road before she entered the house. It was surprisingly tidy, she thought as she wandered from the living room into the kitchen, her gaze sweeping over all the familiar items that filled each room. She wouldn't have thought a girl Astrid's age would be so thorough in her cleaning. At the parsonage, Astrid had always . . .

Inga froze in midstep. Her heart nearly stopped, too.

Astrid had been at the parsonage that morning to welcome Thea and Karl home. But Astrid couldn't have known they were coming. Why had she been there? Maybe she'd been homesick. Or maybe she was visiting for the day. Dirk had said he would be back tomorrow to see Inga. Margaret's cousin—what was Mrs. Trent's first name?—had probably volunteered to watch the girls.

Inga left the kitchen and walked quickly to Hattie Bridger's old bedroom. Nothing was out of place. No luggage was in sight. Her heart began to beat a little faster as she hurried toward the stairs and climbed to the second floor. She checked all three bedrooms. There was nothing in any of them to indicate either Astrid or the Trents had been at the Bridger farm.

She forced her racing heart to slow as she squared her shoulders in determination. She wasn't going to slip back into the doubts and fears. She wasn't going to live that way any longer.

Still, despite her resolve to be calm and patient, the hours of afternoon moved slowly. Inga lost track of the number of times she went to the door to stare down the road, waiting for the wagon to appear.

Where are you, Dirk?

Snippets of memories played in her head. Dirk's expression when Martha had entered his bedroom on Saint Lucia's Day morning. The snowball fight when they'd gone looking for an evergreen tree to brighten Hattie's last Christmas. Dirk's proposal of marriage. The night they'd stood before the mirror and he'd told her she was pretty. The tenderness of his touch. The sweetness in his kisses. The moment she'd realized she was pregnant with his child. Dirk climbing the maple tree. Dirk pushing her in the swing.

Dirk . . .

Her life in Sweden had been one of familiar routine. Inga had welcomed the adventure of coming to America. She had reveled in it, like a starving woman at a banquet table. Once in Uppsala, she had longed for another adventure. Dirk's need of help had seemed an answer to that longing.

But then she had fallen in love, and she had let fear seep into her heart. Fear of the day the adventure would end. Except, how could it end, when life itself was the adventure? She wondered how she had failed to see that before now.

She longed for Dirk to hurry home; she had so much to tell him.

—

"Are you certain you won't change your mind?" Allison asked above the *hiss* and *whoosh* of the waiting train.

"I'm sure," Dirk answered firmly.

The woman glanced at the girls, each with a hand clasped by her uncle. "But you cannot raise them alone. What if their aunt never—"

"My wife's gonna be home tomorrow."

Allison must have seen that further argument was useless. With tears in her eyes, she bent to give Martha and Suzanne each a kiss good-bye.

As she did so, her husband said, "This doesn't mean we're going to be strangers, Mr. Bridger. We'll be back to visit."

"And you'll be welcome." Dirk let go of Martha's hand, then offered it to Harvey. "You're family. Family's always welcome."

Allison couldn't control her tears any longer. They were running down her plump cheeks as she straightened. "You must let us know if the children need anything. Anything at all."

Dirk nodded.

"My dear," Harvey said, "it's time to board the train." He took her arm. "Come along."

Allison wiped her eyes. "Perhaps, when they're older, you'll allow them to spend a few months with us. We have a beautiful summer cottage in New England."

"Perhaps," Dirk answered.

"Allison, we must get on the train."

"Good-bye, Martha. Good-bye, Suzanne." She waved her handkerchief as she walked backward, pulled by her husband.

"Good-bye, Cousin Allison," the children called in unison just as she disappeared into the waiting passenger car.

Martha slipped her hand back into her uncle's. "She sure did cry a lot."

"She's gonna miss you." He looked down at her. "They're nice people."

Suzanne tugged on his arm. "Can we go home now, Unca Dirk? I wanna see Aunt Inga."

"I want to see her, too." He squeezed their hands. "And we will. Soon."

—

"I don't know when they'll be back, Inga," Sven had said as the two of them stood in the barn. "Dirk asked me to see to the milking tonight, and I said I would. He said they were all going down with the Trents to catch the train."

That had been many hours ago. The house was dark now. Dark and silent. Inga had prepared herself an evening meal, but it had gone uneaten. She had tried to sew on her new quilt, but she was too restless to sit still.

There were moments when doubts came again. What if Dirk had decided to accept the Trents' offer? What if Inga had come to her senses too late? But she shoved those thoughts aside. He would be back. He had told her he would, and nothing would ever again make her not believe him.

The house grew cold as the hour became late. Exhausted and lonely, Inga climbed the stairs. She entered the bedroom she'd shared with her husband. She felt his absence most in here, she thought as she crossed the room and undressed for the night.

The sheets on the bed were cool, and the bed seemed too large. She buried her face in his pillow, but the loneliness only increased when she noticed it carried Dirk's scent. Had she ever noticed that before?

She had been blind to many things, it seemed.

For some reason, as the wagon drew closer to the farm, the road ahead of them lit by a full moon, Dirk had begun to feel a new urgency to reach their destination. Anticipation had welled up in his chest, although he hadn't known why.

Now I know why, he thought as he leaned against the doorjamb and stared at his wife, asleep in their bed. He could never have described the surprise, the joy, the hope, or the wonder he'd felt the moment he discovered her there.

He stepped into the room and closed the door. The children had been carried to their room and tucked into their bed. The horses had been rubbed down and put out to pasture. And now the rest of the night belonged to his wife.

He crossed to Inga's side of the bed and knelt there, his gaze never moving from her face. He hadn't made a sound, yet her eyes opened, as if she'd sensed his presence.

"Dirk," she whispered. If there had been any lingering doubt about why she was here—in this room, in this bed—it was dispelled in the loving way she said his name. She sat up. Her hair tumbled about her shoulders, a pale and silky waterfall that glimmered in the moonlight. "I have been waiting for you."

He smiled. "I've been waitin' for you, Inga Bridger." His voice was husky with emotion. "All my life, I've been waitin' for you."

Her fingertips on his cheek were cool. "I know." She cradled his face between the palms of her hands, drew him toward her. "And I am not afraid any longer."

Dirk wished he had the words that would tell his wife how much he loved her. He wished he could make her see all she had given him.

He drew her from the bed, setting her feet gently onto the floor before him, holding her tightly against his chest.

"I love you, Inga."

"As I love you."

"It's not gonna be easy. We're always gonna be short on money and long on problems."

"It does not need to be easy. We need only to have each other and our faith in God. He will see us through."

"Yes," he answered. "Yes, he will."

He felt, more than heard, her sigh, and somehow he understood it was a sound of contentment. He pressed his cheek against the top of her head. After a few moments, he said, "I've always liked the way your hair smells."

"And I have always liked to hear you say it."

Dirk stepped back, holding her at arm's length so he could look at her. "You're beautiful."

Inga felt his gaze upon her. She was warmed by it. She felt … beautiful—just as he'd said.

"My wife," he whispered.

"My husband," she replied softly.

There was a beauty in this moment, in the way their hearts communicated beyond the words that were spoken. A beauty in the love they'd found in one another, a love that transcended everything that had gone before.

A love that caused a twining and tangling of all their tomor-rows.

A love that wove together all of their hopes and dreams.

And where there had been two, now there was only one ...

One more pattern of love.

Epilogue

Saturday, July 30, 1898
Uppsala, Iowa

Dearest Mary,

I pray this letter finds you well and happy. I have been remiss about writing to both you and Beth, my dear friends.

I will always be sorry Thea could not visit you while she was living in New York City, for then she could have brought me more news from you. But, of course, we did not know where you were at the time.

Margaret Bridger's cousins, the Trents, have been most generous, sending gifts to the children from wherever their travels take them. They are planning another visit to our farm next spring, and we are looking forward to it now. I believe I will like Allison Trent a great deal.

My quilts continue to sell beyond my wildest expectations, and thanks to the money these sales have brought us, we now are the proud owners of two beautiful Thoroughbred yearlings. Although Dirk insists they will be no more than saddle horses for us, I think the future holds something else in store for them. There is a chance Dirk is actually beginning to believe it, too.

Karl is working for Dirk on the dairy, and it seems he has found his true calling. There is great enthusiasm in his voice when he discusses his ideas for the future with Dirk. Thea has changed and seems much happier now, especially as she watches her new home being built on the piece of land Dirk gave to them.

As for the rest of my sisters, Kirsten falls desperately in love with someone new every month. Astrid is nearly as bad. Thea says they are both empty-headed and much too flirtatious for their own good. This coming from Thea made us all laugh. Except for Pappa. He did not laugh. I think because he fears it is true.

Gunda recently surprised us with her good news. She is engaged to marry Valdemar Dolk. His parents own the general store in Uppsala, and it was his brother who drowned last March. Valdemar has decided to study medicine rather than go into the family business. The couple plan to marry and then move to Boston where they will stay until he is ready to begin a practice of his own. Then they will return to Uppsala. Dr. Swenson is counting the days until his retirement.

We thank God daily for his grace and mercy, for the lovingkindness he has shown toward us. I have seen the love for our Savior growing in my husband's heart, and I rejoice over what that has wrought in our love for one another. Only God himself could have brought all this to pass.

There is one more miracle for which I praise God, and I shall try to express my gratitude in my newest quilt, one that I shall not finish until next February. For until then I shall not know if our child will be a son or a daughter.

But God knows, just as he knows every stitch, every thread in the patterns of our lives.

Fondly yours,

Inga Bridger

Dear Lady
Robin Lee Hatcher

Dear Mary,

New Prospects, Montana, is nothing like England—so terrifying and beautiful at the same time, and much larger than I dared imagine when you and I first embarked on our adventures in the New World.

I have had the good fortune of becoming the town's schoolmistress. Young Janie Steele is as precious as I imagined from her letters. As for her father, Garret Steele ...

Oh, I feel like such a fool! I've run halfway around the world to escape a man I loathed, only to discover I'm losing my heart to a man still in love with the wife he buried.

The mayor, kind man, has been most attentive. But I wish he were someone else. I wish he were Garret.

With affection,
Your friend Beth Wellington

In the big-sky country of Montana, the past doesn't always stay buried. Circumstances have a way of forcing secrets into the open, sometimes bringing hearts together in unlikely ways, and sometimes tearing them apart.

Dear Lady is book one in the Coming to America series about three different women who come to America to start new lives. Set in the late 1800s, these three novels by best-selling author Robin Lee Hatcher craft intense chemistry and conflict between the characters, lit by a glowing faith and humanity that will win your heart.

Softcover 0-310-23083-7

Available June 2001

In His Arms
Book three in the
Coming to America series.
Softcover 0-310-23120-5

Pick up a copy today at your favorite bookstore!